BLOOD SONS

A MAFIA THRILLER

DAVID LISCIO

DAVID LISCIO

This book is dedicated to good fathers everywhere in the world.

———

1

I PLEDGE MY ALLEGIANCE TO THE MOB

JUNE 1988

MEDFORD, MASSACHUSETTS

Hannah Summers yawned cavernously, adjusted her shoulder holster, crumpled an empty bag of Fritos corn chips and flung it at her partner who was sprawled and dozing on a sleeping bag at the rear of the surveillance van.

Serpentine blue eyes slowly opened and a hand reached up to touch his cheek where the cellophane wad had struck him. He pretended it had caused pain and interrupted his sleep. "I've killed people for less," he said groggily. "I hope you know that."

Hannah raised her hands above her head as though being held at gunpoint. "Please don't shoot me, Agent Decker."

"I'd never do that. Too much paperwork involved."

Hannah feigned relief, lacing her fingers together and pressing them to her lips.

Emmett Decker crawled on his hands and knees toward where Hannah was sitting Indian-style in front of an array of electronic equipment.

"Anything?"

"Your turn," she said, handing him a set of headphones. "The mobile unit reported activity on the street near the house ten minutes ago."

Decker swept aside the honey blonde strands that had fallen across Hannah's face, tucked them behind her ear and gently kissed her lips. "Get some sleep."

Hannah tugged off her black tactical boots and socks and wriggled into the sleeping bag. "This reminds me of fishing with my dad in Missouri. We'd thread a bunch of corn kernels on a hook and just wait for hours until some big-ass carp struck the line."

A bemused grin crossed Decker's face as he stroked the black stubble on his chin. "Is there some sort of Midwestern parable that I'm missing?'

"All I'm saying is, those were good times, even when we didn't catch any fish," she said, squeezing his hand as she yawned again. "Just nudge me if you pick up something."

"Should a big-assed carp give a tug, you'll be the first to know. Now get some sleep."

Hannah had barely drifted off into a pleasant dream when Decker gently tapped her sleeping bag with his boot. She peered around the dark van interior, illuminated by red night-vision lamps.

"It's Vinnie Merlino," he said, gesturing toward his headset. "I'd know that fat fuck's voice anywhere. If they stay in the living room, we'll be all set."

Hannah plugged in her headphones, a huge grin forming across her face when she realized they were eavesdropping on a Mafia blood oath ceremony.

"The candles you see burning are the holiness of what we do," she heard Vinnie Merlino telling the others in a priestly voice. "Before this, you were nothing. But after tonight, you will be made men. You will be one of us."

Noises followed. Shifting feet. Mumbling. "St. Jude makes impossible things possible. As I touch a match to this saint card, watch the flames until there is nothing but ash in my hand. Rub these ashes and make the sign of the cross on your forehead."

Static. Muffled sounds.

"Now it's time to become brothers in a society that comes before everything else, before your family, your wife, your children. It must always come first and you must always be ready, no matter what you are doing when you are called. And now, we must stand in a circle and join hands."

Hannah rolled her eyes at the amplified flick of what sounded like a spring-loaded folding knife. Switchblade? Stiletto?

"Hear that?"

Decker pressed a finger to his lips and touched his headset with his index finger, cueing Hannah to keep quiet.

The priestly voice crackled over the airwaves. "I open my veins for you and for this thing of ours. Blood drips from my thumb. When you have all done the same, we will press our fingers together and we will be one."

Decker combed back his dark hair with spread fingers as he studied Hannah, who was beaming like a schoolgirl. He lifted the left ear cushion on his headphones. "What?"

She shrugged her shoulders and flashed a radiant smile. "Italian version of the Boy Scouts? My bullshit detector is going off. I can't believe these streetwise guys are actually falling for this mumbo-jumbo."

"Just listen."

"I'm hoping they say something worth bringing back to Langley. All we have right now is the audio to some very bad theater."

"That's why I love you, Hannah. You're so positive."

She kicked his thigh with her bare foot. "That's for earlier. Sorry. I'm just hungry. Those Fritos were the last of our rations. You ate both sandwiches, all the cashews, and the chocolate bars."

"When this is over, it's my treat – KFC or the BK."

"Please take me somewhere that uses table cloths. That would be a nice change."

More indistinguishable sounds followed. As the voices reemerged, one by one, the men recited a short oath and swore allegiance to La Cosa Nostra. During the ceremony, one inductee stuttered as he repeated the oath, which caused somebody in the room to chuckle. Another taking the vow had a distinct lisp. Decker and Hannah concentrated on the voices, making notes of The Stutterer and The Lisper for future reference.

When it was over the men said their goodbyes in English and Italian and somewhere a heavy door closed.

Decker's new Motorola MicroTac cell phone beeped in his pocket. It was the mobile unit reporting four men were leaving the house and getting into a large, dark sedan, most likely a Lincoln Continental.

"Follow them. At least get the plate number," Decker said. "Summers and I will stay here and listen a while longer."

2

MY TRUE BLOOD SON

Outside the van, the summer sky over Boston glittered with stars, satellites and commercial airline traffic flying in and out of Logan International Airport.

Decker scratched his chin. "Ready to call it quits?"

"Let's give it ten more minutes," Hannah said. "That's when I turn into a pumpkin."

Persistence paid off when they heard Vinnie Merlino pompously say, "So, Nicholas, what did you think of what you saw and heard here tonight?"

A young man's voice, or maybe it was a boy's, hesitantly replied, "I'm not sure what I'm supposed to think. I get it. This is your club. People like ceremonies. When I was about ten, me and four other kids trapped a snapping turtle in a pond. If you wanted to be in the club, you had to kiss it on the head, not just the shell. Only two of us did."

"La Cosa Nostra is not a club."

"Whatever. A kid in my class back in New York said his dad belongs to the Masons and they do lots of weird shit at their temple meetings."

"Ceremonies are very important. You should remember that."

"Oh sure," the younger voice said flippantly. "At home we go to Mass every Sunday morning. It makes Hope and Gary happy. The priests are dressed in fancy robes and they've got all kinds of props -- incense, candles, holy water, the whole nine yards."

The headsets transmitted a loud bang, possibly a fist pounding a tabletop. Hannah glanced at Decker to confirm he, too, had heard it.

"You're a goddamn smartass. Don't you talk like that about the Church. I don't know what kind of people raised you, but have some respect!"

"OK. OK. I'm not singling out the church. Think about it. There are lots of groups out there with ceremonies. The KKK has burning crosses and guys running around in white bed sheets. Hard to top that."

Vinnie's voice filled with anger. "For Christ's sake, I brought you here to show you what it means to have power, to be a leader."

"Leader of what?"

"You've led a sheltered life with those people on that pig farm in upstate New York."

"It's a vineyard. We grow grapes and make some very good wine. We also grow almost all of our own food."

"Forget those people. You aren't Nicholas Cooper anymore. The hospital may have sent you home with them fifteen years ago, but you are my son, not theirs. Blood doesn't lie. How do you think Rocco feels, believing for fifteen years that I was his father, only to find out through fucking DNA that your pig farmers are his real family."

"He could do worse."

"That's not the point. I'm you're father. You and I, we don't need secret ceremonies to join blood. My blood flows through you. I want you to see the organization I've built, trust the men under my command. We have a plan so big that after it's done you'll never have to work a day in your life."

"I'm not interested in your plan. I actually like physical labor," said Nick. "Nothing's better than a day in the fields. It clears out your head. You should try it some time."

Another bang.

Hannah grimaced. In a voice laced with humor, she said, "Doesn't seem like pops and sonny boy are getting along very well."

Decker shrugged, puzzled by the conversation, not fully understanding what was being revealed. He was familiar with the name Rocco, which he surmised was a reference to Vinnie Merlino's teenage son. But the name Nicholas Cooper was new to the list of players and not part of any previous intelligence reports. Decker wondered how they missed that at the task force. *Fuckin' Feebies. A hundred agents assigned to a case and nobody comes back home with the intel needed to crack it.*

Vinnie Merlino cleared his throat. "Nicholas, you are my son. When I was your age, I was already running numbers. I was doing business. I had a lot of respect even back then."

"I'm not trying to be disrespectful. I just don't want to be here."

"Think of it this way. Some day when I'm gone, you'll inherit everything."

"And what if I'm not interested in any inheritance?"

"Then you'd be a fool. You heard what Nunzio Carlucci said during the meeting in my office yesterday. Big things. Very big things are happening. Before the end of the year, we will take control in Cuba. You know where Cuba is?"

"Yes. I know where Cuba is. I'm not stupid," said Nick, rattling off the jingle, "*Christopher Columbus sailed the ocean blue and discovered Cuba in fourteen hundred and ninety-two.*"

"I'm glad they taught you something at school."

"Me too, only the teachers forgot to mention there were people living on the island before Columbus arrived. But that's ancient history. I don't care about Cuba. I just want to go back home."

"You are home. Not here in Boston, but in Providence with me. That's your home now."

"Providence will never be my home."

"Maybe some day you'll understand. You have opportunity. You can be part of something big, something important."

"Going back home is important to me. Seeing my girlfriend Isabella is important to me. I miss my friends. I want to go swimming in the lake, ride horses, pick grapes. I don't want to be here."

"Don't you love your country?"

"What's that got to do with it?"

"America is a great country. That's why the communists hate us. And that's why we want Castro gone."

"And you're going to make it happen, just like that?"

"There are people in our own government who agree it must be done, but their hands are tied. Castro has ruined that island. We're going to make it better." Merlino's voice dropped low with wrath. "May that lousy Commie fuck spend his eternity searching for food in an empty Russian grocery store."

Hannah slowly shook her head, amused by the man's views on life, but she didn't know what to make of him. Few were likely to challenge the notion that Vinnie Merlino was batshit crazy. The man acted like a character from a B-grade Hollywood gangster film, which was perhaps how he envisioned himself. Despite his laughable bravado, in reality he was dangerous.

It was approaching 1 a.m. when the mobile unit reported back with the license plate number on the Lincoln Continental. The car was registered to Nunzio Carlucci, but he was not among the men who left the house.

Hannah closed her eyes and continued to listen. Vinnie was still rattling on about the evils of communism.

"Once he's gone, the field is wide open. It'll be just like when Batista was President, but you're too young to know about that, Nicholas. I'm talking beautiful hotels all along the beach. Rich casinos. Gambling. Fantastic parties. All the rackets and more money than you've ever seen, only this time, it won't be Batista counting the stacks, it'll be us."

"So you plan to wade ashore and expect the people in charge to just step aside and let you take over? Why would they do that?"

"They won't have to make that decision. They'll be with Fidel in the afterlife."

"Jesus. You're talking about murder. I know you're a powerful man, but last I heard, killing people is a crime."

"Listen to me, Nicholas. I'm talking about business. I'm talking about power and numbers with eight zeros. Capisce?"

"I hope you're kidding."

"One thing you should know about me, Nicholas. I never kid. Now you want a sandwich? I think there are coldcuts in the kitchen. Try the sopressata with a slice of Scali. I saw there were hot peppers in there, too, stuffed with prosciutto and provolone."

"I think you're nuts," said Nick. "If my, whatever I'm supposed to call them, my other parents in upstate New York, knew you were planning some sort of foreign invasion, they'd tell me to hop on the nearest bus and get as far away from you as possible."

"But that's the difference," said Vinnie. "I'm your father. You're real father. And I'm not *pazzo*. I'm solid and there's a fantastic opportunity right around the corner that you will be part of because you are my son."

Another twenty minutes passed but no voices were recorded, only what sounded like the clatter and tinkle of dinner plates and utensils in the distance.

Decker was gloating like a child who'd stolen the last cookie when the babysitter wasn't looking. "We need to find out more about Nicholas Cooper. All this intel is new," he said, his voice brimming with excitement. "Now we can head out, get some sleep and do some serious research tomorrow."

Hannah unplugged her headset and switched off the recorder. "I'm not ready to leave," she said, deftly casting aside her black sweater and cargo pants.

Decker marveled at the sight of her charcoal bra and underwear under the red night-vision lamps. He clearly remembered the first time he ever held her. It had been under dramatic circumstances when a serial killer known as the Boston Butcher tied her to a burning cross atop Orient Heights in East Boston. Disheveled, ribs cracked, bleeding from cuts on her face, and nearly unconscious from the grassfire burning around her, she had still asked Decker for his ID and demanded to know what he was doing at the crime scene. He'd never met a woman like her – brave, beautiful, intelligent, sassy, duty-bound. And graced with a sense of humor.

Decker tossed his headset aside. "I thought you were hungry."

"I am, more than you can imagine," she said, executing a theater-perfect come-hither glance as she lithely collapsed onto her sleeping bag and pulled him down with her. "You better work quick before the other team comes looking for us. What's that old saying from the Sixties, 'Don't come a knockin' if this van's a rockin'?"

Decker let out a muffled laugh. Hannah gave him another smoldering glance as she tugged the black T-shirt over his muscular shoulders. She reached out and touched the raised scars made by bullet wounds. Decker nuzzled her ears, a hand pressed against her back, bringing her closer. "Miss Summers," he whispered. "I'm totally shocked by your behavior."

3

THE TROUBLE WITH DNA

Angie Merlino slammed the lasagna pan into the oven and butted the door closed with her hip. Vinnie sat uncomfortably at the kitchen table in the cramped apartment on Federal Hill, a few blocks off Atwells Avenue. He was about to light a cigar but decided against it, knowing Angie would make a fuss.

"Why the hell are you acting like this? We need to be united in how we handle this situation."

"You shouldn't have let Rocco go with those people."

"He needs to find out who his real parents are."

"We're his real parents. I'm his mother. We raised him. Fifteen years we raised him. He adores you. He thinks you're a god."

"Rocco is a good boy, but he's not mine."

"How can you say that? We're talking about Rocco. For fifteen years Rocco has been the one thing you and I had together that was good, that was just ours. If you hadn't gotten mixed up with that little slut, life would have gone on. We wouldn't have thought twice about any DNA."

Vinnie stood, knocking back the kitchen chair. Angie backed toward the stove, startled by the abrupt show of force.

"Don't you ever call Ruby a slut. She's the mother of my child, my beautiful little daughter. My Carla."

Angie adjusted her apron and patted her bouffant hair with her fingers, which seemed to give her courage. "I'm just saying if you trusted her, you wouldn't have made her prove the baby was yours. I never needed any tests. I was always loyal."

Vinnie moved fast as a jungle cat and slapped Angie across the face, sending her spiraling into the hutch where she displayed her Hummel collection. One of the figurines crashed to the floor, shattering into dozens of ceramic fragments. It was Goose Girl -- her favorite. It always reminded her of the trip to Boston with her parents when she was in elementary school. They'd visited Boston Common and gone for a ride aboard the Swan boats. A goose had waddled over and snatched the candy bar from her hand. Angie thought it hilarious as the bird struggled to swallow the lump of chocolate and nuts. It was years ago, but she could still feel the goose's tug. She brought her hands to her face and began to sob.

"I'm sorry. I'll buy you another one tomorrow."

"I don't want a replacement. That one was special," she said, kneeling on the floor to pick up the shards.

"Look, I got more on my mind than a fuckin' statue of a goose. I'm thinking about what we got to deal with. I'm talking about fuckin' DNA. Who the Christ would have guessed?"

"That's right, Vinnie. Fuckin' DNA."

"How come all these years you never gave me a straight answer about Rocco being the only one in the family with blond hair and blue eyes? Why is that, Angie? You fed me a line of bullshit about some great uncle back in the old country, a guy who supposedly looked like that. You were always going on about how the people in northern Italy had blonde hair because they were fucked by the Vikings."

"I always believed he was the baby that came out of my womb," said Angie, making the Sign of the Cross, her voice laden with sincerity. "With all the trouble I had delivering, and having to end up in that big Boston hospital, what did it matter his hair didn't match? That was the least of my worries. I thought I was going to die. I thought my baby was going to die."

Vinnie draped an arm around Angie's shoulder but she recoiled and dried her eyes with her apron.

Angie glared at him, bracing for another slap. "You only think about yourself. I'm worried about Rocco and about Nicky as well. I don't think either one of them is happy."

"I'm going to show Nicholas how the business works. He seems like a very smart boy. He's as handsome as I was at that age. He'll do fine."

"And what about Rocco? When you told him he wasn't your son, you took away his whole life. Now he doesn't know who he is. He's lost."

"Hey, at least we learned the truth. It cost me a lot of dough, but it was worth it. My lawyers had to bribe those miserable pricks at the hospital, twist their arms to admit they'd made a big mistake and covered it up. The hospital knew the public would go nuts if the story went to the press."

"I wouldn't have cared. I would have gone on raising Rocco as our own."

"But he's not. Some stupid nurse put the wrong ID bracelets on two baby boys. I hope she rots in hell."

Angie buried her face in her hands and sobbed. "All of this is so awful," she said. "I wish you'd never done it. We were better off not knowing the truth."

"For Christ's sake, Angie, we're talking blood here. The private eye I hired was the one who suggested Ruby get tested to make sure Carla was my daughter. It's not that I don't trust her, but some people were saying things that now they'll regret."

Vinnie poured himself a bourbon from the bottle of Jim Beam on the kitchen counter and swirled it in a lowball glass. "Angie, I hope you understand what's going on here. My lawyer kept saying this is modern science. The way he explained it, positive test results would clear the air, eliminate any suspicion and make things better between Ruby and me, which they did. In the long run, it made sense to do it. Carla is mine, not somebody else's. I know that for sure. I always trusted Ruby but I wanted that ace up my sleeve in case anybody challenged it. And that's why I ordered the DNA tests for you and Rocco. It's modern science."

"Did Ruby agree to the test, or did you force her?"

Vinnie sipped his bourbon. "Let's just say she knows when something is for her own good."

"And what about Rocco? The boy was crying in his room before he left here last week. He cried for hours. Did you know that? Probably not. You were too busy playing house with your..."

Vinnie raised a fist, stopping Angie from finishing her sentence. "Rocco will make his way with his real family. He'll learn to love the country life. Cows. Pigs. All those fields."

"You know that's not true. Rocco loves all the things you taught him. His world is racetracks and show horses, fancy restaurants and playing cards. He likes expensive cars and riding around in limousines. He thinks people should do whatever he says, like his word is God's."

Vinnie smiled broadly. "Angie, take a breath. He'll be OK. It'll be like *Little House on the Prairie*," he said, trying to make a joke.

But it was lost on Angie who was in no joking mood. "You've always been a bastard," she said. "You can let go of people without a second thought, just like that. Well, I can't. Rocco will always be my son. Fifteen years, Vinnie. Fifteen years!"

Vinnie downed the entire three fingers of bourbon in one

gulp and wiped his lips with the back of his hand. "Rocco can't keep up in my world. Even as a little kid he couldn't run fast, couldn't catch a ball. You fed him so much pasta he was fat as my Uncle Sal. And you remember Uncle Sal. Big as a battleship. It's no wonder Rocco couldn't ride his bicycle without getting winded. Don't you remember? He had training wheels until he was ten. It was an embarrassment."

"Oh, for god's sake, Vinnie. What's he going to do up there in there in the woods?"

"It's no longer our worry."

"How can you say such a thing? You're so cold sometimes it frightens me."

"Nicholas will be coming to live with me and Ruby."

"Does he know that? He's only been here a week. No time to adjust. He already wants to go back to upstate New York. You think it's good to shake him up again by moving him in with you and Ruby?"

"It doesn't matter what he thinks. And he's not going back to the Finger Lakes. We have a judge's signature, a court order. The law says a judge can decide what's in a kid's best interest, at least until the kid turns sixteen here in Rhode Island," said Vinnie. "Believe me, that signature didn't come cheap. Cost me ten times what the private investigator did. Fuckin' lawyers who handled this bled me for six figures."

Angie wiped the tears from her eyes. "And what about me? Now I have no son. Rocco is gone, and you're going to take away Nicky, too."

"You're Nicholas's mother, so that puts you in the picture. Maybe you still feel like you're Rocco's mother, but Nicholas has your blood. Blood is what matters."

4

SORTING OUT THE SONS

JUNE 1988
  FBI FIELD OFFICE
  BOSTON, MASSACHUSETTS

Hannah played the audio recording of the blood-oath ceremony three times from start to finish for Decker and the four federal agents seated at the conference table at the FBI field office in Boston's Government Center.

On the wall behind them were maps of Boston and Providence, pinned with colorful tabs of tape that marked businesses, government offices and home locations related to the organized crime investigation.

Hannah was still smirking as she clicked off the recorder. She scanned the faces at the table with her deep green eyes. "Nick Cooper seems like a nice kid. Maybe he'll realize he doesn't want to live a life of crime. If we play this right, he could become a vital asset."

Hannah opened the manila folder on the table. "You've all had a chance to read Decker's briefing. I'll just go over the highlights," she said, holding the sheaf of documents near her face as she read aloud. "Nicholas Cooper. Born December 23, 1972 in Boston, Massachusetts, son of Brent and Hope Cooper from upstate New York. Brent Cooper died tragically in a farm machinery accident on the family vineyard when Nick was only three, so the boy never really got to know him."

Hannah glanced around the room to make certain the others were paying attention. She recognized the ever-charged dissonance between her organization and the FBI, one she tried not to foster despite her personal feelings. "In that sense, Nick had no father figure. Hope Cooper ran the vineyard with help from a few trusted employees. She remarried several years later. Apparently to somebody she knew from childhood, a funeral director who also happened to handle her late husband's wake and burial."

Hannah continued. "The second husband's name is Gary Schneider. We don't know if Nick is close to this guy. But we do know Hope Cooper didn't change her last name to Schneider and there's nothing on file in New York State to indicate the funeral director ever tried to adopt the boy."

Hannah paused as the federal agents scribbled notes on yellow legal pads. "And then there's Rocco Merlino, also born December 23, 1972. He's the son of Vincent 'Cocktails' Merlino, who, as you all probably know, is a high-profile Rhode Island gangster so nicknamed because he purportedly prefers to poison his victims."

Hannah looked around at the faces for a reaction. FBI Special Agent Peter Barba pantomimed drinking from a glass and holding his neck as though he could no longer breathe. Hannah appreciated the gesture. She sensed Barba wasn't the typical guns-and-badges type.

"Pete you get a star for that and the bureau will forward your resume to the Screen Actors' Guild," she said, flashing a smile.

Hannah sipped from her water glass before continuing. "Vinnie's wife, Angela Merlino, aka Angie, seems to have drawn the short straw in this new arrangement," she said. "The poor woman had to send away the son she raised for the past fifteen years, and just when she might hope to see the return of her biological son, she finds out her philandering husband wants the kid to live with him and his young girlfriend, one Ruby Salerno. Age 26."

Decker cleared his throat and simultaneously raised an index finger in the air. Hannah acknowledged him.

With a wry smile, he said, "In case any of you were wondering, Ms. Salerno is a hairdresser and holds a cosmetologist license from the state of Rhode Island, although she is no longer practicing. She previously was a pole dancer at the Crystal V, a well-known strip club owned in part by, you guessed it, Vinnie Merlino. So take from that whatever you will. Ruby has a new baby to care for, also courtesy of one Vinnie Merlino."

A couple of the agents snickered.

"At least for now," said Hannah, "Merlino has put young mother and baby daughter up in an apartment in Providence, not far from his headquarters on Federal Hill. Apparently he has been staying there most nights."

Barba shook his head in disbelief. "What a mess. How the hell did this happen at the hospital? Don't they write a name on these babies with a marking pen when they pop out of the womb? At least give them a number in case they don't already have a name?"

Hannah blew back a strand of blonde hair but it quickly fell before her eyes. She ignored it and set her gaze on everyone at the table. "Not quite, Pete," she said. "But they do put ID bracelets on them. In this case, human error got in the way."

Barba scoffed. "And nobody figured it out until now?"

Hannah shrugged her shoulders. "We know both boys were born the same day in the same Boston hospital, apparently around the same time," she said. "The Coopers were visiting friends in Nahant, a little seaside town just north of here, when

Momma Cooper's water broke. The Coopers were a nine-hour drive from home, so the baby was born here in Boston."

"This story is definitely made for daytime television," said FBI Special Agent Sally Parker, pushing aside a pile of sunflower seeds in order to open her own folder.

A tall, coltish brunette in her early thirties, her personnel file contained several decorations for bravery that she seldom acknowledged. Just about everyone at the Boston bureau liked and respected her.

"Well, if it turns out that way, I'm sure the producers will be looking for a law-enforcement consultant on the set. Might be the perfect gig for you," said Hannah, her lips twisting into an appreciative smile. The day before, she'd read Sally Parker's confidential FBI profile and felt an unexplained bond with her, as though they might one day become friends.

Hannah shuffled the documents on the table in front of her as she continued. "Nick apparently has been steadily dating the same girl for over a year. Her name is Isabella Marceau. Same age, same class in school. Very pretty. They spend a lot of time together. If you look at pictures in the school's most recent yearbook, you'll see they're very much a couple."

Agent Parker raised one of her freshly-manicured fingernails. "So what are you implying?"

"My best guess is that a horny fifteen-year-old boy isn't going to be a happy camper if you keep him from his equally-horny girlfriend for too long," said Barba.

Hannah rolled her eyes. "Pete, you're so eloquent."

Barba let out a friendly burst of laughter. "I can still remember what it feels like to be fifteen. Rage of hormones. Off-the-charts amounts of testosterone. Fight or fuck, it don't matter, just bring it on."

Decker raised both hands in the air and placed them over his ears. "Save your trip down memory lane for someone else. I don't want to hear about it. Too much information."

"Neither do I," said Parker, a feigned look of horror pasted across her chiseled face. "Pete, I'm sure you were a real stud muffin."

Barba flexed his biceps. Both women rolled their eyes and laughed. Barba could always be counted on to lighten even the most somber situations.

"We don't know much about Rocco Merlino, other than he occasionally accompanies Vinnie on errands, both day and night. We have no idea what those might entail. We do know the boy voluntarily helps out whenever his church holds a food or clothing drive, and we've heard stories of him handing out scads of money to the homeless on the streets."

"I like him already," said Special Agent Parker. "Maybe his mother was a good influence."

Decker crossed his arms over his chest. "Let's get back to work," he said, his tone all business. "When Hannah finishes, we'll figure out the best way to move on this. We need to know what Merlino intends to do about both boys. But more than that, we need to find out who he's going to target in Cuba. The only way we want that island destabilized is if there's some high-level plan in place in Washington to quickly establish order under the American flag. If there is, we certainly haven't been told about it."

5

A CUBAN BUSINESS PLAN

Vinnie Merlino walked brusquely into the brightly-painted building on Federal Hill in Providence, Rhode Island where he kept a suite of offices, stopping momentarily to inspect his toupee in the full-length mirror. Six men varying in age from early thirties to late sixties were seated at a rectangular wooden table laden with plates of cheeses, hams, salami, fresh-baked breads, beers on ice and open bottles of wine. They stopped talking when Vinnie entered the room.

Vinnie raised his arms in a mock gesture of disapproval. "What? You started without me?"

The men chuckled nervously and made some neutral comments. One of the younger men, whose job was to oversee the numbers runners and the bookies, said, "The sun was already over the yard arm. Isn't that what you always say, boss?"

"No," said Nunzio Carlucci, an enforcer known from Maine to

Florida for his effectiveness. "He says you gotta wait until sundown so that you can have sundowners."

More laughter.

"Is that what we're having? Sundowners? I thought this was wine," said Vinnie, clutching one of the bottles on the table by its neck.

Nunzio Carlucci stood and hugged Vinnie, patting him vigorously on the back. "Good to see you."

"And you, Nunzio. Glad you could make it. How's the weather in Boston today?"

"Very nice. Sunny. I brought you some cannoli from Mike's in the North End."

"I love the North End," said Vinnie, who easily joined the others at the table and soon the talk became animated, the conversations ranging from loan sharking and extortion to arson, bookmaking, horseracing, and hijacking tractor trailers.

"I hope to Christ this place was swept before you fellows got here," said Vinnie, his tone humorous but his intent unmistakably serious. He looked for the answer to a lean, muscular man dressed in black from head to toe, who had quietly entered the room and stood near the door with his arms crossed.

"Swept cleaner than the linoleum on my grandmother's kitchen floor," said Alfredo "The Animal" Ponzi. "If there's a bug around here, our pest control people will make sure it's dead."

"I like your attitude," said Vinnie, whose wide-spanning role in the Rhode Island mob family, headquartered in Providence, included oversight of organized crime activities in Boston.

Five years earlier, Jerry Garafalo, aka Jerry the Joker, the Mafia's underboss in Boston, had been arrested by the FBI for racketeering and remained in prison following his conviction and lengthy federal sentence. The arrest had created a power vacuum, and though The Joker tried to maintain control from his jail cell, several up-and-comers were eager for him to step aside.

The old-timers were satisfied with the proceeds from loan shark-ing, sports betting and prostitution, while the new guys were more interested in the drug trade with its unrivaled profit margins -- cocaine from the Colombians, meth from the biker gangs.

Until all was settled, Nunzio Carlucci would handle matters in Boston, taking his orders from Vinnie who answered directly to Raymond Patriarca Jr., the boss of all New England.

Alfredo was leaning against the wall near the door to the room, which featured extravagant velour draperies, majestic floor-to-ceiling windows and a ceiling three times the height of the tallest man in the room. A three-foot long black plastic tube, like those carried by artists and architects, lay on the conference table where Alfredo had tossed it.

"Jesus Christ, another fuckin' map," said Carlucci. "If I tell Jerry the Joker all we do is look at maps, he's going to tell me to have my head examined."

"It's the same fuckin' map I showed you last time," said Vinnie, who was having difficulty spreading out the rolled map of Cuba.

One of the men at the table set two wine bottles on the upper corners of the map so it wouldn't curl.

"Jerry said we don't need maps. We just go there once busi-ness is taken care of and take what we want," said Carlucci. "You guys know about Jerry's time in Cuba?"

A few of the men moved closer to the table, hoping Carlucci would tell them.

"The way I heard it, Jerry and his hot young girlfriend went over to Cuba just as Castro was coming out of the mountains with his guerillas and taking over. I'm talking 1959. Jerry wanted to show her where he was putting his money from the sports betting and other rackets. He wanted to bring her to the big casinos, introduce her to the high life, but when they got off the boat,

Castro's soldiers pointed their guns and ordered them to get back aboard, to go back to the United States."

The other men at the table were listening intently. "Jerry's girlfriend was only about twenty-seven at the time, a stunner in a short dress looking to party," Nunzio said. "She was probably more pissed off at Castro than Jerry, and she wasn't the one who'd lost millions and would have to start over in Boston."

Gino "Fingers" Terranzetti, the most senior man at the table, wore a serious expression as he peered out through thick, black-framed eyeglasses that were perched on the bridge of his long Roman nose and topped by his mop of white hair. "That's a very touching story Nunzio, but what we need to know is, are you and your people ready?"

"My people can go any time. And we have plenty of hard-ware," Carlucci said proudly. "If we drive to Florida, we can take whatever goods we need with us. The trucks are always gassed up."

Fingers smiled, which was rare and so indicated his solemn approval. "Boston is part of our crew and ready to go," he said, directing his attention at Vinnie. "But what about New York? Are they going to want a piece of this?"

Vinnie bristled for a moment but quickly recovered with a charming smile. He knew better than to question Fingers, his most trusted advisor and confidant, his consigliere, the shrewd man who had helped him rise to power.

Fingers was known for his bluntness. With a knack for various forms of cruel torture, he had earned his nickname by snipping off people's fingers with a pair of bolt cutters. He seldom spoke, but whenever he did, the room fell silent. Most people in the closed family of La Cosa Nostra feared and respected him, understanding he had progressed from a hands-on street guy to one of the inner circle.

"When the time comes, we'll let them know what we're doing.

If they want in on the action, we'll lay out the details and show them how they can get a piece," Vinnie said.

Fingers vigorously shook his head in disagreement. "I think it's a mistake to leave New York out of the plan. John Gotti is nobody to mess with. You want to have him and the Gambino family on your side."

Vinnie grinned sheepishly. "Ah, yes. The Dapper Don. Mr. Teflon. God forbid we don't bow to him every morning. He can't stay out of the newspapers. His mug is everywhere."

Fingers lowered his eyes and without looking up asked, "And what about the boys in Miami? They're the closest to Cuba. Ninety miles. They're not going to be happy if we come into their backyard without telling them."

Vinnie stared intensely at Fingers. "You know how I feel about this. Same deal with Miami. Once we're in place, we can cut them in."

"But the boys in Miami will be looking for their share from the start. They still haven't gotten over the fact that Castro stole Sam Trafficante's casinos in Havana."

"I don't give two fucks about the Trafficantes," said Vinnie. "The Trafficantes are both dead, father and son. We know the kid worked with the feds and tried to take out Castro almost thirty years ago. We all heard Trafficante tried to poison the communist bastard, but it didn't happen. That's ancient history. He should have come to me for advice. And the feds didn't help him much later on when he was out there dangling on a hook after the invasion went sour."

"If I may," said Fingers, slightly raising his right arm and index finger. "Santos Trafficante, god bless his soul, sided with the feds to bring down Castro. It didn't work out, but at least he tried, and for that he had the respect of some very powerful people in Washington."

The room was silent as Fingers continued. "And now, Patsy

LoScalzo is running the Miami operation. We could use him as a friend."

Not one to be upstaged, Vinnie Merlino added, "As always, I appreciate your advice and your concerns Fingers, but when you have too many people involved, the stew pot gets split up into smaller and smaller portions. Pretty soon, there's not enough to eat."

"Agreed," said Fingers. "But for the record, I'm saying we shouldn't move on this until we know for sure that both Gotti's people in New York and LoScalzo's in Miami are on board. And we should also talk about bringing in Sammy Wings and the Chicago Outfit. Otherwise, it could be very messy."

Vinnie Merlino knew Samuel "Wings" Carlisi would want two of the larger casinos. He was also aware the Chicago Outfit had been involved in the CIA-Mafia venture aimed at over-throwing Castro in 1961, in return for access to the former casinos the gangsters had run under the Batista regime. Unfortunately for the Chicago Outfit, the joint operation had failed and ironi-cally resulted in increased federal prosecution of organized crime. It was no secret that the Chicago Outfit blamed then U.S. President John F. Kennedy for sanctioning the pile of indictments and subsequent prison sentences that came out of Washington the following year.

Vinnie lifted his chin smugly. "We'll know very soon if it's going to get messy," he said respectfully to Fingers, making certain all present understood he valued the opinion of his consigliere. Clapping his hands once, he added, "Now let's do some business."

Vinnie delicately set down the sheet of paper he'd been holding and ran his index finger along a list of names. "These are people we need in Cuba. If they cooperate, that would be beauti-ful. If not, well, they'll be out of a job."

A couple of the men snickered. Vinnie had their attention.

"Raul Castro, brother of the maggot President Fidel, is at the top."

Vinnie poured himself a glass of Sangiovese, his favorite Italian wine. "If Fidel was gone, we think Raul would boot out several of his brother's buddies, and those guys would be very unhappy about that. Believe me, they've given this plenty of thought already and at least one of them is ready to help us. As we all know, vengeance can be sweet. What's that old saying, something about revenge being best served cold? Well, these bastards are ready to serve it up frozen."

Vinnie grabbed a fork, stabbed a slice of roast beef and pushed it into his mouth. "Nice stuff. Not too much fat. Who brought it?"

The men all looked over at Martino Bianco, aka Marty White, handsome and athletically fit in his early forties. He wore a two-piece navy tracksuit with a double white stripe down the pants, the top unzipped just enough to reveal a hairy chest and a gold necklace with small crucifix. Marty White saluted with two fingers.

Vinnie continued. "Raul has made some enemies, mostly people who are loyal to his brother -- the foreign minister, the top finance guy, the labor guy. All of them may be helpful."

Marty White spoke for the first time. "Do we promise to let them stay in office?"

"Something like that," said Vinnie. "As long as they agree to play on our team. We also need to deal with some big American investors who are already planning to build high-rise hotels and casinos on the beach. They need to know we'll be in on the action."

Fingers Terranzetti ran his intact fingers through his thick mane and loudly cleared his throat. He looked to Vinnie for a wink, permission to share what was on his mind, and quickly received it. "The businessmen we can deal with. They pay or they don't play," he said. "But Cuba has its own military. How do we deal with that? It's a much bigger problem."

"Let's not call it quits before we get started," said Vinnie. "We have personal information about Cuba's most-powerful general, Octavio Sanchez. Very damaging material. We're certain he wouldn't want his wife, family and friends to know these things. Now let me go down the list and we'll see who's the best fit to take out each one of these big shots."

6

RHODE ISLAND DAZE

JULY 1988

PROVIDENCE, RHODE ISLAND

The only tuna Nick had ever eaten came from a tin can the size of a hockey puck. As a result, he hadn't given much thought to how insane a wild Bluefin tuna might feel when hooked to a strong line and a fiberglass rod jammed into a cup on a belt strapped to his waist.

Vinnie Merlino sipped his bourbon as he studied Nick, enjoying the sight of his son fighting this big mad fish out in the Northeast Canyons aboard a gleaming white Viking sport fisher. He puffed his cigar as the first mate poured water on the open Penn reel to keep it from overheating.

"Coming around," the charter captain shouted from the fly bridge. "We don't want to lose him now. He's getting tired."

Nick felt as though his arms were about to pull out of their sockets, but he wasn't about to let go or give up. This was his fish, his action, which began the moment the first mate had yelled, "Fish on!" That was two hours earlier and the tuna was still struggling for its life, fighting to toss the hook with every bit of energy left in its muscular body.

When the tuna was finally brought aboard, Alfredo snapped a photo of Nick with his catch, framing the fish in the foreground so that it looked even bigger than the 350-plus pounds estimated by the captain. It wasn't anywhere near the biggest Bluefin ever landed, but it was still impressive.

"When we get back, I'm going to have that picture made into a poster you can hang on your wall to remember this special day," Vinnie said. "You did a great job, kid."

Nick smelled like fish guts and the sea, his hands and face crusted with salt spray. Being out on the water was exhilarating, the scents so different from the farms and woods and freshwater lakes of upstate New York. The adrenaline rush was almost enough to make him forget how much he missed home.

As the yacht reversed course and began the run back to Providence, Alfredo took out his Glock 17 handgun and fired several rounds at nothing in particular in the water. The captain, his face a mask of disapproval, looked back from the fly bridge but made no comment. Alfredo also test-fired his new Mini Uzi machine pistol. The weapon made a racket that pasted a grin on Vinnie's face.

"Alfredo, are you happy with that noise maker?"

Alfredo, dressed in his trademark black trousers and black T-shirt, blasted away at the open sea, firing hundreds of rounds as he swapped magazines. He offered to let Nick shoot, but the boy showed no interest.

"Most kids your age would give their left nut to fire a weapon like this," said Alfredo.

Nick shrugged, turned away from Alfredo and gazed out to sea. The first mate, with a trace of foreboding in his eyes, scurried about the deck, picking up and tossing the spent brass shell casings overboard.

"I hope you weren't planning to recycle these," he said apologetically to Alfredo, who burst out laughing.

With the harbor again in view, Nick thought of Isabella and wished she could see him standing on the bow, proud of his skill and strength that had brought in the tuna. Nick admitted to himself he had had fun spending the day alongside the blunt and cruel man who was responsible for keeping him in Rhode Island. He fell asleep on the ride home, a smile on his face for the first time in months. In the morning, $500 in cash was piled on the nightstand next to his bed, his share of what the tuna had brought at market.

The summer ticked by slowly. Vinnie and Angie argued about where to enroll Nick for his sophomore year of school. Angie preferred a private academy, but Vinnie was adamant Nick attend the city's public schools where he would "meet the rough and tumble, the real people" whom he would someday have to deal with as an organized crime boss.

Although she wasn't consulted, Ruby suggested Nick be home-schooled, a trend that was becoming popular, based on a People magazine story she read at the beauty parlor. Vinnie told her to shut up and stay out of the discussion.

Not every day was a challenge. Nick discovered the beauty of Rhode Island's beaches. He occasionally rode a bus to Narragansett Beach where he bodysurfed in the waves until he was nearly too weak to swim to shore. On several of those days, a group of teenage girls in bikinis flirted with him and though they were undeniably attractive he couldn't get the image of Isabella out of his mind. He thought it might be beneficial to get to know these girls and make a new start, forget about Isabella and his old life, but in his heart he knew he was kidding himself.

The next time he talked to Isabella, he'd tell her all about his day at sea and how it felt to reel in a tuna. He wouldn't mention the bikini girls.

7

A DAY AT THE TRACK

SEPTEMBER 1988
BOSTON, MASSACHUSETTS

Nicholas Cooper couldn't hide his contempt as he watched his biological father and the three men accompanying him on the excursion strut like kings toward the row of betting windows at the racetrack. He had no idea why anyone would drive three hours from Providence, Rhode Island to Belmont, New York to watch horses run in an oval. He preferred horses grazing in the fields, the kind you could befriend and eventually ride along country trails.

Nick looked with amusement at Vinnie, who puffed a Cuban cigar and sipped from a plastic glass of bourbon. He disliked the man's shiny Rolex watch – one of at least seven expensive time-pieces Vinnie often bragged about. But more so, he knew the sparkling pinkie ring would be an embarrassment among the folks on the vineyard. It was gaudy. But Vinnie treasured it.

"Do you think people are fooled by the wad?"

Vinnie was clutching a roll of currency that showed a

hundred-dollar bill on the outermost layer. He scrunched his eyebrows and scowled at Nick. "What the fuck is that supposed to mean?"

"The wad. Isn't that what you call it? I saw you wrap a hundred dollar bill around the outside, but the rest of the bills are tens and twenties. And your friends, they've got a fifty wrapped around the outside, but underneath there are mostly fives and ones."

"It makes it easier to keep track of what you've got," Vinnie said.

"So it isn't just for show?"

"What the hell is the matter with you? I bring you to Belmont, to this beautiful track so that we can have some fun betting on these fantastic horses. But all you do is whine and mope."

"I just don't get it. I'm not into gambling. It seems like such a waste of money."

"This track is where Secretariat broke a world record in '73, finishing the mile-and-a-half in 2 minutes, 24 seconds. He beat the nearest horse by 31 lengths. Imagine that – 31 lengths. He was like a rocket ship."

Nick appeared unimpressed. "I guess that's fast. I really wouldn't know. Most of the time I ride horses that like to go along at their own pace, and usually we're in no hurry."

"All those years living with those pig farmers and you never went to the Finger Lakes track? You never heard of Secretariat?"

"My mother and her friends don't care about horse racing. They grow grapes. If they ride horses, it's just for fun."

Vinnie swung a backhand at Nick but the teenager's reflexes were quick and he ducked.

"I'm your father. Angie is your mother. We're your real parents," Vinnie shouted. His face reddened, his eyes filled with rage. "We brought you into this world, so don't forget it. Those pig farmers got you by mistake."

"Please don't call them pig farmers."

"OK. No pig farmers. But cut me some slack here. You're my son. I want us to be like a father and son. You want a cigar?"

"I don't smoke. Let's just start with you not calling people names. No more Micks, Chincs, Dykes, Kikes, Queers and Steers, Rag Heads and Jungle Bunnies and every other group you've got a name for."

The tinny racetrack speakers blared across the stands, announcing *No Can Do* as the winner. Vinnie's facial expression changed from serious to celebratory. "That's my horse," he said, gripping Nick by the shoulders and shaking him with enthusiasm. "We just hit it for the night. Now we can eat."

Nick shuffled his feet, gazing around at the hundreds of discarded tickets, a landfill for losers. He was about to say something sarcastic but decided to give his mobster dad a break.

"Did you win enough to buy me a steak?"

Vinnie glowed with pride, thrilled that Nick might be finally recognizing something in him good and worthwhile. "A steak? You want a steak? I'm going to buy you the whole cow tonight and we're going to eat it at the best steakhouse."

Nick tried to smile, coughing on the second-hand smoke from Vinnie's cigar. His eyes were stinging as they walked together to the car, followed closely by Vinnie's companions.

"Do you always have bodyguards?"

"They aren't bodyguards, they're friends," said Vinnie. "Very loyal friends."

Nick ordered a premium Delmonico steak, baked potato with sour cream, and three different sides. Although he was only fifteen and didn't look much older, Vinnie's clout with the restaurant owner was evident. While Vinnie and his two bodyguards drank wine, Nick was served a cold beer in an opaque glass.

"It's there if you want it, " Vinnie said. "If not, I'm sure they have Coca-Cola."

Nick appreciated the gesture and nursed the beer during dinner. Mostly he just listened as the three men talked in vague terms about the recent goings on in their criminal world. Someone they knew was now serving a life sentence at Walpole State Prison in Massachusetts. Another acquaintance was on trial for killing his wife with a hatchet. To Nick, it sounded like a litany of despair. He would rather have heard conversation about which horse needed new shoes, when the tractor engine parts were arriving, or why the grapes on the southern hillside were growing larger and juicier than expected.

After dinner, Vinnie instructed his driver to head back to Providence. Father and son sat in silence for most of the ride. Vinnie used the pull-down vanity mirror to comb over his hair. He had a big grin on his face as the car pulled up in front of an unmarked, redbrick warehouse along the banks of the Woonasquatucket River, which flows through the city.

"You in the mood to have some fun?"

"What kind of fun?"

Vinnie opened the car door, turned back and winked at his son. "Follow me."

Once inside the lobby doors led to a freight elevator, which was open but protected by a metal grate. A clean-shaven man wearing an orange leather waist jacket, bluejeans and alligator loafers snapped to attention.

"Good evening, Mr. Merlino," he said, slightly bowing his head as he pushed open the grate.

Vinnie barely acknowledged him as he stepped inside and motioned for Nick to join him.

Nick could hear music as the elevator came to a halt on the third floor. It was Bobby McFerrin's latest hit, "Don't Worry, Be Happy", emanating from down the hall, and it sounded as though several out-of-tune voices were singing along.

Two young women wearing little more than high heels, fishnet stockings, lacy underwear and transparent camisoles, approached Vinnie, slipped their arms through his and rested their painted cheeks against his shoulders. A third woman, similarly attired but a bit younger, reached for Nick's hand, but the boy pulled it away.

"He's shy," said Vinnie, chuckling. "Take good care of my son. Let's go girls."

An hour later, Vinnie found Nick sitting alone on a couch near the elevator. "You didn't like the girl I picked out for you? I heard you were both the same age."

"I don't need her. I don't need any of them. I have a girlfriend. Her name is Isabella and she isn't a slut," said Nick, his mind awash with images of Isabella riding her horse through the vineyards, of stealing away with him to the hayloft, of skinny dipping in the clear stream that sliced through the green hills and fed the lake.

"Some day you'll understand. I was trying to do something nice for you."

"I don't need to pay for sex," said Nick, his tone filled with distain.

"Suit yourself. You're being a little prick. If Rocco was here, he'd be with a half dozen girls and I'd have to drag him out of here."

"I don't care about Rocco. Can we go back to the apartment now?"

Vinnie banged the elevator grate with his fist. Seconds later, an electric motor whirred and the same man in the orange leather coat who had greeted them upon arrival was standing aside the metal grate as they entered. He wished father and son a pleasant evening as they left the building.

Vinnie's driver was leaning against the car trunk, smoking a cigarette. The street was dark and quiet, most of the city asleep. "To Ruby's," said Vinnie.

"Yessir."

"Why are we going there and not to your apartment where my mother lives?"

"Because that's where Ruby and your new baby sister Carla live."

"That baby isn't my sister."

The anger returned to Vinnie's reddened face. "Carla is your half-sister. She's my flesh and blood, and that makes her family. She's your family. You're both part of me."

Nick stared out the window as the car wended through the streets of Providence. He was thinking about Isabella and missing her so much it caused a pain in his chest. Summer was over and she was back in school. He hoped she wouldn't forget about him. It was September and the grape harvest had begun. It was his favorite time of year, but there was no sense of fall's magic in Providence.

8

WELCOME TO THE CIA

SEPTEMBER 1988
BOSTON, MASSACHUSETTS

When the strike force assignment was first unveiled, Hannah and Decker were antsy about working with the FBI in Boston. But they didn't have much choice.

William "Wild Bill" Carrington, their handler since they'd joined the CIA, insisted they cooperate with the organized crime investigation because it involved Cuba. As Carrington put it, the matter was international and indisputably linked to national security, placing it within the agency's purview. They all knew, by law at least, the CIA couldn't get involved if the matter was strictly domestic.

Despite the new orders, Hannah and Decker were eager to wrap things up in New England and return to their previous assignment, which had been to infiltrate eco-terrorism groups in the Pacific Northwest. There had been solid intel regarding a plan afoot among at least one of those groups to hijack a tractor trailer loaded with radioactive waste. It remained unclear whether the eco-terrorists intended to use the dangerous cargo as part of a protest, or sell it outside the country to another terrorist organization and use the proceeds to fund their ongoing anti-logging operations.

From Carrington's perspective, both situations had international implications – American mobsters venturing into Cuba, and eco-terrorists crossing the border into Canada. So inserting two operatives was within the agency's scope of influence.

Months earlier, Hannah had completed advanced surveillance and weapons training at two of the CIA's farms in rural Virginia and flown to Oregon on a private jet with Decker and Carrington to get the Pacific Northwest mission under way. Hannah especially appreciated Carrington's tutorials and his refreshing company. He was an easy companion, witty, talkative and sensitive. It was Carrington who opened the path at the agency that allowed Hannah and Decker to function as a team, despite their obvious romance. Occasionally he wondered whether that had been among his less prudent decisions. He was well aware love between field operatives could undermine in a clutch situation and negatively affect the outcome. Whenever emotions came before the mission, danger usually was not far off.

9

A CITY BOY IN THE COUNTRY

SEPTEMBER 1988
  FINGER LAKES REGION, NEW YORK

Rocco lay in bed, thinking about the first time he was awakened by the rooster outside his window. That was back in June, the first week of what was supposed to be the start of summer vacation. He thought he was having a bad dream, remembering how he had peered out at the strutting bird with its puffed feathers and loud crow.

When the bird let loose another cock-a-doodle-do, Rocco formed his fingers into the shape of a pistol and pretended to shoot it. Twice. Three times. Blasted into a cloud of feathers. Despite the death wish, the rooster – who everyone on the vine-yard called Foghorn Leghorn after the 1940s Warner Bros cartoon character -- had continued to wake him every morning at the crack of dawn for the past four months.

Hope Cooper was trying her best to make Rocco feel welcome. She bought him whatever food he requested and stock-piled the refrigerator with soda and snacks. She was still adjusting to the surprise news, delivered by certified mail in May, that her beloved Nick was really not her son at all, while in fact, a boy named Rocco Merlino was her flesh and bone and would soon be joining her family.

An attorney had arrived at the vineyard shortly thereafter to affirm the news and to make arrangements for the switch. He had shown Hope the court order, which she quickly challenged through the vineyard's law firm, only to learn that until the boys turned sixteen, they would have no say in the matter, nor would she. And sixteen was merely a starting point for what might happen next, said the lawyer, because Vinnie Merlino might use his money, power and political connections to engage in a lengthy appeals process, one which might a take year or two to resolve. By then, the boys would be eighteen and perhaps resigned to living in their respective homes.

For Hope, there was also the fear of violence. She'd heard tales of Vinnie Merlino, read about his alleged activities in news-paper clippings at the public library in Ithaca. It seemed many people were afraid of him, a fact more influential than the actual law.

A week after the mob attorney's visit, a trim and muscular man dressed completely in black, with eyes so intense they sent shivers down her spine, deposited an angry 15-year-old Rocco Merlino on her doorstep, along with an envelope containing $5,000 in cash. The man in black, who identified himself only as Alfredo, said the money was for expenses. Other than mentioning he was a friend of the Merlino family, he offered no other explanation or information before climbing into the back seat of a Lincoln Town Car.

What happened next can only be described as an ugly period in the lives of just about everyone involved.

Upon learning what was about to become of him, at least temporarily until his sixteenth birthday in late December, the normally calm Nick emotionally exploded. He accused Hope

Cooper of purposely trying to get rid of him, speculating it was her husband, Gary, secretly behind the effort. He accused Gary Schneider of marrying Hope as a way to steal the sprawling vineyard, upon which the man would construct hundreds of cheap homes for a hefty profit. He shouted that the funeral director should keep his business in town and not stow his supply of caskets in the stable because it was creepy.

When Nick finally calmed down and realized his speculation bore no weight, he profusely apologized to Hope and Gary. He was feeling crazy. The thought of being without Isabella for the summer sickened him. He knew Isabella was equally upset, and together they cried and fell into each other's arms whenever possible, in the fields, the stable and in Nick's bedroom. Not long ago, it seemed impossible that anything could tear them apart, but now it was happening and beyond their control.

Hope was equally depressed. Like it or not, Rocco was her true son, blond and blue-eyed just like her and her late husband, while the very different Nick with his glossy chestnut hair, warm brown eyes and dazzling smile, belonged to someone else. She felt awful for having such thoughts, but as much as this was no fault of Rocco's, she found it difficult to love him. She sensed, too, that Rocco felt no affection for her. She missed Nick and cursed the judge who had ordered him taken from her.

Although she had tucked her favorite photograph of Nick into the top drawer of her bedroom bureau, she often took out the plastic frame and held it close to her heart. Nick was handsome, helpful, smart and polite, the envy of many other mothers in the area whose offspring seemed less promising. It pained her to think she hadn't seen him since school let out in June.

Despite the mix-up, Hope Cooper was determined to set things right, bring Rocco under their roof and into their family as though he'd been there all along. In moments of pure inflective honesty, she recognized both boys as her sons, but her heart pulsed louder and quicker for Nick. It was a sensation she would never admit to anyone. After all, what would people think of a mother who loved a biological stranger more than her own offspring?

The days started early and ended late on the vineyard. Rocco had been shocked to learn the field hands began harvesting grapes shortly after sunrise and continued until sunset. It was the beginning of harvest season and he admired their stamina, but he had no desire to join them. Rocco had never owned a pair of work boots, or what he called shit kickers. His closet back in Providence was overflowing with brand-name sneakers and far more expensive leather shoes, the latter often crafted from the hides of alligators and other protected species, a fact he liked to point out to friends and strangers.

Rocco relocated in summer when the weather was at its best, which definitely helped his mood. But when his sophomore year began in September he made little effort to fit in with the other students.

Dressed most days in his distinctly urban style, he stood out. He was one of the new kids, a stranger who had arrived from the big city. And he didn't care what the others thought. He didn't want to blend. He wasn't about to buy himself faded jeans, a flannel shirt and work boots so that he resembled some hillbilly. He was Rocco Merlino. No farm would change that.

Hope urged him to take the bus to school because it would give him opportunity to meet other students and make friends, but Rocco insisted on being driven by her or her husband, Gary. He sorely missed the town cars and limos, the plush leather interiors and quiet rides. Although there was something admittedly cool about Hope's Jeep Wagoneer, he would have preferred being dropped off in a new Lincoln.

Barely a week into the school year, Rocco found himself in a heap of trouble. He had paid a down-and-out local resident $40 to buy him a couple of sixpacks of Budweiser and a bottle of Jack Daniels. He let the guy keep the change. Shortly before school let out for the day, Rocco sat on the fieldstone wall at the rear of the property and handed out beers and cigarettes to every boy who would accept one. He also urged the boys to take a long sip of bourbon and several did.

Phones began ringing in the community when one of the boys arrived home seeming a bit wobbly and vomited on the livingroom rug while his parents looked on in horror. Quickly interrogated, the boy confessed to having consumed a beer and three shots of whisky, courtesy of a new student named Rocco. An impromptu administrative hearing was held the next morning, at which the vice principal issued a stern warning to Rocco. The admonishment was repeated by Hope and her husband, Gary, once they arrived back at the vineyard where all three dogs were barking wildly.

Rocco told Gary to go fuck himself and reminded the funeral director he was not his father -- biological, through adoption, or otherwise.

"Why don't you go drain some dead bodies or do whatever it is you do all day? Maybe you should go fuck a corpse," he said.

Gary stepped forward as though about to cuff Rocco on the side of his head. The dogs continued barking. Hope raised a hand. "Don't do it, Gary. We'll get through this. Violence doesn't solve anything."

At that, Rocco chuckled. "Sometimes it does."

Yet another confrontation ensued when Rocco was caught smoking cigarettes in the small bedroom that had once been Nick's. When Hope attempted to grab the pack of Marlboro's off the bedroom dresser, Rocco was quicker, snatching and crushing the box until broken cigarettes and loose tobacco spilled to the floor.

"I'm only trying to do what's good for you," she said.

Rocco ordered her out of his bedroom and slide-bolted the door, adding an extra measure of security on the inside by installing a padlock he'd purchased at a local hardware store.

The first time Rocco set eyes on Isabella it was an unseasonably warm day and he thought he was hallucinating. Isabella was on horseback, trotting through an open field where the grapevines ended. She wore a flouncy white peasant top, faded bluejeans and brown leather boots to the knee. Her long blonde hair spread down her back, rising and falling as she rode.

Rocco was sitting on a split-rail fence, smoking a cigarette, when Isabella passed by on the tall Appaloosa, its warm brown tones spattered with marbleized patches of cream.

Isabella brought the big animal to a halt.

"For a minute I thought you were some fairy princess, or maybe Lady Godiva."

Isabella giggled. "No. She rode naked."

"Nothing wrong with that."

"I thought that's what you'd say. Do you ride?"

Rocco's facial expression showed he didn't understand the question. "Horses?"

Isabella rolled her eyes. "Well, I wasn't talking about your bicycle."

"Sure," he lied. "I've spent a lot of time around thoroughbreds."

"Well, this is Chance. He's an Appaloosa. The Coopers have five horses on the vineyard. Maybe they'll let you take one out and we can go riding."

"Looking forward to it. Hope you can keep up."

"Oh, don't you worry about that. You'll be eating my dust," she said, laughing easily.

Rocco stared boldly at Isabella with his sparkling blue eyes, taking in every curve of her body. "I'm glad you decided to stop and talk. When I see you around the school, you don't even say hello."

"Why should I? I don't know you. You sort of just showed up. But you looked lonely sitting on the fence just now."

Rocco hopped down from the split rail and smoothed back

his blonde hair with both hands. "Well, I guess it's time we formally meet. Rocco Merlino at your service," he said, bowing deeply before extending a hand.

Isabella laughed and shook it with her gloved hand but only for a second. She had heard about the drinking incident. Other girls at school had mentioned it, adding they thought the new boy was cool because he had managed to buy alcohol, cigarettes, land himself in the principal's office for disciplinary action, and generally cause a stir. His good looks hadn't gone unnoticed. They'd also heard bits and pieces of a rumor circulating about Rocco being raised by gangsters in Providence, Rhode Island. He was quickly labeled a bad boy and many of the girls at school gravitated to him like moths to a candle.

When people asked Hope Cooper what had become of Nick, she told them to mind their business. Nor did she offer to explain why a teenager named Rocco Merlino was now living with them, while Nick was apparently gone.

"It's obvious you like living here," said Rocco. "Not every girl has her own horse."

"Of course I love it. It's beautiful along the lake and there are all sorts of trails in the hills. Don't you think it's beautiful? Or would you rather be in a place with skyscrapers? Lots of shadows."

Rocco dropped his cigarette to the ground and crushed it with his sneaker.

Isabella's eyes locked on the cigarette and the tiny curl of rising smoke. "Make sure it's out. The grass is so dry around here, you could easily start a fire."

"Is that so? Well, I'll be very careful," he said mockingly, again twisting his sneaker on the ground.

Isabella ignored his tone. She didn't know much about him, but admitted to herself that he radiated some sort of dangerous charisma. She appreciated the fact that Nick was a wonderful person, kind and earnest. But standing before her was the bad boy and she was intrigued. She'd never dated a boy with blonde hair and blue eyes, or one who had been raised in a large city and who went out of his way to defy authority.

"I heard you got some of the kids in class drunk. Is that true?"

Rocco grinned, pleased with himself. "They haven't learned to handle their liquor. It's an important skill."

"And you know how?"

"Of course. Back in Providence me and my friends drink every weekend. If anybody gets sloppy, they hear about it. And what about you? Do you like to drink?"

"Only in the winter. When we go horseback riding in the snow or tobogganing. Some of the girls bring brandy."

Rocco looked boldly into her eyes. "Well, if I get some brandy, maybe we can drink some before winter, which I'm told arrives around here with a foot of snow just after Thanksgiving."

Isabella didn't reply. She seemed suddenly uneasy and her horse shuffled, as though sensing her discomfort.

"I'd better go," she said.

Rocco feigned surprise. "You just got here," he said, tossing up his hands. "Why not get off your horse and we'll take a walk? It's a beautiful day."

Isabella clicked her tongue and flicked the reins, signaling the horse to start moving.

Rocco shouted. "When will I see you again?"

Isabella glanced backward over her shoulder. "I ride this way almost every day after I get out of school."

"Then I'll see you soon," he said, flashing a flirtatious smile.

10

A COUNTRY BOY IN THE CITY

OCTOBER 1988
  PROVIDENCE, RHODE ISLAND

Nick studied the judge's decision, an official-looking document that had ordered him to leave his home on a bucolic upstate New York vineyard and move to a strange apartment in Providence, Rhode Island, a rundown industrial city of 160,000 residents.

Nearly five months had gone by since the switch and he wasn't happy. Although some of the kids at his new school were friendly, he remained an outsider, partially due to his unwillingness to forge bonds in a place where he had no intention of staying.

Once he turned sixteen in late December, he'd do whatever it took to reverse the circumstances. He marked it at two months and counting. Until then, he'd try to adjust and, if opportunity arose, escape, though he wasn't sure where he might go. He wanted to tear the copied document to shreds but decided to keep it because it contained case and file numbers, information he might need.

Nick lay back on his new bed and tried to think of ways to better his situation. He hated Providence. The people were generally friendly, but he loathed the traffic, the congestion, the smells, all so different from the green hills that rolled down to meet Cayuga Lake, one of the long, slender Fingers Lakes carved by glaciers a million years earlier. He missed the horses, the cows, the fields, the pungent manure and the rich aroma of grapes on the vine. But most of all he missed Isabella Marceau. She was what made him feel most alive.

The Marceau family – Tom and Sophie and their three daughters -- lived in a restored farmhouse less than two miles from the Cooper vineyard. A web of horse trails connected the properties, the paths well trodden. On weekends, Nick and Isabella often rode for hours, laughing and talking on the trail. Routinely they brought along water bottles and sandwiches and spread a blanket beneath their favorite tree where inevitably they made love. Isabella habitually collected tree leaves on these outings – Northern Red Oak, Mountain Ash, Sycamore, Red Maple, Poplar, Birch, Black Willow, Horse Chestnut and many others. She slipped them between wax paper and ironed them so they were preserved as sheets, which she labeled, dated and inserted into a ring binder.

More than a year had elapsed since they first began dating, a pairing which quickly developed into a serious relationship. At school, Nick and Isabella were a known commodity who could more often be found together than apart. Friends referred to them as Nikabella.

Nick wondered if Isabella still wore the turquoise ring he'd bought from her from a shop in Ithaca that stocked Native American jewelry. She'd gushed when he'd given it to her for her fifteenth birthday and spent the day showing it to her friends as though it were some rare diamond.

11

FAMILY VIDEOS OF A DIFFERENT SORT

OCTOBER 1988
BOSTON, MASSACHUSETTS

Hannah and Decker watched intently as the projector played the silent video on a white wall in the FBI conference room in Boston. The image was grainy but clear enough to see a man in a long black trench coat, wearing black gloves, savagely beating someone in an alley.

Two much larger men were holding the victim as the trench coat slammed fist after fist into the man's torso. Whenever the trench coat stopped punching, he shook the victim by the shoulders, pointed a black gloved-finger an inch from the man's face, and followed with an uppercut to the jaw. The man's head rolled back each time, but he didn't collapse, his body kept upright by the trench coat's burly accomplices.

FBI Special Agent Sally Parker stood in front of the projector so that some of the moving images played across her white blouse. "Meet Alfredo 'The Animal' Ponzi, one of the top enforcers for the New England mob. He works directly for Vinnie

Merlino in Providence. They used to steal cars together when they were kids. Ponzi was probably about ten. Later on they ran numbers, sold meth cooked by an entrepreneurial motorcycle gang, and tried their hand at hijacking tractor trailers filled with cigarettes, electronics and other goodies," she said.

Agent Parker used the remote control to freeze the video and display a mugshot of Alfredo Ponzi, a series of numbers visible on a black and white placard across his chest. The man had black hair and intense dark eyes that showed no sign of kindness, sincerity or understanding.

Agent Parker shined her laser pointer on the projected mug shot. "Alfredo Ponzi. Age 43. Six feet tall, approximately 220 pounds. Muscular. Fit. Almost always dresses in black. It's his trademark. Most of his associates are deathly afraid of him."

Decker passed out printed copies of Ponzi's mugshot to the agents at the table as Agent Parker continued her briefing.

"Ponzi went to jail for hijacking tractor trailers at rest stops all along the East Coast, but he only served two years and was released early for good behavior," Parker said. "The first thing he did when he got out was nearly beat to death a kid who'd taken three cases of whisky off one of the stolen trucks without his permission. The kid was in the hospital for months but wouldn't say a word. Ponzi never forgets anybody who did him wrong."

"Sounds like a great guy," said Hannah. "Is he single?"

A couple of the agents in the room snorted.

"He really is an animal," said Parker, her voice filled with distain. "These days, his job responsibilities bring him to Boston quite often. The situation there is unstable. Last we heard from our sources on the street, several young Turks are trying to take over the No. 1 spot while underboss Jerry Garafalo is behind bars. This video came from a camera we had hidden in the front headlight of a parked car in the North End."

"Nice work," said Hannah. "Makes it easier for us to see who we're dealing with. An animal."

"It took two tries," said Agent Parker. "The car was parked on Prince Street for more than a week with no action before it got ticketed and towed. We didn't want to expose our involvement, so we had to let it go. The second time, we had agents keeping an eye on the meter maids."

Decker asked, "Do we know why Ponzi was in Boston and whether this particular beating is related to the Cuba plans?"

"We don't," said Agent Pete Barba. "We believe Ponzi was in town to meet with people from the Boston organization. Most likely he had some discussion with Nunzio Carlucci, who has been trying to keep a lid on the power keg. Those two seem to have a lot in common. As for beating the guy in the alley, Ponzi probably used the occasion to send a message to anybody and everybody who owes Vinnie Merlino money."

"Ponzi's a multi-tasker," quipped Agent Parker. "No sense in making two separate trips to Boston."

"An all-around handyman," said Hannah. "Do we have a workable file on Ponzi?"

"More video than paperwork," she said. "Except for his prison and school records, information about him isn't easy to find."

Agent Parker again clicked the remote so that the video showed the victim toppling to the cobblestones. Alfredo Ponzi repeatedly kicked the man in the head and stomach with his black boots. Seconds later, Ponzi could be seen exiting the alley, peeling off his black leather gloves with a grin on his face as he unknowingly walked toward the hidden FBI
camera.

"Alfredo Ponzi has a bachelor's degree in political science from BU," said Agent Parker, referring to Boston University. "At one time he hoped to run for public office in Providence but was talked out of it, apparently by Vinnie Merlino. We know he speaks fluent Spanish, which could be why he was along in Puerto Rico when General Sanchez visited Vinnie aboard the yacht."

Hannah interjected. "We know Ponzi was aboard, but we don't know if he was part of whatever discussion went on between Vinnie and the general. He might have been there simply as muscle."

"We also know Vinnie is trying to line up people in Castro's regime who might be willing to cooperate out of fear they'll be left out once their leader is removed," added Decker. "That's where Ponzi's ability to speak Spanish would certainly come in handy."

12

THE GENERAL'S SECRETS

November 1988
San Juan, Puerto Rico

The oldest of the three dark-haired men standing on the dock was clearly nervous, smoking a thin cigar and glancing in all directions. He wore wraparound sunglasses, which he continually adjusted on the bridge of his nose. The two others were younger, their muscular frames nearly bursting under tropical two-piece suits.

The older man, whose face was bumpy and pockmarked, wore loose-fitting pants, sturdy sandals, and a guayabera shirt unbuttoned at the neck to expose a necklace with shiny gold cross. The younger men tensed as a rigid inflatable boat rapidly approached. The driver expertly nudged the pontoons against the dock and signaled for them to step aboard. Seconds later they were being whisked to a white yacht that was at least seventy feet long and anchored at the mouth of the harbor.

Hannah studied them closely through the 800-millimeter telephoto lens steadied on the thick stone of the San Cristobal fortress overlooking the harbor in Old San Juan. The two body-guards were trying to act casually, but the outline of their suits showed weapons bulging. Although General Sanchez was not in uniform, Hannah recognized him from the agency files.

General Octavio Sanchez, the most powerful Army officer in the Castro regime, tossed his cigar into the water as they climbed the gangway. Hannah, wearing a flowery summer dress and flip flops, clicked the camera shutter repeatedly to capture the image, pretending she was a tourist and bird watcher photographing the harbor and cruise ships.

She was thrilled to be part of the CIA operation in Puerto Rico. It was far more exciting than the small-town, undercover cop routine she had once known, and exotic compared to her days on the State Police homicide squad. She loved assuming disguises and false identities.

Hannah monitored the activity on board, wishing she could hear the conversation. For the first time in her life she felt like a spy instead of a cop and it was exhilarating.

Fingers Terranzetti met the visitors on deck. He didn't attempt to shake hands. He simply said, "Follow me."

Just before opening the door leading to the yacht's interior, Fingers gave an almost imperceptible signal and instantly Alfredo "The Animal" Ponzi, dressed fully in black and accompanied by two other men in dark blue trousers and long-sleeve jerseys, appeared along an iron railing about ten feet above them. All three carried Micro Uzi machine pistols.

"If you have any weapons, please leave them on the chair here. You can get them back on your way out," Fingers said with absolutely no emotion in his voice.

The general's bodyguards looked alarmed.

"Do as they say," Sanchez said. "Put down your weapons."

Reluctantly the men rested their Glock pistols on the lounge chair.

"Is that everything?"

Again they looked at the general.

"Everything," he said.

Two knives and two smaller handguns that had been strapped to the bodyguards' ankles were set on the chair.

Hannah clicked the shutter, hoping to catch more of the action.

"Now we can go," said Fingers.

Vinnie Merlino was seated behind a mahogany desk in a room laden with nautical décor. The walls were filled with photographs of white yachts, cigarette boats, smiling men posing with trophy fish or beautiful women. A series of round portals allowed diagonal tubes of sunshine to create patterns on the rich teak floor.

Vinnie wore a yellow polo shirt, white chino pants and tan canvas shoes. He glanced at himself in a mirror and adjusted his toupee, pleased by the reflection despite the drooping jowls and potbelly. A cigar burned in the ashtray but he ignored it as the visitors entered. "Please sit down," he said in a business-like tone. "Gino, get these gentlemen something to drink. They're probably thirsty."

"No thank you," said the general. "We won't be staying long."

"Then let me get to the point."

The general raised a hand. "One moment," he said. "I think this conversation should be between you and me and no one else."

"That's fine," said Vinnie, motioning for Fingers to leave the room and cocking his head toward the door. "*Vas afuera (go outside)*."

When Vinnie and the general were alone, neither spoke for more than a minute, but the span of time seemed much longer as the seconds dragged by. It was a little game to see who would speak first. The general removed a handkerchief from his front pocket and dabbed the sheen of perspiration on his forehead. It was he who broke the silence.

"So what is it that you want from me, Señor Merlino?"

"Your cooperation."

"You want me to become a traitor?"

"I'm giving you a chance to come out on the right side of something that is going to happen, with or without you."

"And if I refuse?"

"Your wife and the rest of the world will know what you do with young homeless boys," Vinnie said smugly with an unmistakable hint of disgust in his voice. "Maybe she'll get to see your private film collection."

The general squirmed in his seat, narrowed his eyes to slits and pursed his lips as he considered his options. His mind whirled as he tried to imagine who had given such private information to these gangsters. Once he found out whose tongues had wagged, the guilty would pay – slowly and painfully.

Vinnie Merlino leaned forward on his desk, his hands braced on its inner edge. Smoke from the untended cigar wafted in front of his face as he spoke. "Imagine what the men under your command will think," he said. "How old were the youngest ones? Seven? Eight years old? Nobody ever missed them."

The general adjusted his posture in the uncomfortable seat. "Why are you trying to ruin me?"

"It's nothing personal. Just business. When Fidel is gone, we're going to need somebody who can keep the military under control and show them the benefits of change."

"What's in it for me?"

"You get to salvage your marriage and your reputation. You get to go on being the invincible General Sanchez."

"That's it?"

"You want more?"

"I thought there might be a payment involved."

Vinnie stared at the general as if the man was a mouse whose tail was already caught in the trap. "How much would it take to ensure your cooperation?"

The general closed his eyes as though calculating what sort of post-Fidel lifestyle he could afford.

"Enough to live comfortably," he said. "I have financial responsibilities."

Vinnie chuckled quietly, enjoying the general's discomfort. "Give me a figure."

"I have two houses, cars, bodyguards, a few servants, a family to feed and clothe, and like you I have a boat that requires maintenance and fuel."

"It seems like you have a good life. It would be a shame to lose it. Starting today, you'll be on the payroll. You'll have enough to cover your expenses month by month. Are you agreed to that?"

The general pursed his lips. "Tell me precisely what you want me to do."

"Gladly," said Vinnie, withdrawing a list of names from his pants pocket.

Vinnie stepped out from behind the desk and walked through the door leading to the upper deck where the harbor was alive with ships coming and going. The general followed close behind. Although the general's bodyguards attempted to join them, they were ordered to stay put.

"Now would you like to have that drink, General Sanchez?"

The general looked defeated but greedily downed the cold beer. He didn't clink bottles with Vinnie, nor did he offer a toast. Fingers returned the bodyguards' weapons and within minutes the rigid inflatable was headed back to the dock. Hannah photographed the men aboard the yacht and those returning to shore.

Later that afternoon, Hannah strolled along the waterfront, heading for San Felipe del Morro Fortress, better known as El Morro, where she hoped the height would provide a better vantage point from which to watch Vinnie's yacht. She slung the 35mm camera with its weighty telephoto lens across her back, wishing it wasn't such a conspicuous piece of equipment. It made her a prime target for muggers.

Her concerns materialized as she walked through a waterfront shantytown called La Perla, nestled beside a cemetery between the El Moro and San Cristobal fortresses. The rough neighborhood stretched for about 600 yards, as long as six football fields. Some of the buildings were ramshackle and boarded up, others so covered in political graffiti it was difficult to tell where the windows and doors were located.

Hannah spotted the glint of a machete as a paunchy, middle-aged man wearing torn bluejeans and a Bob Marley T-shirt, a greasy baseball cap pulled down to his eyebrows, stepped from an alley to her left. He stood in her path, round face with droopy eyes and thin lips, smiling menacingly. A second man, probably no older than eighteen, wiry and darker in complexion, suddenly appeared beside him. His wife beater shirt and frayed shorts were grimy, as though he'd been working on a car engine. He flashed a butcher knife, wiping the blade back and forth across his open palm. There was no one else in sight.

"Good afternoon, señorita," said the moustache. "I hope you are enjoying your walk through our neighborhood."

Hannah's senses were on full alert, her heart pounding. She considered using the lens as a weapon.

The moustache took a step toward her, still smiling. "Anyone can walk here, but there is a toll. In your case, it is that very nice camera and lens you are carrying and the few dollars you may have in your pocket. For that small sum, you can move along unharmed."

"Maybe I'll want a little bit more. Maybe something else," said the younger man, flicking his tongue lasciviously while grabbing his balls. "But don't worry, you'll like it."

"Now if you please, hand me the camera and lens," said the moustache.

Hannah raised the carrying strap over her head, bending at

the waist as though momentarily struggling to relieve herself of the heavy glass. Just as the moustache grabbed hold of the lens, he screamed in pain. With lightning speed, Hannah had gripped the compact commando knife – which she often kept strapped to her upper thigh when wearing a dress – and sliced across the man's palm. Howling, he ignored the blood coating his fingers and again reached for the camera. Hannah twisted her body, throwing the assailant off balance as he held onto the lens strap. She thrust her knife outward once more, and watched with satisfaction as blood spurted.

The younger man charged, his butcher knife poised over his head and ready to plunge. The muscle memory ingrained by Hannah's extensive martial arts training kicked into gear. Using the wiry man's forward momentum against him, Hannah tripped him onto his back. The instant he hit the pavement, she made her move, repeatedly smashing his knife-wielding hand against the ground until his fingers released it.

Still holding the man's wrist, Hannah pressed her blade against his throat, prepared to sever his windpipe. She might have done just that if the moustache hadn't chosen that moment to resume his attack.

Hannah lost her patience. The moustache, his T-shirt soaked in blood, was again clutching his rusty machete, but his gait was unsteady, the blood loss already affecting his balance and sending him into shock. As he swung the deadly tool in a chopping motion toward Hannah's neck, she blocked it with the telephoto lens. The machete bit deeply into the metal casing, causing the glass elements to shatter. The moustache had meant business. If Hannah had not acted quickly, she'd be dead, and she knew it.

Filled with rage, she kicked the moustache squarely in the face, which sent the flip flop on her right foot flying. He staggered and fell to the ground, hands cupped over his nose. Hannah lifted the heavy camera lens to eye level and brought it down on his head, knocking him unconscious. The younger man, his eyes wide with fear, ran toward a dark alley. Hannah was too exhausted to follow.

The lens was beyond repair. She wouldn't be taking any more surveillance photos until a replacement arrived. Instead of continuing on to El Morro, she wandered back toward the more gentrified streets of the old quarter, near La Fortaleza – the governor's house – and the small hotel where she was staying under an assumed name. She wasn't scheduled to make contact with Carrington, her CIA handler, until 11 p.m. She needed a piña colada and a hot shower. She also wanted to mend her toenail, which had split when she kicked the mustachioed assailant. She was really pissed about the cracked nail because she'd just had an expensive manicure and pedicure at her favorite spa in DC. But not quite as pissed as she was about the blood spattered across her brand new sundress. After she pulled herself together, she'd find a decent restaurant. The one that caught her eye was called Barrachina. She'd seen it mentioned in a travel guide. It was close by, boasted authentic Puerto Rican food, and offered live flamenco dance shows.

A few blocks away, Vinnie, Fingers and Alfredo wandered through the narrow streets of Old San Juan, looking more like jovial tourists than plotting gangsters. Whenever they passed a young woman whose attire showed the least bit of cleavage or thigh, Vinnie stopped to admire her and cluck his tongue approvingly.

"I can't afford that kind of trouble any more," said Fingers. "Women are too much maintenance."

Alfredo, dressed like Johnny Cash despite the heat, slapped him hard on the back. "You sound like a guy with cobwebs on his dick."

All three men were still laughing as the Barrachina maître d escorted them to a table on the far side of the dining room archway.

Although seated no more than ten feet away, Hannah couldn't see the men. But if she concentrated and listened carefully, she could catch snippets of their conversation.

Vinnie was showing off, telling his companions the Barrachina restaurant was birthplace and home the piña colada.

"It was invented right here, in 1963," he said, exuberantly enough for those seated at nearby tables to look over.

Alfredo was impressed, his expression filled with astonishment and admiration. "How did you know that, boss?"

Vinnie stared at him with mock distain. "What? You don't think I know a lot of important stuff?"

"Of course, of course," Alfredo stammered, fearful of offending the man whose quick-fuse temper was known to blow without warning. "Everyone knows you are a very smart man."

"I'll tell you something else," said Vinnie. "The bartender who invented it was named Don Ramon Portas Mingot. You don't believe me, ask our waiter."

As the spaghetti-thin waiter approached the table, Vinnie snagged him by the cuff of his black serving jacket. He tweezed a $20 bill between his thumb and forefinger, holding it up to where the waiter could see it. "My friend, I want to ask you a question. If you get the answer right, you can keep the twenty. Is that a deal?"

The waiter, flushed with discomfort, answered in a gentlemanly tone that seem to harken from a different era. "I can most certainly try, sir."

"You ready?"

The waiter clasped his hands together and leaned toward the table in order to better hear the question.

"What was the name of the bartender who invented the piña colada?"

Without any hesitation, the waiter proudly said, "Don Ramon Portas Mingot."

Vinnie clapped three times, slowly, and handed over the

twenty. "*Muchas gracias, amigo*," he said. "I'm glad you know your history."

"I didn't doubt you, boss," said Alfredo. "I was just amazed that you knew it."

Fingers had been perusing the menu since they sat down and suddenly he started to laugh. Twice he lightly slapped the table-cloth with his right hand as he extended his copy of the menu so that it was almost in Alfredo's lap. With a knowing look, he grinned at Vinnie and said, "You were always a fast reader."

Slightly embarrassed, Alfredo joined in the laughter as the waiter returned with three piña coladas.

Looking down at his menu, Vinnie said, "Don Ramon Portas Mingot. Now that's some name. Who the hell could remember that? If he was one of us, we'd have to call him Rum Boy or Piña Alotta."

Hannah sipped her drink slowly, not making eye contact with anyone. She had found Vinnie's stunt somewhat amusing. She noted his sense of humor and the camaraderie of the men. She left when the flamenco show ended, sensing there would be little to gain by remaining longer.

On the short walk back to her hotel, she imagined herself as a flamenco dancer and tapped out a few impromptu steps on the cobblestone.

13

A NECESSARY ROAD TRIP

November 1988
Finger Lakes Region, New York

Nick quietly locked the door to the small bedroom in the apartment where he lived with Vinnie, Ruby and baby Carla. He spread the highway roadmap on his bed and studied the routes from Providence to the vineyard on the northwest end of Cayuga Lake. He followed the colored lines, trying to make sense of the map, and traced his finger along those that led to Ithaca, New York.

A backpack stuffed with a change of clothing, food snacks, a folding knife, flashlight, down jacket and other items was hidden behind his bed. It was already almost 8 a.m. but he waited until Ruby had left with the baby before he shouldered the backpack and headed out. He sensed Vinnie would have men check the bus and train stations, so he avoided both, choosing to walk toward the highway and put out his thumb. He yearned for a driver's license and his own car, but both would be out of reach until he celebrated his sixteenth birthday, and that was more than a month away.

Two days earlier he had called Isabella from a pay phone. He left a message on the Marceau family answering machine, not knowing whether she ever heard it. He wanted to let her know he was coming, but didn't say as much, just in case the phone was tapped, which he wouldn't put past Vinnie. Instead, he had simply left the phone number to the apartment, hoping if Isabella called back and Ruby answered she would hand him the receiver or at least relay a message.

Nick was still stewing from the previous phone conversation they had, during which Isabella told him Rocco was "acting weird" but "kind of cool in his own way."

Isabella's description had left him uneasy. The green monster of jealousy crawled along his spine. He knew then he had to head back to the vineyard as quickly as possible.

There were two weeks to go before Thanksgiving, a holiday celebrated on the vineyard with friends from the neighboring farms, and enough fresh food to feed a village. The mood was always festive and the people truly thankful for what they had – friends, family and a robust life connected to the regional soil, to the grapes that sprang from it, and to the wine fermenting in thousands of wood barrels at locations all along the Finger Lakes. The celebration was a big thank-you to nature for the annual harvest.

If Nick were there, Isabella would be at his side, talking and laughing and sharing in the special day. If the opportunity presented, they might slip away to his bedroom and kiss until their lips were puffed and exhausted. If time allowed, and nobody noticed their absence, they might slip beneath the sheets.

Nick imagined Rocco taking his place at the Thanksgiving table and, though he tried hard to not see it, envisioned Isabella seated next to the boy from the city. He tried not to think of Rocco kissing or touching her. The mere possibility of it was driving him mad.

A cold, relentless rain drenched him as he held the cardboard sign that bore the destination: Ithaca, New York.

Nearly an hour passed before a stake truck pulled onto the road shoulder. It was filled with wooden crates. Three men were squashed in the front seat. The skinny man nearest the passenger window shouted out. "If you want a ride, climb in the back and pull one of the tarps over your head to keep out the rain."

Nick hauled himself into the truck, slapped the rear window of the cab to let them know he was aboard, and squeezed between two wooden crates draped by a tarp. The crates smelled of diesel fuel. It was chilly and unpleasant under the tarp and he was completely soaked, but thoughts of Isabella warmed him. He tried to sleep but the truck rocked and bumped as the miles ticked by. At one point during the climb over the Berkshires, the truck hit an icy patch of road and nearly spun out of control. Nick hung onto the wooden stakes, his pulse racing. He pressed his face against the cab's rear window and was given a thumbs-up sign.

Somewhere near Albany, New York the driver pulled into a rest area and announced they would be continuing north on Interstate 87, a major route most motorists referred to as The Northway. Nick had studied the map and knew he needed to go west. He thanked the driver and trudged to the entry ramp, glad the rain had finally stopped. It was mid-afternoon. Nick knew he had at least two more hours of daylight. After that, his chances of catching a ride would diminish -- drivers were less apt to pick up a hitchhiker in the dark.

The second ride was a chatty salesman whose rotund body rubbed against the steering wheel of the aging Buick sedan. He told Nick he was planning to stop at several hardware stores along Route 20, a secondary road running parallel to the New York State Thruway. Nick felt lucky because if Vinnie's men began searching for him, his chances of remaining undetected were better if he stayed away from the major highways.

The salesman was eating a massive roast beef sandwich that was spread across the dashboard on a sheet of waxy paper. Without asking, he ripped off a generous portion and handed it to Nick, who took it and surprised himself by ravenously eating it in three bites. The salesman grinned.

"Thanks," said Nick, who slumped against the passenger side door, emotionally and physically exhausted.

"Mind if I listen to some music?"

"Absolutely not. I'm so tired it won't keep me awake."

The man inserted a cassette tape and *Last Train to Clarkesville* by the Monkees blared out the tiny speakers. "Can't get enough of The Monkees," he said, explaining how the song came out in 1966, the year he had graduated from high school.

Next came *Cherish* by The Association, followed by *Ballad of the Green Berets* by Sgt. Barry Sadler – all hits from the same year.

Nick smiled, figuring the man must be about forty. "Great choice of tunes," he said, but truly didn't recognize the songs until *We Can Work it Out* by The Beatles began to play. That one he knew and it made him think of Isabella. He hoped they could work it out. The Beatles were still singing when he fell asleep.

After making sales calls in Duanesburg and Sharon Springs, the man tapped Nick awake and explained he was detouring to the small town of Cherry Valley for the day's final business stop before spending the night in Cooperstown, better known as the birthplace of baseball at Doubleday Field and home to the Baseball Hall of Fame.

It was early evening by the time they arrived at the shores of Lake Otsego and an icy wind was exhaling across the water. They ate burgers at a roadside diner where the warm food put Nick in a more cheerful mood. His clothes were still damp but he no longer cared.

Things got a bit weird when it came time to find a motel, but

once Nick was convinced the friendly salesman wasn't a
pedophile or serial killer, he agreed to split the cost of a room
with two beds.

Nick changed into dry clothing and quickly fell into a deep
sleep. He awoke just after dawn and learned the salesman had
paid for the room. The man had already eaten the complimen-
tary breakfast and brought Nick a carton of orange juice and two
glazed doughnuts. He was packed and ready to go. A late-
morning appointment in Syracuse awaited him.

En route they listened to more music from the mid-1960s.
Nick said goodbye where the road intersected with Interstate 81,
another major highway leading north. Thumb out once again, he
hitchhiked west along Route 20, knowing it would eventually
bring him to the northern tip of Cayuga Lake, the vineyard, and
his real home.

14

THE GIRL FROM ARGENTINA

NOVEMBER 1988
HAVANA, CUBA

Hannah was determined to find out more about General Octavio Sanchez. She tried to discuss the situation with Decker but he wasn't keen on her going to Cuba undercover and alone. His reluctance made her feel second-rate, B-team, and she didn't like it one bit. She presumed Decker was against the idea out of need to protect her, some ingrained caveman attitude, but there was always the slight chance he didn't want her to show him up.

Instead, while at Langley for a full briefing on Cuba, she approached Bill Carrington to pitch the idea. The affable Carrington listened as Hannah explained how she intended to get an audience with the four-star general.

Since the United States had broken off formal diplomatic and trade relations with Cuba following the Bay of Pigs incident in 1961 and subsequent Cuban Missile Crisis in 1963, she would have to pose as a representative from a neutral country. She decided upon Argentina mostly because of its relatively neutral political stance regarding Fidel Castro. She also was forced to take into account her physical appearance – tall and thin, with blonde hair and green eyes. She could easily have been an American or Scandinavian movie star, maybe an Australian, although that might have required mastering an accent. Fortunately, Argentina was full of Germans who had settled there after World War II, in many instances to avoid prosecution by the United States and its allies for war crimes in Nazi Germany.

Carrington agreed Argentina was a good choice. They'd have to work on creating her new identity – passport, driver's license, credit cards, professional resume.

"And what do you intend to offer General Sanchez, presuming you get to meet him?"

"We can't very well supply him with little boys, so what's the next best thing? What's the one thing every general thinks he needs?"

"You tell me," said Carrington, amused by the amount of thought Hannah had put into the proposal on such short notice.

"Weapons. Every general wants weapons, and right now Argentina is full them. Our own intelligence reports bear that out," she said.

"Tell me more."

Hannah launched into her elevator pitch, noting the public's confidence in Argentina's military had eroded ever since the outcome of the Falklands War in 1982.

"The people of Argentina are tired of buying weapons for their generals and then losing battles. So now there are tons of weapons still greased and packed in their shipping crates, sitting in the country's warehouses."

"And you want to offer them for sale to General Sanchez as an enticement?"

Hannah smiled irresistibly. "Something like that."

Carrington had to admit she had guts. "You think General Sanchez wants more guns, but he can't afford them?"

"Correct."

"And you also think he'll meet with you if you can offer him a discount price?"

"Yes. But not just any weapons. From what I've been told by a couple of my contacts at a Washington think tank, the general has been talking nonstop about the need for an advanced field arsenal, specifically the Red Arrow 8, which as you know is made by the Chinese and provides formidable firepower on the battlefield."

Carrington reached for an oversized, four-inch thick book on the shelf next to his desk and flipped it open. He pointed to the image of an olive-green tube mounted on a tripod. It appeared the device could be easily loaded with a lethal missile and was relatively mobile.

Carrington whistled. "I forgot about the Red Arrow 8. I believe they're also made in Pakistan these days. At least the knockoffs are." He leaned closer to the page in order to read the fine-print specifications. "Tube-launched, optically-tracked, wire-guided."

"And don't forget armor-piercing," she said.

"The perfect anti-tank missile system."

Hannah looked self-satisfied, thinking her father would be proud of her knowledge of weapons. She'd learned to ride horses and shoot his hunting rifles, shotguns and pistols while still in high school and she quickly became what was arguably the best marksman in the Summers family. She was also the star of her high school equestrian team.

"If Cuba was attacked by an invasion force of mechanized infantry, General Sanchez could be the country's hero, presuming he had access to this kind of weaponry," she said.

"Good point."

Carrington promised to consider the idea and investigate whether any funds were available for such an operation.

A week later, Hannah had a new Argentinian passport under

the name Mariel Becker. It listed her home address as Buenos Aires and her occupation as industrial product consultant. She didn't tell Decker about the passport or her travel plans. She feared he would storm into Carrington's office and demand she be given a safer assignment. She didn't need his protection, or him screwing with her credibility at Langley.

Upon arriving in Havana, Hannah's attempts to contact General Sanchez were twice rejected. When she learned the general frequented the El Floridita bar in the city's old quarter almost daily, she bought a couple of snug-fitting dresses, expensive high heels, and began wearing more eye makeup and lipstick than she'd imagined possible. Working undercover was part of the job that got her heart racing and made her feel more alive. She knew it was living on the edge and she embraced it. Some days she still couldn't believe how far she'd come – from chasing leads at a small state police department to spying for arguably the best spook organization in the world. The Central Intelligence Agency was the Harvard of black ops. And Hannah was an eager student.

On the third day in Havana she spotted General Sanchez in uniform at a corner table in the bar made famous by Ernest Hemingway and other writers. He was seated with two other men who wore cream-colored tropical business suits. The epaulets on each of the general's shoulder were oversized and gold, which made Hannah chuckle because they reminded her of the brushes on floor polishing machines used by janitors at her high school.

All three men were chatting candidly and sipping piña coladas. She purposely sashayed her hips as she walked slowly toward the ladies' room. The general saluted as she made her way back to the bar, where a fresh drink was waiting.

Hannah held up the glass to thank him and sipped the cold daiquiri. She allowed the dress to slide up her shapely thigh as she dismounted the bar stool and approached their table. The general's two companions were mesmerized and undressed her with their eyes. Sanchez appeared interested, but not in a sexual way.

"Please join us," the general said, waving a hand at the unoccupied chair. "We are just three old men talking about football. It would be a pleasure to hear your thoughts on a more interesting subject."

15

THE SOUTHERNMOST CITY

November 1988
Key West, Florida

Making the most of their time in the sun, Vinnie Merlino, Fingers Terranzetti and Alfredo Ponzi sat in a booth at Sloppy Joe's Bar on Duval Street in Key West. The place was packed, mostly with tourists. Jimmy Buffet tunes, pumped at mid-volume through a system of massive speakers, blended with the barroom chatter and made for a pleasant atmosphere.

"Just think. Less than ninety miles from where we're sitting, there's a goldmine," said Vinnie, plucking a pink umbrella from his drink and crushing it in his hand before taking a sip. He didn't like girly touches on his drink -- paper umbrellas and too many pieces of fruit laced onto a plastic straw. "Gentlemen, I have a very good feeling about this. I can hear the roulette tables spinning in my head."

"I'm glad you came to your senses about Miami," said Fingers, who had ordered a double of straight Kentucky bourbon. "We need them. They know the Cubans living in the city who still want nothing more than to return home after nearly thirty years."

"Point taken, Gino. I put out a feeler to LoScalzo. When he got back to me, I told him we wanted to cut a deal," said Vinnie. "I asked if we could meet in Miami. I figured he might be more comfortable in his own city."

Fingers Terranzetti offered up a tired smile, eyes squinted and nearly closed behind the thick, black-framed glasses. "To bringing in the boss from Miami."

Alfredo Ponzi raised his beer bottle. "Cin cin."

Vinnie bristled. "Just don't forget I'm the big boss of the whole operation."

The men, chastised, stared into their drinks. They were well aware of Vinnie Merlino's short fuse, and while he was actually underboss to Raymond Patriarca Jr., who oversaw all mob activities in New England from his office in Providence, he liked being referred to as the boss.

In an effort to lighten the mood, Alfredo proposed another toast. "To the best boss in the world."

"Salute!" said Fingers, brushing back his thick white mane.

Vinnie nodded agreement. "Salute."

With cat-like quickness, Alfredo rose from the table and grabbed the arm of a pretty young redhead standing nearby. The woman was in her early twenties. She was so thin her ribcage was visible through her taught skin. She had short spiky hair highlighted by a streak of pink, dozens of freckles, and purple lipstick covering her pouty lips.

Alfredo put on his most charming smile as he tugged the woman toward their table. The woman was slightly off balance, most likely due to the tequila shots she and her friends were doing.

Alfredo quickly explained he meant no harm and was only out on the town with friends to have some fun. He pulled a wad of cash from his pocket and peeled off a fifty-dollar bill, which he held up near the woman's eyes.

"You can keep the money if you pull up your halter and shimmy your tits," he said, his white teeth flashing a harmless smile.

The woman's four friends, who had been pounding back the tequila shots, gathered around and dared her to accept the challenge. Seconds later, amid their exuberant cheering, and with the fifty-dollar bill in hand, she delivered a quick performance.

"See that, boss," said Alfredo. "Now doesn't that make you feel better?"

Vinnie smiled at the woman endearingly. "They're a little small for my taste, but maybe they'll grow," he guffawed, causing his companions and the woman's friends to clap and join the merriment. Vinnie admitted to himself he suddenly felt much better.

"Give her another fifty, you cheap fuck," he said to Alfredo, his belly still jiggling from laughter.

Alfredo peeled off another fifty. The woman's companions were all giggling as they edged toward the bar, eager to spend the money.

"I'm glad we came to Key West," said Vinnie. "It was a good idea, Alfredo. I haven't been here in years. It's a shame we gotta go back tomorrow, but business is business."

"And then there's Thanksgiving," said Fingers, rolling his eyes. "The way things are going, if the specialists are right, it might be my last one."

Alfredo didn't want gloom to overshadow the sunny day they were enjoying. "Don't you worry, Fingers. You're going to outlive us all," he said. "Half of those doctors are quacks."

"We'll see," said Fingers. "My wife has been making wedding soup, meatballs, ravioli, you name it. She goes out of her mind on the holidays."

"Christ, I hate the fucking holidays," said Vinnie, who

glanced at himself in a wall mirror and carefully patted his toupee so that it covered the bald spot on his forehead. "Angie wants me to come over but I told her I'm going to be with Nicholas, Ruby and Carla. Maybe I can go over later for a drink. Otherwise, she might be alone. I feel bad for her, but what the fuck can I do?"

16

MY SON IS MISSING

November 1988
Boston, Massachusetts

Vinnie Merlino was a wild man when he touched down at Boston's Logan International Airport and found out Nick was missing. He slammed the pay phone receiver so hard it broke into two pieces and hung limply from the metal-shielded wire. He had hoped to spend a few days relaxing in Florida after meeting with General Sanchez in Puerto Rico, and he had done just that, but suddenly the static from the homefront was giving him a migraine.

After interrogating Ruby, he burst into the apartment he still occasionally shared with his wife, Angie, and accused her of meddling in his affairs. But neither woman knew where Nick had gone or why he wasn't in Providence.

Several thoughts crossed Vinnie's mind as he went into panic mode. Did one of his enemies kidnap the boy as an act of revenge? If so, would they harm Nick, or worse?

All his cars were accounted for – the Lincoln, the Bugatti, the Caddy -- and Nick hadn't contacted any of the usual drivers to request a ride.

Vinnie went into overdrive and tore apart the bedroom in Ruby's apartment where Nick slept. He looked for items that might be missing, anything to provide a clue to the boy's disappearance. It hurt when he realized he didn't know Nick very well, nor did he have a clear picture of the boy's clothing or other possessions. It was Ruby who noticed the blue backpack, the kind that could be used for a two-week hiking and camping adventure, was gone from its spot at the foot of the bed.

A flurry of phone calls dispatched men to train and bus stations around Providence where a photo of Nick was shown to various ticket agents and other personnel. Vinnie also called in favors with a few local police officers and they, in turn, reached out to their State Police contacts to learn whether any of the troopers had spotted a 15-year-old boy hitchhiking alone in the rain.

That night, Vinnie was inconsolable and everyone gave him wide berth. He drank several bourbons on an empty stomach and at one point punched a hole in the plaster wall of the apartment. Ruby swept up the white dust and broken bits of sheetrock, but no word arrived about Nick.

Vinnie had a suspicion Nick might head back to the vineyard to see his girlfriend, Isabella. He ordered two of his best men to head upstate to watch the property and call him immediately if they spotted Nick. He also called Hope Cooper, allowing the phone to ring more than twenty times, but nobody picked up and no answering machine clicked on to take a message.

Boiling inside, he ripped the phone from the wall and hurled it across the room.

Vinnie put on an overcoat and walked to his Federal Hill office at a quick clip. He knew these rock-bottom moments of despair could be dangerous, causing him to act without thinking. In such times he'd often mull over a list of those who had somehow wronged him, after which he'd think of ways to even the score.

The list inside his head rolled like a slot machine and stopped at the name Percy Myles, a wiseguy wannabe who'd served time for burglary and spent most of his days drinking in the dive bars along the Providence waterfront.

The way Vinnie heard it from several witnesses, Myles had drunkenly announced to a packed crowd at his favorite strip club that Ruby Salerno was an exotic-dancing whore, adding it was doubtful Vinnie Merlino was the father of her baby because too many others had been riding down that road around the same time.

Vinnie reached for the bottle of bourbon in his desk drawer and took a long swig. He summoned two trusted associates and together they waited until Myles left the grubby bar where he had played Keno for three hours.

It was well past midnight when they whacked him on the head with a blackjack, tossed him into the car trunk and drove to a boarded-up warehouse where stolen goods were routinely stored.

The two lackeys tied Myles to a chair with rope and duct tape and stuffed a dirty rag in his mouth. Vinnie put two fingers beneath the man's chin and lifted it, looking him squarely in the eyes.

"Do you like to drink?"

Myles' eyes grew wide.

"Percy, I asked you a question. You spend a lot of time in the bars. Do you like to drink?"

Myles hunched his shoulders and grunted, pulling against the ropes that bound him to the chair.

"That's good. Because we're going to do a little drinking here tonight."

Myles watched attentively as Vinnie filled a tumbler with equal parts bourbon and green automotive antifreeze.

"Do you know why they call me Cocktails?"

Myles shook his head affirmatively, his eyes filled with apprehension.

"It's because I enjoy making them, special ones for special people. Now drink."

Vinnie yanked out the rag and pressed the rim of the glass against the man's mouth. Myles locked his jaw but one of Vinnie's associates pried his teeth open and inserted a wooden stick. Vinnie pushed back the man's neck and poured the concoction. When Myles tried to spit it out, Vinnie covered his mouth with the rag, forcing him to swallow.

"You're a loudmouth punk. I understand you had some not so nice things to say about my girl Ruby. I heard you even mentioned my baby daughter Carla."

Myles immediately understood what this torture was all about. He planned to run home when it was over, force himself to vomit, and drink a gallon of milk to coat his stomach. He'd heard Vinnie was crazy but he just had to get through it.

"A man like you must get very thirsty after telling so many lies," said Vinnie, holding up a clear shot glass so that the overhead light shown through it. He filled the glass mostly with drain cleaner and added a dash of anisette.

"It's cocktail time again. Better drink up," Vinnie said, forcing the caustic liquid down the man's throat while his associates stood behind Myles and held the wooden stick in place. "I think the anisette is a nice touch."

Myles coughed and moaned, choking as he wriggled in the chair.

"Sounds like you have something stuck in your throat. Maybe we should try some bleach to break up the clog," said Vinnie, twisting the cap off a plastic quart jug of Clorox. "That's what my plumber always tells me."

Myles was gasping for breath. "Please don't," he said, the words garbled as his lips desperately worked to expel the wooden stick. His eyes bulged, his chin sunk to his chest as a foamy substance drooled from his lips.

"I'd say that was his last call," said Vinnie, chuckling at his own humor. "Let's get rid of this useless piece of shit."

17

LOOSE LIPS WILL GET YOU KILLED

November 1988
Boston, Massachusetts

Agent Sally Parker's desk phone began ringing minutes after the FBI got word of what had been found behind a waterfront nightclub in the nearby city of Lynn. She sensed the victim was somehow related to the investigation into Vinnie Merlino's plan to take over underworld activities in Cuba.

Agent Parker was scribbling furiously with a pencil on a yellow legal notepad, the receiver cradled between her neck and shoulder. Hannah heard her repeat the words *Lynnway, hog-tied, in the car trunk, stolen, shit, god dammit.* Parker snapped the pencil between her fingers.

"What's that all about?"

Agent Parker's typically cheerful face bore an expression of deep concern as she looked across the desk at Hannah. "We got a body in the trunk of a stolen car. It's parked behind an abandoned nightclub off the Lynnway in Lynn. Looks like an OC hit.

The State Police from the Essex County DA's office are already on scene. We need to go now."

"I had the feeling something like this was going to happen," said Hannah, who was on her feet in an instant. "It was too quiet."

Before joining the CIA, she had worked as a State Police homicide and major crimes investigator in Suffolk County, a jurisdiction that included Boston and some surrounding cities and towns. She'd been to several grisly murder scenes and knew what to expect. Three of the killers in those cases were serving life sentences because she relentlessly tracked them down. Such extraordinary police work had earned her a stack of commendations and promotions but caused friction with her co-workers, who were either plagued with professional jealousy or simply male, and thus disapproving of a woman among the department's top investigators. She wasn't allowed into the boys' club.

Slipping into her shoulder holster and an insulated navy blue windbreaker with the letters FBI prominently stenciled on the back, Agent Parker was eager to leave. Hannah was right behind her as they bolted for the elevator that would take them to the gray, unmarked cruiser parked beneath the bureau's office in Government Center. Her clothing bore no agency letters or affiliations.

The troopers on scene were surprised to see an FBI agent approach. Agent Parker flashed her credentials and ducked beneath the yellow crime scene tape. Hannah followed close behind. She didn't offer to show ID and nobody asked. The less people who knew the CIA had agents involved in the anti-organized crime strike force, the better.

The trunk of the battered and rusted Oldsmobile Delta 88 was open. A man's grotesquely twisted body lay in the trunk, the tightly-cinched rope around his neck creating a web that extended behind his back to his bound wrists and ankles.

Hannah understood immediately how death had occurred.

As the victim stretched to relieve the discomfort, the ropes pulled tighter. The victim unintentionally strangled himself but was helpless to avoid it, which was precisely the intention of those who hog-tied him. It was standard procedure for many under-world hits.

"Poor bastard," said Agent Parker. "Such an awful way to go."

"I can't imagine how it must have felt, being all alone in the dark trunk, and knowing you were killing yourself and there was nothing you could do about it," said Hannah. "The people who do this sort of thing are so sick. Sadistic."

The trussed victim was clad in faded bluejeans, beat-up work boots, and a Boston Red Sox sweatshirt, its hood nestled atop his shoulders. He appeared to be in his twenties, maybe early thirties, though it was hard to tell because his face was bloated.

The troopers at the scene had no ID on the victim and wouldn't until the fingerprints were processed. The Oldsmobile Delta 88 was unregistered and likely stolen, as were the license plates. Agent Parker leaned into the trunk, holding a handker-chief over her nose. She wanted a closer look at the victim's face. Although it was November, the decomposing body gave off a stomach-wrenching stench. It was very possible the victim had been hog-tied elsewhere and left to die, the car with its stolen license plates later driven to the shadowy lot behind the aban-doned Lynn nightclub where the weeds grew taller than most men.

A forensic team arrived and began gathering equipment from the State Police van while a department photographer took pictures of the victim from all angles, the car, and the overall location.

Thankfully none of the troopers from the Essex County DA's office recognized Hannah. Otherwise she likely would have received a cold reception and some vile remarks for having reported and ended the career of a corrupt FBI agent who had supplied Irish mobsters with vital police information during an international search operation.

Agent Parker nudged Hannah toward their cruiser. "Let's got out of here," she said.

As they walked away, one of the troopers shouted, "Too much for you ladies?"

"Don't look back. Don't say anything," Agent Parker whispered to Hannah. "They don't deserve a response."

But Hannah couldn't resist. "We're just grateful you got here before we did," she said sarcastically. "Don't know what we would have done without you."

Once inside the cruiser, Agent Parker calmly radioed the FBI dispatcher to say she was returning to headquarters to file an incident report. She returned the microphone to its clip on the dashboard and then burst into tears.

Hannah remained silent as she waited for Agent Parker to regain control of her emotions.

"I know him."

"Who?"

"The victim. His name is Anthony Balducci. People on the street call him Tony Bags because he went to prison a few years ago for selling bags of heroin in East Boston."

"So who killed him? And why?"

Agent Parker dabbed her eyes with a tissue. "I don't know for sure, but he was one of our informants. He was a snitch. A month after he was released, he got caught in an undercover sting. Same deal. Selling bags. He definitely didn't want to go back to prison so we gave him an option."

Hannah wasn't surprised. Such arrangements were commonly made by law enforcement, especially at the federal level.

Agent Parker explained that Tony's older brother, Reno, was murdered a couple of years earlier. Stabbed to death with an icepick at a campground in New Hampshire. He had been hanging with a tough biker crowd. There was no telling what might have led to the stabbing. Could have been nothing more than a fistfight that turned serious.

"In Tony's case, everybody will know it was a hit. Word on the street was that he owed money to Nunzio Carlucci," she said. "Tony was a junkie. He spent most days figuring how to get enough heroin to shoot in his veins, not worrying about how to repay his debts."

Hannah remained quiet. Such savage street violence depressed her, which was part of reason she became a cop. She wanted to do her part to stop it.

"We'll ask to see the 302 file on Tony Bags when we get back to the office," said Agent Parker, referring to the highly-guarded, confidential files on each of the bureau's thousands of informants. The 302s were mostly transcripts of interviews. "Maybe something will pop up and give us a lead."

Lost in deep thought, Hannah thrust out her lower lip and raised it so that it covered the upper. "Could this Tony Bags have heard something he wasn't supposed to and passed it along?"

"That's always a possibility, but even if he did, it might not be in the file. We'll have to talk to Pete. He was Tony's handler."

18

NOT EXACTLY A HOMECOMING

NOVEMBER 1988

FINGER LAKES REGION, UPSTATE NEW YORK

Hope Cooper was stunned and undeniably thrilled to see Nick standing outside the front door. It was six days before Thanksgiving. The mid-morning sun was basking the hills around the lake in a warm glow, the November temperature unseasonably warm.

Hope pushed the door open and threw her arms around Nick, hugging him tightly. "Oh my god. What are you doing here? How are you, honey? Let's go in the house."

Nick stepped inside and glanced around the familiar front room, as though he expected to see Rocco lounging on the well-worn couch. He heard noises coming from the rear of the house.

Hope's husband, Gary Schneider, poked his head out from behind the archway to the kitchen. He was peeling an apple with a jackknife. "Hey! We weren't expecting you but we're glad you're here."

"Set down your backpack," said Hope, struggling to pull the straps off his shoulders. She took two steps backward so that she could scan him head to toe. "You look tired. Come sit down. Is everything all right?"

Nick's eyes were glassy but he quickly dried them with his jacket sleeve. "I just thought I'd stop by," he said, as if he were routinely traveling through the area and had decided to visit some friends.

"You must be cold. Would you like a cup of coffee? Gary, get him some coffee. There's a fresh pot perking."

Before he could answer, Hope wrapped her arms around him again and pulled him close, tears welling in her eyes.

Nick's shoulders flinched with emotion, making it difficult to swallow. Once under control he twisted away from Hope's embrace and set down his backpack. He didn't know what to say. They sat at the wood plank kitchen table where a steaming cup of coffee was set in front of Nick along with a waxy cardboard carton of light cream.

Hope looked suddenly fearful. "Do the people you're living with know you're here?"

Nick sipped the hot coffee. "Not really," he said.

"Then won't they be looking for you?"

"Probably. I just didn't want to be there any longer. I wanted to be here."

Gary nervously picked at a scab on his lower lip and poured himself a cup of coffee. Hope stepped behind Nick and rested her hands on his shoulders, massaging them lightly. Nick was shaking. He turned his head sideways and buried his face in her sweater.

"So you just disappeared? I'm sure they're very worried about you, honey," Hope said. "Do they know where you are?"

"They're not my family. To me, they're just Vinnie and Angie and Ruby. I don't know them and I don't want to get to know them. I don't want to live in Providence. I want to live here."

"It's not a matter of what you want. A judge has ordered it," Gary said matter-of-factly. "You've got to do what the court says."

"I know. But that doesn't make it right. And I miss Isabella. Has she been around? I tried calling her."

Hope and Gary exchanged uneasy glances and Nick got the feeling they were not going to tell him the truth. "She comes by on her horse now and then, but not like when you were here," Hope said.

Nick looked around for signs of Rocco. An expensive two-piece suit that definitely was not his style hung from a wall hook near the pantry. The shiny material was draped inside a clear plastic bag with a dry-cleaning tag stapled near the top. A pair of expensive leather shoes sat on the floor directly beneath it.

Nick finished the coffee and pushed the cup toward the center of the table. "Thank you. I should probably go," he said, feeling like a stranger who'd knocked on someone's door to get out of the storm. "I just wanted to see you and say hello."

"Oh, Nick. I wish you could stay. I want you to stay," said Hope, sobbing as she again wrapped her arms around him. "We love you. But you're going to be in a lot of trouble if you don't tell somebody in Providence that you're here."

"My so-called mother and father don't even live together. Vinnie got his girlfriend Ruby pregnant and she just had a baby. I've been living with them."

"I'm so sorry," said Hope, wiping the tears from her eyes. "We haven't been given much information even though we've asked. If there was something we could do, we would. We tried. There's nothing we can do until you turn sixteen, and even then, this man might fight it. He can appeal, which could take years. And we've heard he's a very scary person with lots of important connections."

Gary remained silent and remote, as though calculating the odds on how Nick's presence might somehow bring more chaos into their lives.

At that moment Rocco burst through the front door. Isabella was right behind him, long blonde hair swaying, their laughter filling the room. Nick recognized Isabella's bubbly giggles, a sound he treasured, and suddenly his chest felt tight. He couldn't inhale a full breath. Paralyzed by the sound, he just stood there, eyes wide, jaw slightly agape.

"Nick! What are you doing here? What a surprise," said Isabella, enthusiastically slinging both arms around his neck and hugging him tightly.

Nick was a statue. Cement. He felt like saying, I'll bet it's a surprise, considering you're here with Rocco having a great time. Instead he smiled half-heartedly and said, "I was just leaving."

Isabella's expression crumpled, eyebrows turned down, face scrunched. "Can somebody tell me what's going on?" She glanced at Hope and Gary for a clue. They both cast their eyes at the floor.

Nick hefted his backpack onto his shoulders and clipped the waist strap. Isabella grabbed his arm. "Where are you going?"

"Not sure. Just not back to Providence," he said, observing she was not wearing the turquoise ring. She had promised to always wear it. So much for promises, he thought.

"Don't go," said Hope, stepping forward and stretching her arms like a street crossing guard to prevent Nick from leaving. "We love you. I love you. You're everything to us." When he brushed past her, she let her arms fall to her sides and sank into one of the kitchen chairs, where she began to weep.

Isabella set a hand on Hope's shoulder in a show of sympathy and solidarity. "Nick, what the fuck is going on? Why are you leaving? Didn't you just get here? And now you've upset Hope," she said.

"If he wants to leave, let him," Rocco shouted from the living room.

Isabella snarled. "Be quiet, Rocco."

"Yeah. Fuck you, Rocco," said Nick. "Nobody needs your shit around here. You should go back to Providence and those gangsters who raised you."

Hope curled her fingers and pressed them against her lips,

deeply perplexed by the goings on. "Please stop, Nick. Maybe everyone can be friends when all of this gets straightened out."

Rocco took a few steps into the kitchen.

"Go back into the front room," Hope commanded.

Nick got himself into fighting position, a three-point stance despite the heavy backpack. "Bring it on, Rocco," he said. "I'd like nothing better than to beat your ass to a pulp."

Rocco didn't move. Isabella yanked at the backpack, trying to pull it off. "Nick, talk to me," she said. "You can't just walk away."

"Why not? Seems like you're doing just fine without me."

Nick looked at Hope and then at Isabella. "I always thought this was my home. I guess it isn't anymore."

A dairy farmer and his wife gave Nick a ride in their rattling Chevy van to the outskirts of Syracuse. They tried to make polite conversation but Nick couldn't bring himself to talk. His insides were churning. He felt lost and sick. He imagined Rocco touching Isabella and it made him want to puke.

It was cold outdoors, the temperature hovering around freezing. Nick tugged his watch cap down to just above his eyebrows as he climbed out of the van and took up position on the road shoulder near the New York Thruway tollbooth. He didn't have any plans or any real destination in mind, but knew he couldn't stay on the vineyard.

A long-haul trucker gave him a lift almost all the way to Boston, depositing him at the intersection of I-90 and I-495 just west of the city. The trucker had barely spoken and smoked unfiltered Camel cigarettes nonstop. Occasionally the man chatted into his CB radio microphone to ask about the location of any bears, which was code for State Police cruisers. He also asked his fellow truckers about traffic accidents and weather conditions along the route. Nick tried to sleep in the truck cab but mostly he listened to music on his Sony Discman. He was glad he remembered to toss a dozen CDs in his backpack. He felt half-crazed by his emotions when he got out of the truck and began hitchhiking south toward Providence.

When Nick showed up at Ruby's apartment, she quickly pulled him inside. "Your father is going to kill you," she said. "He's been out of his mind looking for you. Where have you been?"

Nick stood silently, still wearing his backpack, his clothing drenched.

Ruby turned a full circle as though unsure where she should go or what she should do. "I've got to call him and tell him you're safe," she said, hurrying to the kitchen phone.

Nick shrugged, shuffled to his bedroom and set his backpack at the foot of the bed, then collapsed on the mattress in his wet and soiled clothes. Just before falling off to sleep, he heard Ruby tell Vinnie on the phone that Nick was home and unharmed.

"He's coming right over," she shouted, cursing herself for waking baby Carla who immediately began to cry. Seconds later, the phone rang.

Nick assumed it was Vinnie.

"For you," said Rudy. "It's not your father."

Nick seemed surprised. "Who is it?"

"A girl."

Nick rolled off the bed and grabbed the receiver. "Who is this?"

Isabella began firing questions like a machine gun. "Who do you think it is? What's wrong with you? Why didn't you stay? Why did you just leave without saying a word? What's going on with you?"

"I didn't want to interfere with you and Rocco."

"I don't like Rocco."

"But you hang out with him."

"Not in the way you think. He's just a friend, a new kid at school. That's all."

Nick felt betrayed, although he truly had nothing solid on which to base those suspicions. "Goodbye, Isabella. Have a nice life," he said as he hung up the phone.

The phone rang again but he told Ruby not to answer it.

"What if it's Vinnie?"

"Don't answer it," he growled.

As though on cue, Vinnie opened the door and marched toward Nick. "Where the fuck have you been?"

"Nowhere special. I thought I'd take a road trip."

"A road trip? You aren't old enough to drive."

"I hitched."

"And where did you go?"

"I went to Newport, and then to Mystic. The aquarium was so cool. Have you ever been there? Lots of dolphins."

"Sounds like a lot of bullshit. Where did you sleep?"

"At a motel just outside of Newport. It was really nice. And cheap."

"What was the name of it?"

"I can't remember."

"Where's your receipt?"

"I didn't ask for one."

Vinnie's face was crimson and sweat glistened on his forehead. His neck jowls quivered as he spoke. "Tell me where you really went."

"I just told you."

Vinnie's slap was so forceful it knocked Nick to the floor.

"Stop, Vinnie. Don't hurt him," said Ruby, rushing out of the back bedroom with the baby in her arms. "He's just a boy. He misses his girlfriend."

Nick was bleeding from the nose, the drops forming dark spots on his shirt. "You happy now?"

"We'll talk about this later," said Vinnie, glancing in the hallway mirror to adjust his toupee. "I'm glad you're back home safe. You should get something to eat."

19

THE SNITCH FILES

NOVEMBER 1988
BOSTON, MASSACHUSETTS

FBI Agent Pete Barba never relished opening the bureau's FD-302 files. He was among a select team at the FBI's Boston field office who held a key to the cabinet and it was a responsibility he didn't take lightly. He knew well that any leak could result in the immediate death of the confidential informant. But in this case, the informant was already dead.

"We wouldn't ask if we didn't think it was important," said FBI Agent Sally Parker. "But both Hannah and I got the feeling Tony Bags' death was somehow linked to Vinnie Merlino."

Barba cleared his throat before speaking. "I didn't share this because I wasn't sure it was relevant," he said. "As a member of the strike force, I wanted nothing more than to tell you all Anthony Balducci didn't die in vain, that he provided us with enough vital information to put a hose to Vinnie Merlino's aspirations. But that just isn't the case."

Barba opened a small vault and returned with a manila file

folder. "Here it is," he said, tossing it toward Hannah and Agent Parker. "Take a look, but you can't leave the room with it."

Hannah asked, "Aren't these files stored on your computer?"

"No. If our system got breached, it would be a bloodbath."

"I see," she said, appreciating the reason. Over the years, she'd seen too many police files and pieces of evidence compromised or simply go missing without explanation, starting with her days as a college campus security intern.

Agent Parker fanned through the notes in the file, an elegantly manicured fingernail tracing back and forth along the notes. When her index finger suddenly stopped, Hannah and Agent Barba focused their attention and waited in suspense.

"Pete, it states here that the informant was often seen over the past six months on the East Boston waterfront in the company of people with links to the IRA," said Agent Parker. "Doesn't that increase the possibility that gun shipments were involved?"

Barba was willing to acknowledge only a slim connection. "Even if Tony Bags was somehow involved in gun-running, what does that have to do with Vinnie Merlino?"

Hannah burst into the conversation. "Maybe he was helping Merlino equip an army? One getting one ready to invade Cuba."

Barba rubbed his chin between his thumb and forefinger. "We need more intel on what's aboard certain boats in that neighborhood, but no judge is going to give us a search warrant unless we have probable cause."

Hannah smiled sheepishly. "I'll deny I ever said this, but sometimes it's more effective to just go have a look without asking for permission."

Both FBI agents returned expressions of incredulity. "Maybe the organization you work for operates like that, but here at the bureau we still abide by the law," said Agent Barba in a tone that carried a slight reprimand.

Hannah rolled her eyes. Agent Parker sensed Hannah was

thinking about the turned FBI agent who almost succeeded in defeating their search for the Boston Butcher.

"Pete's partially right," said Parker. "Most of the time we try to stay within the law, but there have been occasions when the bureau has stepped outside those lines. Wouldn't you agree, Pete?"

"But those occasions are very rare," Barba grudgingly conceded. "And always with the right intention."

Hannah let the agent's comment pass. She knew he was a loyal FBI man who had difficulty saying anything negative about the bureau, even if the facts suggested otherwise.

The next day, Hannah and Decker set up surveillance overlooking the East Boston waterfront. Amid huge tankers and freighters were dozens of smaller fishing boats, mostly draggers and purse seiners in the forty to sixty-foot range. Some were seaworthy enough to carry a shipment of weapons for great distances along the coast or to a larger ship waiting offshore.

Although Decker had lived in an East Boston apartment when he returned home from deployment in the Middle East, he hadn't maintained a strong list of neighborhood contacts and his ties had weakened since moving into a downtown condo with Hannah. Nemo's Bar was the one place where he still felt connected, mostly because he'd spent hours drinking there prior to his recruitment by the CIA. He wondered if Bubby was still bartending.

Decker walked into Nemo's alone, hoping Bubby would be pouring drinks, open and friendly. He purposefully didn't bring Hannah along because her beauty often made other women uncomfortable.

Sure enough, Bubby was wisecracking as she topped off drafts for three sullen fishermen. She was still wearing her trademark *Flashdance* bandana. She immediately recognized Decker and inadvertently allowed beer to spill over the glass she was holding beneath the tap.

Bubby batted her eyelashes. "See what you do to me?"

Decker flashed a smile. "Good to see you, Bubby."

"You haven't been around in what, close to a year, maybe more."

"Been out of town," said Decker, getting comfortable on the bar stool. "But it's good to be back, especially here. Nemo's was like my second home." He ordered a Bombay gin, tonic and lime.

"Well, that part of you hasn't changed," said Bubby, who rattled off the local goings on, filling Decker in on mutual acquaintances, marriages, deaths and, of course, arrests. When talk turned to the street, Decker asked about Tony Bags. In a hushed tone Bubby said she'd heard about how he had ended up in the trunk of a car in Lynn.

"Never did learn to keep his mouth shut," she said, wiping lipstick from the rim of a washed wineglass before sliding it into the overhead rack.

"Looks like he may have ticked off the wrong person."

"Nunzio Carlucci," she whispered. "At least that's what people are saying. No matter what, you don't cross that guy, because he'll find you and you'll end up like Tony Bags. Carlucci is a cement shoes kind of guy."

"What do you think he opened his mouth about?"

"Who knows? Could have been bookmaking, loansharking, drug dealing, or maybe something to do with guns. Every time he was high, he'd talk about seeing boats down at the dock filled with more guns than the soldiers had in World War II."

Decker ordered another Bombay. "Maybe he was hallucinating. Who was Bags hanging out with? I don't think he was part of a crew."

"No. Bags was usually alone. Once in a while he'd come in with a girl named Anita. We called her Anita Fix because she was always saying she needed a fix. Get it? Anita Fix?"

Decker chuckled. "I got it. So is Anita still around?"

"Last I heard she was homeless, living in some cardboard box in the North End. Why do you care?"

"I don't. Just seems like a waste of a life. I know people who might be able to help her."

"That's nice of you, Decker. I recall Bags saying she slept most nights under the Central Artery."

It didn't take Decker long to find Anita. She was asleep under the Southeast Expressway beneath three tattered blankets and atop a pile of rags. Hypodermic syringes, condoms and cigarette butts littered the area. At least four other bodies were asleep nearby, though with their heavy clothing it was difficult to tell if they were male or female.

Anita looked frightened when Decker nudged her awake. He said he was an old friend of Tony Bags and that they'd gone to high school together. Anita's hands were shaking from the cold temperature or her need for drugs, probably both.

"I need a fix," she said, peering out at Decker from beneath the blankets, her face smudged with ash and grime.

Decker started to laugh but caught himself. "I'll give you money for that, but first tell me about Tony Bags. We were good pals and I want to know who killed him."

Anita's eyes filled with fear. She began fidgeting with her thin gloves. "I don't know anything," she said.

"But you were his closest friend, the one person he spent time with every day."

"They were after him."

"Who was after him?"

"Nunzio."

"Nunzio Carlucci?"

Anita shook her head.

"For what?"

Anita looked left and right before speaking, pulling her head beneath the blankets like a turtle seeking shelter in its shell. Her voice was barely audible, forcing Decker to kneel and lean closer. The blankets were damp and smelled of vomit and cigarette smoke.

"Bags was down on the waterfront," she said. "He had passed out and when he woke up, there were guys loading guns onto a boat. Lots of guns."

"And?"

"He wasn't supposed to see that."

"But they knew he did?"

"You got it. They punched him in the face and kicked him in the stomach, made him promise not to say nothing to nobody. It took me a long time to stop his nose from bleeding. I think they broke it."

"And he tried not to do that, tried not to talk about what he'd seen, but something slipped out?"

Again Anita nodded, her face emanating a profound sadness.

"Did he tell you about the guns?"

"He told all of us. We were sitting around a heating grate, trying to stay warm, and people were telling stories like they always do. I don't know if any of them were true. Probably not. But Bags told a story about the boats and the guns."

"How do you know Nunzio Carlucci wanted him dead?"

"Because two guys came to get him and brought him over to a car. A man rolled down the window and I heard Bags apologize. He was crying real bad when he came back. They told him his day was coming and that it was too late to do anything about it. It was right after that they beat him up."

"You think he died because he told a story?"

Anita gazed up at Decker with an expression that said she agreed.

"And all he said was, *I saw guns being loaded onto a boat*?"

"Something like that. He heard the fishermen talking. They

were taking the guns to a bigger boat, some kind of ship that was headed to Miami or somewhere down south."

"He specifically mentioned Miami?"

Anita didn't answer. She yanked the outermost blanket to her neck and let her chin sink into her chest. "I need to get high."

Decker knew she was done talking. "Let's talk again tomorrow, Anita. I need to find out who did this to Bags." He tucked two twenties in the front pocket of her overcoat and disappeared into the night, wondering if she'd ever find the money.

20

THAT'S NOT A TURKEY

November 1988
Finger Lakes Region, New York

Hope Cooper was drying dishes with a cloth when Rocco approached the back door to the farmhouse, holding the vineyard's celebrity rooster upside down by its legs. The burly bird was limp.

"Oh my lord, what happened to Foghorn?"

Rocco was grinning. "Now we don't have to buy a turkey," he said. "We can have chicken."

Hope dropped the plate she was holding and it shattered into hundreds of fragments on the kitchen floor. Her mouth hung open, unsure whether what she was seeing was for real. "You did this?"

"I was trying to help out with the holiday dinner," Rocco said without a trace of sarcasm.

Hope yanked the limp bird from Rocco's grip and hugged it, bursting into tears as she quietly uttered its name. "Foghorn...Oh, my old friend. You won't be telling us to rise and shine any more."

Rocco pretended he was mystified. "What's wrong, Mom?"

"You did this on purpose. You're sick," said Hope, glaring at the boy. "And don't call me Mom. No child of mine would ever do something like this."

"I had no idea the rooster was your pet. I thought it was just another animal around here, like the goats and chickens. A girl at school told me her family had a pet pig for five years and then they ate it. They turned it into hotdogs and sausages and bacon."

Hope laid Foghorn's body on the kitchen counter. She rolled a terrycloth dish towel and placed it beneath the bird's head like a pillow.

"Get out of my kitchen," she shouted.

Rocco raised his arms in the air as though being held at gunpoint and slowly backed out the door, closing it behind him. Hope pulled six fresh flowers from a vase on the kitchen table, part of an assortment she'd purchased earlier in the week at a supermarket in Ithaca. She arranged them near Foghorn, three long stems on each side. Still shocked by what she knew was an act of malice, she wanted to call Gary at the funeral home but couldn't remember the phone number, even though it was one she used almost daily. She couldn't think. Her mind had gone blank. She gently stroked the rooster's colorful feathers. Until that moment, she had not realized the bird's neck was broken. She sat at the kitchen table and cried until her eyes were bleary and she was overcome with the desire to sleep.

When her husband arrived home in late afternoon, he was startled to see Foghorn dead and spread out on the kitchen counter. He found Hope in bed curled into a fetal position.

"Rocco did it," she said.

Gary tensed. "I'm going to bust his head," he said.

Hope sat up on the edge of the bed and wiped her eyes. "He claims he was trying to help get ready for Thanksgiving dinner."

"Bullshit."

"I know it is. But what should we do? He's my son but I don't feel like his mother."

It was two days before Thanksgiving. In keeping with the Cooper's family tradition, which Gary Schneider had embraced upon marrying Hope, dinner invitations to select neighbors and a handful of regional grape growers and vinters had been sent out weeks earlier.

The Marceau family, which included their daughter Isabella and her two younger sisters, was among those invited.

Rocco had disappeared after the rooster's death and the reaction he had received from Hope. He didn't return to the farmhouse that night. Hope and Gary were drinking coffee in the kitchen when Rocco showed up the following afternoon. Neither adult acknowledged his presence as he slowly slunk toward his bedroom.

Hope was nervous about how Rocco would behave around their guests at the holiday dinner. She decided to abandon the freeze-him-out strategy and instead invite him to assist with the food preparation. She and Gary had already buried Foghorn in a shallow grave near the chicken coop where the rooster often stood to show off his most enthusiastic crowing.

When Hope knocked on the bedroom door, Rocco was spread across his bed, playing the new Super Mario Bros 2 video game that had arrived by mail the previous week. The name Angie Merlino, accompanied by a P.O. box number in Rhode Island, was scrawled on the package as the return address.

"What is it?"

"I was hoping you could help me prepare some of the food for tomorrow."

"I'm going to Ithaca. One of the kids I know from school has his driver's license."

"And what are you going to do there?"

"See a movie."

Hope wanted to keep the borderline conversation going. "Which one?"

"*Big.*"

Although she already knew the answer to the question, she asked, "Is that the new one with Tom Hanks?"

"That's the one."

"I've heard it's very good."

"How would I know? It came out in June and it's finally playing here in the sticks. If I was back in Providence, I would have already seen it."

"Well, if you can't help with dinner, I hope you plan on being at the table. We have a lot of nice people coming. Isabella will be here with her family."

Hope felt guilty providing that information. It was as though she had betrayed Nick. But she wanted to do everything possible to ensure the holiday dinner was enjoyable for everyone and if Isabella's presence could lessen Rocco's abrasiveness, then so be it.

The mere mention of Isabella rekindled Rocco's interest in the festivities. "I can help you in the kitchen before my ride gets here," he said, not revealing his passion for cooking that had been dampened when Vinnie poked fun at him for wearing an apron.

As they peeled a mound of potatoes, Hope described the small Thanksgiving Day parade conducted each year in the village by the grape growers, winemakers and sparse social organizations.

"It's so much fun," she said. "It usually starts at midmorning. The growers line up their tractors and wagons, and the 4-H Club kids bring goats and sheep on their float. The Boy Scouts and Girl Scouts march. Of course, so do the veterans. Some people ride horses or use them to pull buckboards. And there's music, not anything like a marching band, but a group of local musicians volunteers every year and they play popular songs."

"Sounds like a blast," said Rocco, rolling his eyes, his tone blatantly sarcastic, although deep inside he wished his previous Thanksgivings had been homey rather than out on the town.

"Well, it might not be like the big city. But we all love it."

"I'm sure it'll be great," he said. "It's just that I'm used to a different kind of Thanksgiving. My father..." As soon as he realized he had referred to Vinnie Merlino, he stopped talking.

"Please tell me what you would normally do for Thanksgiving," said Hope.

"Vinnie and Angie would make hotel reservations. We'd go to New York to watch the Macy's Parade."

"Well, I guess it would be hard to top that," she said. "But you've got a knack for peeling potatoes so I'm assuming you helped prepare dinners in Rhode Island."

Rocco didn't respond. His mind wandered back to the many times he'd helped Angie in the kitchen, stirring the polenta, frying the breaded veal cutlets, laughing together when the scallions made his eyes water.

"Did you argue about how to cook the turkey? Gary always wants to boil it in oil or do some new-fangled thing. But I'm old-fashioned. I like an oven-baked turkey with the stuffing inside. What about you?"

"I really don't know anything about cooking turkeys. After the parade, we'd spend the night in the city. We usually ate at restaurants. Sometimes my father's friends..." Again, Rocco caught himself. "I meant, Vinnie. Sometimes Vinnie's friends would join us."

"Well, that sounds very nice," said Hope. "Preparing a big dinner for lots of people can be stressful. I imagine it would be very relaxing to just enjoy the company without all the other responsibilities."

"This is nice, too," said Rocco. "Maybe we can watch some of the parade on TV."

21

THANKS BUT NO THANKS

THANKSGIVING DAY 1988
PROVIDENCE, RHODE ISLAND

Vinnie showed up at Ruby's apartment carrying a pan of wedding soup his aging mother had cooked in preparation for Thanksgiving. The soup was among his favorite holiday dishes and he was looking forward to eating the tiny meatballs that floated in the broth.

Nick was locked in his room. Ruby looked distressed and haggard, her makeup smeared beneath eyes with dark circles. Baby Carla had cried most of the night so Ruby hadn't gotten much sleep. The turkey had burned in the oven. The mashed potatoes were overcooked into a gray mush. Ruby had tried to follow one of her aunt's recipes for stuffing but the outcome looked nothing like the picture in the cookbook. She wanted to cry.

Vinnie placed the soup pan on the stove and put his arms around Ruby, attempting to smother her with kisses. She made a slight effort to return his affection but she was exhausted and all out of passion. Besides, she felt unattractive and was almost certain she reeked of diaper ointment.

"Not now, Vinnie," she said. "Look at me. I'm a mess."

Vinnie was undeterred. His hands cupped her buttocks and he lifted her so that her swollen breasts pressed into his chest. When she barely responded, he set her down and pawed her bra, trying to slip his hand beneath it.

"Easy. They're sore," she said. "I'm nursing."

Vinnie grabbed her crotch. "Is this sore, too?"

"Please stop."

"What do you mean, please stop? You're my wife, for god's sake."

"We're not married, remember?"

"But we live together. We're a couple. You're the mother of my child."

Wiping the sweat from her brow with a dishcloth, she said, "I'm sorry. I've just had a rough twenty-four hours."

Vinnie's face showed disappointment. "What happened to my red hot Ruby? The girl I fell in love with?"

"That girl is tired today."

"How can you be tired? You're only twenty-six years old. What I'd give to be twenty-six. Even forty-six. And it's Thanksgiving, for Christ's sake. We gotta celebrate the holiday. Give thanks to the Pilgrims and those dumb fuck Indians who were kind enough to feed them."

Nick opened his bedroom door and stepped toward the kitchen. "Can't you ever think about anybody but yourself? Ruby needs some sleep."

Vinnie curled his fists but kept his arms at his side. "Maybe if you'd been out here to help in the kitchen, she wouldn't be so tired?"

"And where were you this morning? Out collecting from your loan sharks, or was it the numbers runners?"

"Listen to me, Buster. You're on thin ice around here after that shit you pulled," said Vinnie, pointing a menacing finger at Nick. "I want you back in school on Monday and no complaints. I don't want to hear a word from that fucking principal again about you being absent. You need to make some friends and get along. Try to fit in."

Nick inspected the food on the stovetop and in the oven. Ruby had definitely made a mess, but in the grand scheme of things it didn't seem like a big deal.

"The inside of the stuffing is still edible, and I can slice the turkey so that we won't taste any of burned parts," Nick said. "The mashed potatoes might be a lost cause, but if there's lettuce and tomatoes in the frig I can whip up a tossed salad."

Ruby hugged him. "You're a good kid, Nicky. I appreciate what you're trying to do."

"Jesus, he gets a hug but not me," said Vinnie, but the gesture seemed to calm him, as if it signified all was well on the home front. He reached for a bottle of Sangiovese, popped the cork and pulled three goblets from the cupboard. Carla began to cry in the bedroom.

Ruby pressed the palms of her hands to her face. "Shit. She's awake again. We're talking too loud."

Nick studied Ruby closely. She was only ten years older than him, but somehow seemed part of a different generation, a different universe. Maybe it was the bouffant hairdo or the heavy mascara. Or else it was the spiky heels, the cow-like gum chewing, or the frequent misuse of English words. It made him wonder what her childhood had been like and what sort of life she'd had up to the present.

"Is there anything else I can do to help?"

"No," said Ruby. "Carla is hungry and right now I'm the only one who can fix that."

Nick blushed. "I'll work on dinner," he said. "If nobody is starving, I'll make more mashed potatoes. It won't take long."

Vinnie poured himself a generous glass of wine. "You want a taste?"

"No thanks. I'll stick with water," Nick said.

"What? You don't like wine? You grew up on a vineyard. Didn't you tell me those pig farmers make some good vino?"

"Please don't start with the pig farmers again. They're good people. And yes, they make some excellent wine. I'm just not in the mood to drink."

Vinnie drained the glass and poured himself another. "Sangiovese is from Italy, not upstate New York. Try it. You'll taste the difference. If you're going to grow grapes, you gotta have the weather. In Italy, they have all the sunshine you need." He held out an empty goblet, poured a couple inches of wine and handed it to Nick, who had busied himself by peeling potatoes and washing pots and pans.

"No thanks," he said.

"God dammit," said Vinnie. "Hey, Ruby, I'm pouring you a glass of Sangiovese."

Carla began crying again. "Shhhhh! I just had her quiet," said Ruby. "I can't have any wine while I'm nursing."

"Jesus, what a dull party this turned out to be," Vinnie muttered to himself, but loud enough for everyone else to hear. "Nobody in this place likes to have fun."

Vinnie abruptly left the apartment when he learned there was no dessert and didn't return until after midnight. He was drunk and his tone was nasty. "Ruby, why don't you make me and Nicholas a turkey sandwich?"

"I'm tired, Vinnie. I want to go to bed."

"You want a sandwich, I'll make you one," said Nick. "Just let Ruby sleep."

Vinnie puffed his chest, though he seemed unsteady on his feet. "Ruby," he shouted. "Get your ass out here and make some sandwiches for me and my son."

Ruby walked shakily toward the kitchen, her nightgown on backward, though she didn't seem to notice.

"Go back to bed, Ruby. I'll take care of it," said Nick, steering the young woman back toward the master bedroom.

"Let her make the fuckin' sandwiches," said Vinnie. "I'm the fucking boss around here. She needs to learn her job."

Ruby turned in a circle as though she had no idea where she was standing. "I need to feed Carla," she said. "She's hungry."

Vinnie lurched toward Ruby and grabbed a fist full of her nightgown, clutching the material until it was tight to her chest. "Don't fuck with me, Ruby. Go feed that fuckin' kid and then come back and make me a sandwich."

Ruby was about to reply when Vinnie cuffed her on the side of the head, sending her staggering toward Carla's bedroom. She cupped a hand over her left ear, tears welling up in her eyes.

Nick set down the pan he was washing and went to Ruby's side.

"Don't," said Vinnie. "Leave it alone."

"You just hit her," he hissed, coming closer to Vinnie until he was an arm's length away.

Vinnie pushed a compact black handgun stiffly into Nick's chest. "One more step and you're my dead son," he said, his intense black eyes focused squarely on Nick.

An uncomfortable few seconds elapsed. Nick remained fixed, hands at his sides. "Shoot me and you'll have no son."

Vinnie kept the handgun pointed at Nick, but the swagger had gone out of his mood and he burst into wild laughter. "What a Thanksgiving this has been," he chortled. "I should have stayed out with the boys."

Shortly before 1 a.m., two uniformed police officers knocked on the door to Ruby's apartment. Neighbors had called to report a ruckus and what sounded like a woman screaming.

When the police officers questioned the victim, Ruby swore she had tripped and fallen down the stairs leading to the front entrance. She was just thankful she hadn't been holding Baby Carla or a hot tea kettle or a sharp knife when she so clumsily lost her balance.

Before the officers could radio the police station dispatcher with a report, Fingers Terranzetti arrived at the apartment. He knew both police officers and their families.

"Good evening, gentlemen," he said, setting his fedora on the kitchen counter and draping his overcoat on a chair before kneeling in front of where Ruby was seated. "You know how these things go," he said aloud. "Those steps can be very unsafe, but we don't want the building inspector down here."

Fingers stood and produced two white envelopes. "So please accept this as our gratitude for your coming down here on this cold night to make sure everything was all right."

Each envelope contained $500 cash. The police officers glanced at each other but remained still until one tucked the cash into his jacket pocket.

"Let's get out of here," he said to his partner, handing off the second envelope.

22

JUNGLE ATTRACTIONS

NOVEMBER 1988
BELIZE CITY, BELIZE

Decker followed the instructions Carrington gave him during their briefing at Langley. Dressed like a gringo tourist, he boarded a cheap commercial flight from Boston and after one layover landed in Belize City, where he began searching for the mercenary recruiter easily identifiable by a black patch over his right eye and a deformed left hand.

Carrington's orders were simple yet vague: use the alias Jared Malone, ex-Special Forces, complete with civilian passport showing recent travel to Europe and South America. Join the mercenaries as part of the anti-Castro force, learn the attack plan and relay that information to Langley. Also, if possible, prepare to eliminate Vinnie Merlino if he unexpectedly shows up during the operation and causes problems, but with the understanding no action should be taken unless instructed by Langley because the target could be of future use to the agency.

Decker did a quick head count. Twenty-four sweaty men and

women, dressed in an array of military-style clothing and a hodgepodge of reggae band T-shirts and ratty jeans, were sitting on a concrete wall near the Belize City swing bridge. Several were smoking cigars or cigarettes. The temperature was in the mid-eighties Fahrenheit, but the rainy season had already come to an end so the heat wasn't unpleasant. The pungent smell of marijuana blended with the tobacco. Decker wondered if this is what Brigade 2506 looked like as its paramilitary members trained in Guatemala before attempting to invade Cuba in 1961. He listened to learn what language most of them were speaking. Spanish was prevalent, as was the local dialect Kriol, but English was also heard, especially among the British and Australians.

Decker had shipped his weapons via a confidential carrier with ties to the Belize Defense Forces. He was skeptical about whether he'd ever see those familiar weapons again, but sure enough, two duffel bags bearing his confirmation number were stacked on a deuce-and-a-half military truck parked near the mouth of the river.

Out of habit, Decker immediately hauled the duffels to a private patch of grass behind a stand of trees and conducted an inventory. He smiled at the sight of his favorite Beretta 92FS semi-automatic handgun with silencer, a backup Glock 17 pistol, and a Heckler & Koch MP5 submachine gun. Decker knew whoever had handled his personal weapons shipment had some friends in the right places when he fully unzipped the second duffel and found a .50-cal. Barrett M82 sniper rifle, just like the one he'd lugged as an Army Ranger on countless missions throughout the Middle East and Central America. The rifle was protected by a hard travel case.

Although Decker was certainly glad to have his weapons in hand, he was surprised many of the men were unarmed. There was no sign of the small freighter Carrington told him would be anchored just beyond the shallow harbor. A row of long and narrow wooden skiffs fitted with outboard engines was hauled up on the sand. The locals were seated along the gunwales of the skiffs, casting their fishing lines into the harbor. The entire scene was laid back. It seemed the gun shipment had been delayed.

As Decker took in all the sights, sounds and smells around him, he soon surmised the three men standing nearest, talking and smoking at the bridge, had the sort of combat experience he recognized. None seemed willing to speak to him first, but Decker wasn't there to make friends. He wanted to explore connections and if possible find out who hired them for this dark ops mission. What had those men been told about the upcoming invasion, if anything? Or were they as yet uninformed about the details? Did any of them personally know Vinnie Merlino?

Decker decided he'd try to strike up a conversation with an Australian and a Brit who were wolfing down what appeared to be a limitless supply of sandwiches and fresh fruit pulled from a knapsack. He introduced himself as Jared Malone, ex-U.S. Special Forces.

The men gave their names as Chad Taylor and Trevor Rainsford. The tall and lanky Rainsford offered Decker a Cornish pasty, a lightly-baked pastry with innards of beef, potatoes, vegetables and gravy, and he devoured it with gusto. Decker immediately decided his prejudice against English food had been misguided.

Soon they were talking subjects most professional soldiers find in common – weapons, tactics, incompetent commanders, theaters of operation, bravery, cowardice, women, and the remote possibility of finding the right one of the latter who will convince them to give up soldiering and embrace a more conventional family life they presumably want – wife, kids, dog, house, mortgage, steady paycheck, backyard barbecue.

The conversation caused Decker to think about his family back in Pennsylvania. He realized it was Thanksgiving Day back home, a singularly American holiday that had somehow lost historic meaning over the years, except at elementary school plays where Pilgrims were saved from extinction by kind-hearted Indians who fed them.

If he were back there in the Pennsylvania hills, he'd be either watching football on TV and drinking large quantities of beer, or traipsing through the woods with his uncle, shotguns in hand as they hunted elusive prey. He wondered how Hannah was spending the occasion. He hadn't tried to contact her. Was she still in Puerto Rico on a recon? Did she head west to her hometown of Kansas City, Missouri to enjoy Thanksgiving with her parents and two sisters? Did she decide to go it alone, back at their Harbor Towers condo on the Boston waterfront? Or was she already onto another mission, whatever the agency might have required since his departure to Belize. He hadn't seen or heard from her and he wondered if she had tried to reach out through Carrington.

Sometimes he didn't know what to make of Hannah. At times she could be lovingly attentive, or totally aloof, to the point where he often felt she didn't like him. He knew he often behaved the same way – cold-blooded. Whenever images of Beirut came back to haunt him, he'd retreat far into himself and form a thick, impenetrable shell. He'd switch on his damage-control button and wait out the bad feelings. How many people had he killed? Did they deserve it? Were all of them the enemy? Why had he felt nothing when he pulled the trigger all those times?

Maybe he was reading Hannah all wrong, but on the days when her steely-minded logic emerged and she became unapproachable, he wondered how long their relationship would last. He yearned for the sizzle he'd felt with a woman named Kaleigh whom he'd met in Boston shortly after his discharge from the service. Whenever they'd gone out on a date, the sexual tension between them was undeniable, electric, buzzing, alive. If Kaleigh hadn't had a steady boyfriend, they might have taken things to new heights. He wanted to feel that way with Hannah, but the baggage they both carried usually got in the way. Some days, he just didn't know how to light her fire, and so he found himself gratefully alone in Belize on a secret mission designed by men with nebulous motives.

Although Decker was nearly fluent in Spanish, he was glad his two companions at the bridge spoke English. It made things easier. He wanted to ask many of the men why they carried no weapons. Why didn't they wear sturdy boots or clothing made to withstand hiking through dense rainforest? Most wore sneakers or sandals and seemed to Decker more like poor farmers than soldiers. He knew he'd find the answers soon enough.

After five hours of listlessly sitting or pacing near the swing bridge in the blazing sun, a short, balding, heavyset Latino dressed in jungle cammies and sporting a black eye patch showed up at the head of a convoy of four beat-up passenger vans. The vehicles looked more like those used to shuttle tourists to the Mayan ruins at Tikal than transport a couple dozen mercenaries to a jungle camp.

"Good day, gentlemen. You can call me Che," he said, chuckling at his own words.

Several of the mercenaries smiled or laughed at the reference to the late revolutionary Che Guevara, who had been a handsome poster boy with thick black hair and beard, and seemingly always at Fidel Castro's side in Cuba until he was killed while fighting in Boliva.

"Hola Señor Guevara!"

"Hey Che!"

"G'day, Che!

The man touched two crooked and curled fingers to his eye patch. "I may not look like Che, but I can assure you I have complete understanding of military tactics and what we need to accomplish," he said, patting the pistol strapped to his waist. "We should leave here shortly so that we can be at our camp before nightfall. The roads here, I'm afraid, are not always dependable."

Clipboard in hand, he began calling out surnames. When

Decker heard the name Malone, he almost didn't respond, momentarily forgetting his alias. Other soldiers in the group seemed to suffer from a similar temporary loss of memory.

Gathering their belongings, the men boarded the vehicles. Decker tossed his duffel bags on a seat near the back of the van and sat next to a strikingly beautiful Latino woman with dark eyes, long lashes, high cheekbones, full lips and lustrous black hair restrained by a single coarse braid that flopped over her right shoulder and onto her chest. Decker guessed she was in her late twenties. The woman's olive fatigues somehow managed to show off her curves. Her forehead was pressed against a side window as though she were tired or trying to get a better look at the activity outside the van. She didn't look up as Decker settled into the compact seat, trying to keep his body from encroaching.

"I won't be offended if you need more room," she said in Spanish. "You Americanos eat a lot of cheeseburgers."

Decker wasn't sure what she meant by the comment, but he could see a flirtatious smile had creased her lips. A delicate hand the color of cocoa reached across her torso and stretched toward him.

"Selena Delgado," she said, still gazing out the window.

"Jared Malone," he replied, gently grasping her delicate fingers and giving them an awkward shake. "And how did you know I'm American?"

Selena slowly sat upright and turned toward Decker. "I heard you speaking Spanish at the camp. You speak very well, but some of the words you choose are Castilian, or what we Latinos call Castellano. You won't hear it around here, especially among the rebels."

Decker was struck by her beauty and intrigued by her odd manners.

"So, that's what we are, rebels?"

"I assume we are all here for our own reasons. My family is Cuban. My grandparents were both schoolteachers and intellectuals. Because they supported Batista, they were killed by Castro's forces," she said with such sadness Decker had trouble swallowing. "My mother was pregnant. She and my father fled to Miami where I was born. It was a difficult time, but as you can see, I survived. My father died last year. His one wish was to see Cuba again. It's a shame he was unable to do that."

Decker offered understanding and sympathy, briefly looking into her eyes that were glassy with emotion.

"You want to know if I am a rebel, Señor Malone? The answer is, yes, if it means Castro gets pushed out of Cuba. If I had the chance to kill him, I would gladly pull the trigger and put a bullet in his head."

Separated from Hannah for months, Decker hadn't until this moment thought about other women. He quickly forced the imaginary picture of himself kissing the fiery Selena Delgado out of his mind. That effort lasted about six seconds until the image returned. Feeling uneasy, Decker took a deep breath as he stared intensely into her dark eyes, not saying a word. He wished he knew what she was thinking.

The road trip to the river lasted just over an hour, during which Decker and Selena talked mainly about the peasant struggles in Belize and Guatemala, the glitz of Miami, and the day's weather. The seats were compact and several times their thighs brushed together, yet neither pulled away. Decker felt some inexplicable current running between them. Selena Delgado possessed a primal intensity that was unlike any women he'd ever met.

The four vans soon pulled off into a bumpy field where acrid smoke from burning sugar cane made their eyes sting. Fire was the most efficient way to remove the plant's outer leaves before harvesting.

Three low-slung, olive-green military patrol boats were tied to a wooden dock, waiting to ferry the soldiers along a snaking brown river in the Orange Walk District, deeper into the jungle where archeologists were still unearthing a pre-Columbian city called Lamanai, the Mayan word for submerged crocodile.

The coxswain of Decker's boat was more like a tour guide, eager to show the soldiers the wonders of Belize. As the boats rounded a wide bend, the first vessel shut down its throbbing engines and the others followed suit. For the next half hour, the mercenaries floated quietly, treated to the sight of crocodiles dozing on the mudflats, and giant black bats, hanging upside down from trees branches, asleep in broad daylight.

"At night, the bats eat – snakes, mice, big river rats," said the jovial and informative driver in rapid-fire Spanish. "Maybe they try to eat you, too. Fortunately, they sleep like babies during the day."

A couple of the men laughed. Selena and Decker stood close together, not talking, instead taking in the scenery and occasionally meeting each other's furtive glances.

The guide suggested they keep a wary eye out for the larger crocodiles and not fall out of the boat, once again laughing and entertaining himself.

The river wound its way between tall, unbroken stands of brush growing along both shores. For five or six miles it became difficult to breathe as they crossed through more fields of burning sugar cane. It stung the eyes and made nostrils twitch.

When they finally reached the lake near Lamanai, the boats kept in formation as they approached a rickety dock. The young Belizean at the helm of Decker's boat lashed the vessel to the rotted wooden boards and stood on the dock until everyone was ashore. As he untied the lines he laughed heartily, promising to return when the mission was over. A joke – they all knew the soldiers would not be returning to Belize. For the professional mercenaries, it was the nature of the business. Move on to the next job in whatever country it might be.

Just beyond the Lamanai archeological dig were privately-owned expanses of tropical rainforest where the men could practice the art of war. A cluster of tents, each shelter large enough to accommodate six cots, was already erected. Several firing ranges with staggered targets were also in place, awaiting the barrage of bullets.

In a few days, the soldiers were scheduled to join a larger force just over the Guatemalan border for additional training. That was about all they had been told, other than those recruits were mostly comprised of Cuban ex-patriots living in Miami and dreaming of returning to their former lives on the Caribbean island.

Che, the organizer with black eye patch, promised a more thorough orientation in the morning, when he would unveil the details of the attack and explain their individual and team roles in the overall master plan.

23

URBAN COWBOYS DON'T RIDE HORSES

DECEMBER 1988
FINGER LAKES REGION, NEW YORK

Marvel, the largest Morgan horse in the Cooper's stable, had thrown Rocco a half dozen times since he first tossed a saddle over the animal's back. Unwilling to accept defeat, he vowed to get back on the horse that threw him until he could remain in the saddle.

The last unwelcome incident occurred just outside the barn the previous day, leaving Rocco coated in dirty snow, his muscles aching. It seemed to him the horse was mocking his inability to stay in the saddle. He looked Marvel straight in the eyes and when the animal didn't flinch or turn away, he picked up a rock twice the size of his fist and slammed it against the horse's snout. The horse, its reins tied tightly to a fence rail, cried out in pain, but before it could rear up Rocco bashed it again, this time drawing blood. He yanked hard on the bridle, which he had fitted with the sharpest bit in the tack room, knowing it would cut into the horse's mouth if it resisted his commands.

When Hope Cooper asked what had happened to cause the injury to Marvel, Rocco lied that the horse had stumbled on the trail and struck its head on a ledge. An avid horsewoman, Hope knew the story wasn't true. She didn't challenge his explanation. Rocco had a mean streak. She'd been watching him with new wariness since the Foghorn incident.

Rocco hid a bamboo stick under a hay bale next to Marvel's stall. Whenever he entered the stable, the horse became restless, moving to and fro, undoubtedly sensing a beating coming on. Usually it was two or three lashes, until Marvel broke into panicked neighing.

The day Isabella rode up to the barn atop Chance, Rocco was sitting in the metal seat of a rusted John Deere tractor, smoking a cigarette and flipping through pages of a Penthouse magazine.

"I haven't seen you on the trails so I thought I'd come get you," she said, her smile bursting with enthusiasm. "You promised me we'd go riding together."

Rocco tucked the magazine under the tractor seat, crushed his cigarette on the fender and climbed down. "I've been busy," he said.

"You don't look too busy. Let's ride. I'm sure Marvel would be very happy to get some fresh air."

Rocco entered the stable and cautiously approached Marvel, who immediately stirred and began kicking the stall boards.

"This horse is a real asshole," he said to Isabella, who had dismounted and followed him inside.

"He has to know you're the boss."

"Oh, believe me. He knows."

Isabella tossed Rocco a bridle and a saddle blanket. "You want help saddling up?"

"I can do it myself," he said, feeling inadequate as he clumsily draped the saddle across Marvel's spine.

"Back him out first."

"I know what to do," he lied, apprehensive at the thought of bending down near the animal's warm and muscular body and tightening the girth strap.

Isabella held the reins as Rocco did his best to tighten the leather girth and neck straps. Rocco jammed a foot into the stirrup and nearly fell off Marvel as his Italian loafer twisted and tangled in the metal brace.

"Boots or sneakers might work better for you," she said.

"I like these shoes. They're more comfortable than shit kickers."

Isabella grinned. "How often do you ride?"

"Let's just go," he said, hauling himself onto the saddle and giving Marvel a heel kick.

Isabella led the way on the trail. The route zig-zagged up a steep hill, flattening out at the top where the fields stretched to the horizon.

"Time to let them get some exercise," she said mischievously, nudging Chance forward.

Marvel remained inert. "Let's go, you miserable shit," Rocco shouted, digging his heels into the horse's ribs.

When the horse didn't move, Rocco kicked harder, twice punching the animal in the muzzle. "Move," he shouted, rubbing his knuckles. They stung from the impact. Rocco reminded himself to wear brass knuckles next time, a street tool guaranteed to get the horse's attention and show him who was in charge. He might even bring along his favorite stiletto and stab the animal in the eyes if it didn't cooperate.

Isabella slowed her pace and let out a shrill whistle. Marvel immediately began walking toward her, which made Rocco seethe. When Isabella again broke Chance into a trot, Marvel kept pace, causing Rocco to bounce in the saddle. Seconds later he was on the ground, sitting up in the snow and cursing, clutching his right arm, which he insisted was broken.

Isabella laughed. "Riding can be a tough sport."

Rocco swore at the gorgeous young woman under his breath

and vowed to extract revenge on her as well as the stubborn animal.

"We should just walk back to the stable," Isabella giddily suggested. "Might be faster and safer."

Shamed and angry, Rocco completely let go the reins so that Marvel was free to go wherever he pleased. Isabella didn't comment. She led the way back, holding Chance by the reins. Marvel tagged along a few feet behind her while Rocco took up the rear. Half an hour later they were at the stable. Rocco slapped Marvel on the backside, yelling at him to get inside the barn.

"Aren't you going to give him some water? You've got to let him cool down and then brush him," Isabella said.

"That fucking horse can die of thirst for all I care," Rocco blurted out. "He can brush his own goddamn coat."

Isabella saw a part of Rocco that frightened her but she continued to smile. "Well, I'd better be going. I've got lots of homework tonight. I'll see you tomorrow in school."

"Sure thing," said Rocco, barely able to conceal his resentment.

When Isabella returned home, she phoned Hope Cooper and quickly warned her not to announce it was she on the line. Isabella told her about what had occurred along the trail and later at the stable. She suggested Hope take a look at Marvel's muzzle, give him water and brush his coat, if only briefly. She also made Hope promise not to tell Rocco about the phone call, but after hanging up she knew the request had been unnecessary. Hope already understood what she was dealing with. She wished Rocco could be more like Nick, but after hearing Isabella's story, she knew that wasn't likely to happen.

24

TOO MANY CHEFS MAKING THE STEW

DECEMBER 1988
    CIA HEADQUARTERS
    LANGLEY, VIRGINIA

Hannah's personnel file was open on Bill Carrington's desk at Langley when she knocked curtly and entered his office. Carrington was standing near a window overlooking the sprawling campus. He was holding a vintage Walther PPK pistol in one hand while the other swabbed the barrel with a scrap of oily cloth attached to a thin metal rod.

"Did you enjoy your trip to Puerto Rico?"

"Very much so."

"We liked the photos."

Carrington set down the pistol and seated himself on a couch near the window. Unlike some supervisors, he didn't leave the visitor standing, nor did he remain behind his desk. He waved a hand toward a pair of comfortable upholstered chairs.

Carrington listened as Hannah provided details about her

observation of the meeting between Vinnie Merlino and General Sanchez, and also about the would-be robbers in Old San Juan.

"That expensive lens comes out of your pay," Carrington said in the utmost serious tone. "You need to take better care of company equipment."

Hannah's expression of surprise combined with dismay was enough reward for Carrington, who broke into a boyish grin that revealed just how much he enjoyed joking with her.

"Love the La Perla story," he said. "Too bad you couldn't have sent them both to that little above-ground cemetery next door. I'm just glad you were armed, even if it was only with a knife and a camera lens. By the way, it says here you have an impressive knife collection. Care to elaborate?"

"They're all sharp," she said with a feeling of satisfaction. "As for those morons in Old San Juan, if I had killed them, the police would have gotten involved. I highly doubt those two reported being attacked by a female tourist. That would have hurt their machismo."

"I suppose you're right," he said. "By the way, the Deputy Director commented on your photos," said Carrington, referring to Preston Barlow, the CIA's Deputy Director of Operations known primarily for his role in the agency's failed Bay of Pigs invasion. "He said they were exactly what he had hoped for because they put Merlino and General Sanchez together. That's an ace we can keep up our sleeve. Nice to see Alfredo Ponzi was also there, enjoying the sunshine while all dressed in black. At least he doesn't have to think about what to wear when he gets up in the morning."

Hannah blushed. She appreciated the compliment on a job well done. "The shot of Ponzi was a bonus. He had returned to shore with the others in the inflatable. Apparently he had to catch a flight from San Juan to Boston."

Carrington moved slowly toward his desk where he flipped a few pages in her file. "For such a short-timer, you've had an impressive law enforcement career," he said. " Lot's of great investigative work and a knack for going undercover."

"I enjoy it."

Carrington had memorized her file when the decision to bring her into the fold along with Decker was made by his boss nearly two years ago. Nonetheless, he made a show of running his finger down the facing page as if this was the first time learning about her undercover exploits.

"Hmm. Let's see. Student dissident. Homeless person. Prostitute. Waitress and barmaid. And now military hardware consultant from Argentina. You're a woman of many guises."

"My parents always encouraged me to dress up in costume on Halloween. I guess I never got over it."

Carrington appreciated her spunk. "Well, don't be surprised if you're asked to continue your charades. For now, you'll be Mariel Becker, at least when you're in Cuba."

Hannah couldn't hold back another second. She asked Carrington for an update on Decker's whereabouts.

"He's in Belize but he'll soon be in Guatemala, presuming he doesn't run into trouble joining the rag-tag army. After that, there's no telling how things will play out. If they end up heading for Cuba, I presume that's where he'll be."

Hannah wore a look of concern.

"Decker can handle himself. He's been in a lot worse situations than this," said Carrington, attempting to assuage Hannah's fears. "He's there strictly as reconnaissance. He's our eyes and ears on the ground and once he gets what we need we'll pull him back here."

Hannah accepted the explanation but didn't believe a word of it. She knew Decker had stripped and oiled several weapons at their Boston condo before flying to Belize. She hadn't seen which weapons, but the fact that Decker had prepped them for action was indication enough that a rough patch of road lay directly ahead.

"Decker packed kind of heavy for the trip," she said, not revealing she hadn't actually witnessed him prep the weapons for transport.

Carrington turned to face Hannah. "What's that old Boy Scout saying? *'Better to have it and not need it, than need it and not have it.'* Wouldn't you agree?"

"That's what Decker always says."

"Right. But now we need to talk about you. I want you to find out more about who's involved in shipping that load of weapons from Boston to Belize, the one that apparently ended up in the small freighter that Decker spotted just outside of Boston Harbor. I get the distinct feeling that some folks in this building may have had something to do with it."

Hannah briefed Carrington on the death of Tony "Bags" Balducci, former East Boston junkie and occasional resident of the North End, Boston's Italian neighborhood. Based on what Hannah had learned from FBI Special Agent Sally Parker, Balducci's grisly murder was meant to send a message to all the denizens of Boston's underworld. Keep your mouth shut – or else.

"The hit was probably ordered after he stumbled upon crates of military weapons being loaded onto a Boston Whaler and two other small vessels at a dock in Eastie," said Hannah "The weapons were being ferried to an anchored freighter and Tony Bags apparently was dumb enough to talk about it on the street."

Hannah also informed Carrington that Agent Sally Parker, a key member of the Anti-Organized Crime Strike Force, seemed top-notch and could prove helpful. So far, Agent Parker had given her no reason to suspect she couldn't be trusted with sensitive information.

"That's good to hear," Carrington said. "Trust is sometimes a rare commodity in our business."

"Agent Parker knows these players in Boston better than we do."

"Good enough. Let's assume Vinnie Merlino and his crew are

supplying the weapons to the mercenaries. Does Agent Parker happen to know where Merlino may have acquired them?"

"Not yet. There are plenty of people out there selling guns in New England. When I was a state trooper working the serial killer case, we spent a lot of time on the coast and ran across stockpiles of small arms being secretly shipped to IRA cells in Northern Ireland."

Carrington had an uneasy feeling the weapons shipment headed to the mercenary training camp in Guatemala might have received some clandestine support from his CIA colleagues, particularly those at Langley who were a few years older and a few pay grades higher. He wondered. Did his superiors orchestrate the weapons deal for Vinnie Merlino?

If so, was Merlino aware he was buying guns from the CIA?

The question nagged Carrington. If his suspicions were correct, that the CIA was already involved at a level above his security clearance, why had he been asked to make certain Decker was in place to terminate Vinnie Merlino with extreme prejudice if needed? Carrington's lengthy experience in the world of black ops told him this was a clusterfuck in the making.

Only the Deputy Director could provide the answers, and Carrington was quite certain the man wouldn't be entertaining questions any time soon. Barlow, now in his late sixties, was old-school CIA, a former friend of late Miami organized crime boss Santos Trafficante Jr., and among those still at Langley who plotted the bungled Cuban invasion of 1961. The failed mission was embedded in his psyche and played a role in everything he did or considered doing.

"The last time the agency tried something like this, partnering with mobsters, it didn't go well," Carrington said.

"I'm aware," said Hannah. "I was only two years old at the time, so the incident wasn't quite at the top of my things-to-worry-about list, but I read several reports from the company files a few months ago."

Carrington was impressed. Hannah Summers was a mature and capable operative at twenty-nine years old. He wished he'd known her when he was in his early thirties and unmarried. He would have asked her out in a heartbeat. Occasionally he allowed himself to wonder how she would feel wrapped in his arms. But mostly he was glad she and Decker were together, despite the relationship's drawbacks from an operational perspective. They were both quality people and deserved each other. A fine match.

"The Bay of Pigs was certainly not our proudest moment," he said, recalling the stories he'd heard at Langley over the years about how Castro had pushed the 1,400-man, CIA-trained, counter-revolutionary army of Cuban exiles back into the turquoise sea.

"If it's true that the company is back in business with the mob, what do you think Deputy Director Barlow and his confidants expect to gain if Vinnie Merlino is successful?"

"I wish I knew. Like you, I'm just a cog in the wheel. But if I had to guess, I'd say the company's highest priority is the stabilization of Cuba once the current regime has been removed."

"And you think Vinnie Merlino might not be the solution to that problem?"

"Let's just say I think he might be helpful putting things into play and getting some of the needed groundwork done, but it might turn out he's not the right person to represent the world of organized criminals in Cuba. He might demand too much money, or power. His ego might get in the way so that he becomes a hindrance."

"So when will this operation likely take place?"

"All I know is that Vinnie Merlino has been talking to certain people, telling them it's all going to be accomplished by Christmas, but based on the reports I've received about the situation in Belize, not to mention Guatemala, nothing will happen until January."

"Does Decker know that?"

"No. But I'm sure it'll occur to him once he see's how slowly things are progressing. He's a quick study."

"Have you talked to him?"

"No. He's in the bush. He decided not to take along one of the new Sat-phones because it was too bulky and people might start asking questions if they noticed it."

Hannah's lower lip rose to cover the upper one, as it always did when she was nervous or deep in thought. Carrington took note.

"Decker's among the best operatives I've ever seen in the more than twenty years that I've been doing this job," he said in a reassuring tone. "He's resourceful. And won't likely do anything stupid. He knows you'd kill him if he did."

25

HANNAH IN HAVANA

December 1988
Havana, Cuba

During her visit to Havana in November, Hannah had been surprised to find a sealed envelope under the door of her hotel room following her impromptu meeting with General Sanchez and his companions at the El Floridita restaurant.

It was a note to Mariel Becker from the general, suggesting they have dinner the following night at one of the finest restaurants in Havana, where they could talk privately about her consulting business. Hannah knew Sanchez wasn't hitting on her. Sanchez was a pedophile of the worst order, a sadistic killer and hardcore fan of snuff films, but he obviously sensed Mariel Becker could provide something valuable.

Upon meeting Hannah, the general and his two associates had been polite, mostly because she was young and pretty and wearing a dress that showed off her curves. When she told them she worked as a product consultant, they smiled condescendingly as though the title meant little or nothing. She might as well have been selling Tupperware or vacuum cleaners.

Their interest wasn't piqued until they inquired, more out of politeness than curiosity, about what sort of products she consulted on. What was her field of expertise?

When she answered, "Military hardware," they were hooked.

By the time the general's invitation arrived, she was packed for a flight to Montreal, since no direct air travel between Cuba and the United States was allowed in most instances. Once in Canada, she'd return to Boston where she and Decker lived in a high-rise condominium near the harbor. She'd told Sanchez an important client was waiting to meet her in Boston and had promised to take her on a tour of the city's art museums.

Hannah did, however, accept the general's phone call in her hotel room. She told him her schedule was overloaded, but they agreed to meet again in two weeks while on her way back to Argentina. They'd have drinks at El Floridita and later in the evening, a sumptuous dinner at the restaurant the general had suggested.

Still on the phone, Hannah gave the general the name of her consulting firm, which was actually a shell company run by the CIA where field operatives could receive messages without unveiling their true identity. If the general tried to contact her, the system administrators would send out an appropriate response and notify Hannah of the incoming messages.

By the time she returned to Havana in early December, she felt comfortable within the city's old quarter and the layout of El Floridita. She knew the entrances, exits, fields of fire, and even where the main box of electrical breakers was located in case for whatever reason she needed complete darkness.

The general sent a staff car to Hannah's hotel -- a 1950 black, four-door Lincoln Cosmopolitan, part of his private collection. A small Cuban flag was flown from the front fender, and below it a pennant bearing the top-ranking military general's four stars.

Hannah was transported to El Floridita, where the general was seated at a table for two, surrounded by tall vases overflowing with fresh-cut lilies. The natural perfume was pleasantly overwhelming.

"Oh, how lovely," she said as the general stood and reached for her hand, kissing it quickly. "How did you know I love flowers?"

"All beautiful women love flowers. Isn't this so?"

Hannah acted as though she were blushing while the waiter adjusted her chair. Her white tropical dress hung off the shoulders, tapering at the waist and flowing generously outward until it reached her knees.

"*Magnifico*," said Sanchez. "You have a real sense of fashion."

The waiter poured glasses of water and asked the general for the drink order.

"Champagne? A superb vintage."

"Not for me, thank you," she said. "But I will have a glass of Riesling, preferably dry and German."

"Many people here order French wine."

"There are lots of Germans living in Argentina. German-style wine is very popular in Buenos Aires and also with the Becker family."

The general pretended he understood the family reference. He ordered the Riesling and a Zinfandel and when the wine arrived they toasted to mutual business connections. The general asked about her museum tour in Boston. Hannah was careful not to provide too many details of her life that the general could trace. Instead, she kept her statements vague until the talk turned to military hardware, which she knew was the real reason the general had asked her to dinner.

"We can order dinner here if you like, or we can go somewhere even more special," he said. "A close friend owns the most amazing restaurant that overlooks the sea. He has the best chefs and a cellar filled with rare wines I'm sure he would like to share."

Hannah gently pushed back her padded chair, arched her back and lifted her chin, as though lost in the beauty of the place. "I'd like to stay right here if you don't mind," she said. "El Floridita has a certain aura which I can't explain, but just being here fills me with good feelings. Maybe it's all the flowers, so thank you for being so thoughtful."

"Then we shall stay here and dine like kings and queens, like royalty," said Sanchez, signaling the waiter to bring the menus and rattle off the specials.

Dinner arrived as a smorgasbord of fresh seafood, which quieted the talk until the mutual subject of interest was resurrected. Hannah daintily sipped her wine before opening the conversation with a barrage General Sanchez had not anticipated.

"You and your friends asked what it is I do for a living. What is my field of expertise? Well, I sell weapons. Big ones, little ones, economical ones, and some so expensive the number of zeros in the price tag still make my eyes go blurry."

The general raised his eyebrows as though impressed. "And business is good these days?"

"It's a bit like investing in supermarkets and funeral parlors," she said, her lips twisted wryly. "Both unstoppable businesses. People are always hungry or dying to come to you. Seems the same applies to the sale of weapons. People are always killing each other."

"You make an interesting point," said General Sanchez, staring intensely at Hannah as he raised his glass in a toast. "To a woman who understands the world of men and power."

"Well. I don't want to bore you by talking shop," Hannah responded demurely. "I think Cuba is an amazing place, so unspoiled, and you as a military officer are such a part of the culture. I'd like to hear your views on your country."

"That could take some time."

Hannah glanced at her Cartier wristwatch, remembering the special evening when Decker had given it to her. They had been sitting on a bench along the Esplanade in Boston, watching the college crew teams methodically slicing the silver surface of the Charles River. Always more comfortable than she with public displays of affection, Decker had gently fastened it on her wrist, kissed her passionately and asked that she always make time for him. The kiss, which she had returned with equal fervor, was among the best in her life and she still felt giddy inside whenever she recalled it. Some days she wondered if they'd ever feel that spark again.

"Well, I won't turn into a pumpkin until midnight, so give it a go," she said, raising her glass. "To Cuba."

General Sanchez seemed confused by the notion that his dinner guest might at some point transform into a squash, but he didn't mention it and proceeded to tell Hannah about his boyhood in Cuba and how he became the country's most powerful general.

Hannah listened attentively as Sanchez talked of the proud Cuban people living amid extreme poverty, of hypocrisy and corruption in government, of being a baby abandoned on a stranger's doorstep, only to learn much later his mother had been a prostitute and his father unknown.

Hannah recoiled at the image of Sanchez, at age eight, removing the acidic, lead-plated innards of discarded car batteries to help support the family that had informally adopted him. She saw the sadness in his eyes as he talked of hunger and the physical pain it caused, of being forced to steal vegetables from a neighbor's garden. There were other scars as well. A middle-aged man with one milky blind eye and rotted teeth, who worked alongside him in the field where the car batteries were dissected, had dragged him into the forest and abused him. When it was about to happen again a few days later, Sanchez tossed battery acid in the man's face. He had stored the volatile liquid in a rusted tin can for just such an occasion.

When the man reappeared in the fields with horrific burns on his face, he threw himself atop Sanchez, attempting to strangle the boy. Others standing nearby did nothing to help. It was as if they found the whole scene amusing. But Sanchez was prepared. Using the sharp-edged lid from the same tin can that had held the battery acid, he slashed the man's jugular vein. Blood spurted everywhere as the boy squirmed out from beneath the heavy body and watched the man die. The air filled with stench as the man's bowels released. Sanchez was surprised at how easy it was to kill. Nobody among the workers seemed to care. Apparently they were relieved another bully was gone, one less obstacle to deal with as they struggled to eke out a living.

One of the older workers who acted as though he was in charge ordered the others to dig a slit trench for the dead man. A dozen men quickly began digging with shovels and spades. Once the body was rolled into the hole it was covered over with soil and palm fronds, and everyone went back to work.

Nothing might have changed amid this sordid life had it not been for the Canadian businessman seated at a café in the seaport city of Cienfuegos when Sanchez was ten. Sanchez, who took the surname of his adopted family, had kicked a soccer ball with gusto and it had struck the Canadian in the head. Thinking immediately of the punishment that would follow as a result, Sanchez waited for the man to berate him and summon the police. Instead, the man proved kind and eager to talk. The stranger quickly learned Sanchez's formal education would stop in two years, after graduation from elementary school, because his family could not afford to send him to secondary school.

The Canadian offered to pay the relatively meager sum for the boy's education as long as his grades were maintained at the highest level and an annual status report was sent to the benefactor.

After completing high school, Sanchez assumed the payments would cease, but he was mistaken. The Canadian Army officer saw in Sanchez certain qualities that might flourish in the military. He subsidized Sanchez's college tuition, leaving the young man to figure out how to pay for room and board. In return, he expected only top grades and the updates. The rest, as Sanchez explained, was history. Military school followed and Sanchez became a commissioned officer in the Cuban military. He was sent to fight in Angola where he learned to give orders and watch men die. He was taught to value effectiveness, ruthlessness and power. Upon returning to Cuba, he followed a path of marriage, children, home, comforts, all made possible by his ascension through the ranks in the military.

When it seemed the general had finished his story, Hannah said, "General Sanchez, your story is a tragic one but you are the real Cuba, and I think you should do everything in your power to make sure it stays that way."

"Your opinion is very much appreciated," he said. "I, too, love Cuba the way it is, though there are many who would change it, mold it back into the slime that flourished under Batista."

Feigning ignorance, she asked, "But who would threaten your way of life?"

"Argentina is a long way from Cuba, but the United States is not. We are always feeling the threat of Yankee invasion. If it happens, it will not be something new for us."

"And what if you had the weapons to prevent that, would you sleep better?"

"As always, that would depend on the price."

Hannah sipped her wine. " I don't always believe what I hear, but I was informed recently that a shipment of weapons is headed from Boston to Belize, and then overland to Guatemala. If those weapons were to fall into the hands of soldiers who want to make Cuba once again into an island of casinos, luxury hotels and ignorant tourists, your country as you know it would no longer exist."

"And you can provide the weapons needed to prevent this?"

"For the right price, anything is possible."

"Not just small arms, but something more substantial?"

"Like the Red Arrow 8?"

The general glowed as he smiled enthusiastically for the first time. "You can read my mind," he said, a genuine smile forming across his face and exposing his yellowed teeth.

This time, Hannah raised her glass and waited until the general clinked it with his. "If you would like to place an order, I can handle the arrangements. My company has offshore accounts so there is no trace of any transactions, presuming secrecy is of importance to you."

26

LET'S JUST BE FRIENDS

When Rocco first began waiting for Isabella every day after school, she was flattered and her girlfriends made much of it. In those early weeks Isabella found it sort of cool that this handsome, blond, blue-eyed bad boy was devoting his attention exclusively to her. But after a month had gone by she missed her friends, the small talk and gossip, and the solitary bus ride home. She savored those minutes alone because they allowed her to think about her life and the world without interruption.

Although Rocco projected the image of a daring, hell-raising, fun-seeking companion, Isabella couldn't ignore the darkness she felt oozing from his soul whenever they were together. She knew deep inside he was still seething about falling off Marvel on the trail. It had been a moment of monumental embarrassment and Rocco wasn't the type of person who could accept failure and move on. Rocco Merlino took everything personally. If you crossed him, made him look foolish, you were a lifelong enemy, no matter if you were human or animal, prince or pauper.

The day Isabella told Rocco she wanted to sit alone on the bus, he demanded to know what was going on. Why was she rejecting him? Was it because of Nick?

Isabella tried to explain that she and Nick had been a couple for more than a year. Together they were Nikabella and his absence often made her sad.

"Rocco, you're so handsome and all the girls at school are wishing you'd ask them out. They love your long hair and how you bought beer for the guys and got them drunk," she said. "I really like you, too. You're cool and different. But I'm not ready to get involved with anybody. I just can't be crowded right now."

Rocco, exasperated to the core, nonetheless projected an air of calm. "I understand. It's no big deal," he had said, adding they could always be good friends because he was going to live on the vineyard and be her neighbor forever.

The next day he avoided her at school and got a ride back to the vineyard with one of the older boys who'd just been issued a driver's license.

After their seemingly minor confrontation, Isabella noticed Rocco began flirting with the other girls at school, especially those in her friend group. She wasn't in any way jealous and actually wished them well. She really wanted Nick cuddled next to her in bed, just as he'd frequently been when her parents weren't home.

When she and Rocco finally did speak to each other, he pretended nothing was different, that Isabella was the most special person in his life. He put his arm around her, which she found uncomfortable, and when he tried to kiss her she dipped her head to ensure her lips were inaccessible.

Undeterred, Rocco withdrew and instead rested his hands on her hips. Isabella tried to wriggle away, but he held on tighter. "I love you. Do you know that?"

"Oh, Rocco. You just told me you were fine with us being friends. Now you're saying you love me. We're both mixed up. You haven't been here long enough to truly love anybody. And I get that."

"So you don't love me?"

"Will you please stop?"

"Are you coming to my birthday party?"

"I didn't know I was invited."

"I'll be sixteen in less than two weeks," he said. "But so will somebody else I know. Maybe you're already going to Nick's party in Rhode Island."

27

THE BIRTHDAY BOYS

It was no surprise to anyone in the Cooper or Merlino families when December 23 evolved into an unpleasant day. Nicholas Cooper and Rocco Merlino were about to celebrate their mutual sixteenth birthday, despite the fact they lived nearly four hundred miles apart.

Nick spent the day brooding because he was not with Isabella who, in his mind, was very probably in the arms of Rocco Merlino. He was miserable. He had turned sixteen, but it would take months before he obtained a learner's permit and valid driver's license. Besides, he knew Vinnie wouldn't cooperate because a car would provide Nick with new wings. Vinnie had made it clear he wanted Nick to stay close to Providence, unless given permission to travel elsewhere.

Rocco was equally distraught. Hope baked him a birthday cake with sixteen candles and churned out a batch of home-made ice cream. Although there was a part of Rocco that appreciated the gesture, if he were back in Providence and none of this mix-up had ever occurred, he was pretty certain Vinnie would have thrown him a wild party and invited some of his closest school friends. Instead of cake and ice cream, there would have been champagne and steak and girls wearing almost nothing prancing about who would do whatever he asked.

After the lackluster celebration in the farmhouse kitchen, Rocco headed outdoors to smoke a cigarette, setting fire to the tobacco with the gold-plated Dupont Ligne lighter he'd pilfered from Vinnie's impressive collection of rings, watches, necklaces and other expensive items. He looked up at the sky and realized he had never noticed there were so many stars, certainly a lot more than he had imagined. The sky over Providence, Rhode Island had a way of hiding them.

After his smoke he walked into the barn where Marvel and the other four horses were locked in their stalls. Marvel stirred uneasily and kicked the stall boards, sensing Rocco's presence.

Rocco picked up the bamboo stick he kept hidden and whacked it across Marvel's backside, leaving a welt. The horse neighed and stepped side to side in the stall.

"How do you like that?"

Holding the stick above his head, he whacked the horse again. "I'd like to grind you into dog food," he said, returning the stick to its hiding place behind two bales of hay. "Or maybe I'll cook you alive!"

Rocco thrust an arm between the stall plank boards and flicked the vintage lighter. The small blue and yellow flame was enough to make Marvel rear up with his front legs.

Back inside the house, Rocco phoned Isabella, hoping she would agree to meet him. After all, it was still early on a Friday night. The call went into the Marceau family's answering machine. Rocco left a voice message, reminding Isabella it was his birthday and asking if she would like to join him for a celebratory drink of brandy, recalling her comment about occasionally imbibing when tobogganing with friends.

With the receiver back in its cradle, Rocco cursed aloud, angry with himself for having left such a pathetic, loser message. Isabella would listen to it and think he was lame. He also regretted mentioning alcohol, since there was always the possibility Isabella's parents would be first to retrieve their messages. He wondered, too, if Isabella had telephoned Nick to wish him a happy birthday.

Nick wasn't having a much better day than Rocco. He wanted to be left alone in his room. Although his heart told him to call Isabella again, his pride left his fingers frozen.

Ruby bought him a nip of anisette and a box containing two cannoli and a few biscotti from Scialo Brothers Bakery on Atwells Avenue. Although she had only known Nick since summer, she liked him and was certain he'd enjoy her bakery selections more than a slice of chocolate cake.

Nick thanked her and retreated to his room to savor the pastries and the licorice-tasting liquor, intending to go to sleep early and forget it was his birthday. But Vinnie had other plans for the night's celebration. Nick hadn't digested the first cannoli when Vinnie pounded on his door.

Vinnie's voice boomed. "Time to celebrate."

Ruby's eyes opened wide. "Don't shout. You'll wake Carla."

After a deliberate pause, Nick said, "I'm going to sleep. I don't feel like celebrating."

"Come on, Nicholas. You only turn sixteen once. This is a big birthday."

The thought of Isabella in Rocco's arms filled him with bitterness. If she was going to mess around, he wouldn't be caught playing the fool, the loyal boyfriend who pined away until she realized the error of her ways.

"Well?"

"Where are we going?"

"It's a surprise."

"Just not back to that warehouse place."

Ruby scowled. "What's he talking about? What warehouse?"

Vinnie's face flushed pink. "I don't know about any warehouse."

Nick realized he had mentioned a piece of Vinnie's life that Ruby chose to ignore or didn't know about. In either case, he'd have to repair the damage.

"Maybe it wasn't a warehouse. I think it was more like a bar in an old building," he said, knowing it was half-truth. "It was the place where they sold lots of different beers."

Relieved, Vinnie embellished Nick's description of the fictitious bar. "It's a good place. Cold drinks and no sign on the front door. Just the guys. Nice and quiet. The owner wants to keep it local. He doesn't want it to become a tourist joint."

Ruby seemed to accept the explanation. Besides, the baby had begun crying in the back bedroom so she didn't have time to give it deeper thought.

When Ruby was gone, Vinnie said through the closed bedroom door, "Thanks for clearing that up. It could have been a problem."

Later that night, his cheeks smudged with lipstick, his mind awash with whisky and damaging thoughts of Isabella, Nick hugged the toilet bowl and vomited until his stomach was as empty as his heart. Ruby told him in the morning that Isabella had called to wish him a happy birthday but he hadn't been home.

28

IT'S BEGINNING TO LOOK A LOT LIKE CHRISTMAS

CHRISTMAS 1988
GUATEMALA

Decker was antsy. It was hot and buggy at the base camp in the Guatemalan rainforest and it made the men short-tempered. The camp, little more than a cluster of tents filled with cots, contained more than forty soldiers, though many still had no weapons.

It was Christmas morning. Decker missed the snow-capped evergreen trees he had come to appreciate as a boy in Pennsylvania and more recently in New England. One of the Latino soldiers began vigorously strumming a guitar and singing *Feliz Navidad.* Soon several other men cheerfully joined in and the air filled with song. Decker sensed it was going to be a weird Christmas. He didn't feel like singing, but Chad and Trevor, his new Australian and British acquaintances, were belting out the repetitive Christmas tune like schoolboys.

At noon there was stirring in the camp as two military Jeeps came to a mud-sloshing halt, followed by three deuce-and-a-half trucks laden with crates of weapons. The second Jeep carried Cuban ex-patriot Homer Duarte, who stood in the passenger seat, holding onto the windshield and looking like a dashing field general.

Duarte had been designated the unit commander by Vinnie Merlino and his Miami counterpart, Patsy LoScalzo, head of the Trafficante crime family since the death of Santos Trafficante Jr. the previous year.

Duarte was tall for a Cuban, handsome with dark piercing eyes and chiseled facial features. He had the athletic build of a tennis player and a thick mane of black hair combed straight back from his forehead. Wearing olive fatigues, a .45 Colt handgun strapped to his waist, he was brash and pompous as he addressed the men in Spanish, waving his arms to emphasize his words. He told them they would share in the glory of taking back Cuba from a communist shit bum. He had promised the weapons would arrive by Christmas and had kept his word. But he urged the mercenaries to remain patient until more intelligence reports arrived. He wisely posted a guard outside each truck, fearing too many guns in the hands of soldiers already geared up for a fight could be a disaster.

Best of all, he said, the trucks also contained everything needed for a holiday barbecue feast, which would soon get underway. Two soldiers in the second Jeep lifted cases of rum from Cuello's Brothers Distillery over their heads, which brought a round of cheers.

Decker knew plenty about Vinnie Merlino and had been briefed on Patsy LoScalzo, but Homer Duarte was another wild card tossed into the mix. He worried Duarte might be an incompetent military commander and as a result lead the men to their deaths. He assumed Duarte was a Cuban ex-patriot with a score to settle and the ability to muster enough fighting men, albeit for pay or vengeance. He guessed Duarte was about fifty, old enough to have owned property and reaped the benefits of an intellectual profession -- a teacher or lawyer -- until Castro had taken it all away.

At midday the men began drinking rum and cold beer while the pig-roasting fire was tended. More musical instruments appeared – bongo drums, an ocarina, another guitar and a vintage squeezebox. Duarte swaggered among the soldiers, stopping to make small talk. When he saw Selena Delgado he smiled extravagantly and roped his arms around her, planting a firm kiss on each of her high cheekbones.

"My Cuban *compatriota*," he said with gusto. "It's always refreshing to see someone who understands what was taken away by Castro. I was saddened to hear about the death of your father, but I pray your mother is well."

"Still in Miami," said Selena. "As long as there are lots of Cubans in the neighborhood, she'll be fine. I can only imagine the food she has prepared for the holiday table."

Some of the soldiers were craning their necks to see what had held up Duarte's progress as he wended his way through the ranks.

Decker introduced himself in Spanish as Jared Malone and Duarte replied in English. The man asked a lot of questions about Decker's military experience and was obviously impressed with his talents, especially those acquired as a Special Forces ranger and sniper.

"Well, Mr. Malone. You may be just the man I am seeking to remove any wrinkles from our plan," he said. "After today's fiesta, we must talk. There's much to prepare."

Cut off from almost all outside news, Decker was stunned to learn from Duarte that a terrorist bomb had exploded a few days earlier aboard a Pan Am commercial airliner flying over Lockerbie, Scotland. The bomb had killed all 243 passengers and sixteen crew aboard Flight 103. Eleven more people died on the ground.

"This is why we cannot let the communists control Cuba.

They bring nothing but misery and death," said Duarte, expressing his belief the attack was in retaliation for the 1986 U.S. airstrikes against Libya that left Libyan leader Muammar al-Qaddafi's young daughter dead.

Decker clenched his fists as he envisioned hundreds of passengers being blown to bits inside the plane, body parts strewn in every direction. However, he wasn't convinced the Libyan airstrikes were the only reason for the airline bombing. It seemed lots of people were holding grudges against the United States.

Only six months earlier, on July 3, the American guided missile frigate USS Vincennes had mistakenly shot down Iran Air Flight 655, a commercial aircraft flying from Tehran to Dubai. The surface-to-air missile fired from the warship killed all 290 passengers. The Navy captain later said he mistook the commercial airliner for an Iranian fighter plane on the attack.

Decker didn't mention the doomed Iranian flight, not wanting to give Duarte the impression he kept abreast of such matters and by doing so draw his suspicion. But he sensed it was only a matter of time before a counter strike was launched by Iran against the United States, either directly or through a proxy.

Their friendly conversation was interrupted by commotion amid the soldiers. A wild boar had attacked three mercenaries gathering coconuts along a thickly-forested trail. The youngest soldier, still in his teens, had been gashed by the boar's sharp tusks and was badly bleeding from the thigh. The tusk had nicked the femoral artery. Shouts went out for a medic. When nobody moved to help, Decker ran toward the boy and fastened a tourniquet above the wound. He had patched up plenty of fellow Rangers in firefights on three continents. Trevor was right beside him, his personal first-aid kit opened and ready with blood-clotting bandages. The Brit began applying direct pressure to the wound and monitoring the boy's vital signs.

After several tense moments a medic arrived and inserted an

IV, pushing meds as the boy writhed in pain. Decker high-fived
Trevor, acknowledging a job well done.

29

HOLIDAY ANGST

CHRISTMAS 1988
UPSTATE NEW YORK AND PROVIDENCE, RI

Christmas had fallen on a Sunday and the mood at the Cooper house was dreary. Rocco was ornery, mostly because Isabella had done her best to ignore him during the Thanksgiving dinner a month earlier, choosing instead to play board games with the younger children. When the school break was over, she barely spoke to him on the bus. If he asked her a question, she'd answered it, but nothing more.

Two packages had arrived at the vineyard by delivery truck the previous week but remained unopened beneath the illuminated holiday tree. Hope and Gary had urged Rocco to come with them into the fields to cut a tree, but he declined, claiming he was too tired. Nor did he help decorate it.

"What's with all these silly fucking ornaments? It's such a stupid holiday," he had said. "Nobody believes in Santa Claus."

To which Hope, trying to spark his interest, had replied,

"Some of them have been in our family for years. A few of them are older than you are. It's a tradition."

Hope suggested Rocco open the gifts that had been delivered, as well as the one she and Gary had purchased for him and wrapped in colorful paper. But as Christmas morning turned to afternoon, the gifts lay untouched.

Through the bay window that looked out at the hills, Rocco could see it was snowing lightly, magically transforming the rolling fields into a glittering white blanket. He put on a pair of short leather boots with a side zipper that were better designed for urban streets than snowy rural roads. He smoked three cigarettes as he walked along the road shoulder toward the Marceau farmhouse. He stopped beneath an enormous hemlock tree, its branches heavy with snow, and watched the activity inside the house. The lights were on and he saw Isabella laughing and talking to her mother in the kitchen. They were making pies.

Isabella's father opened the front door to let the dogs out – two Labrador retrievers that Rocco despised, mostly because they slobbered on his pants and vied for attention he would never give them. The animals stopped to sniff the air and Rocco feared they might detect his scent and start barking. The night was quiet and windless, the snow falling in big flakes. A light went on in the barn. Rocco heard Chance whinny. Isabella crossed the open yard and entered the barn, the heavy metal hinges complaining. She wasn't wearing a coat. Her arms were crossed as if to retain body heat.

Rocco kept to the shadows as he stepped closer to the barn. Again the horse let out a gentle sigh as Isabella tossed a blanket across its back. The door to the house opened again and Isabella's father stepped onto the farmer's porch. "Isabella. Phone call," he shouted. "It's Nick."

Rocco felt an uncontrolled fury course through his body as his fingers gripped the tree bark. He ran part of the way back to the Cooper house, cursing as he slipped and fell flat on his back in the middle of the icy road. His anger for the countryside grew as he walked, imagining the bare and salted sidewalks of downtown Providence.

Nick was equally restless in the city. When Isabella's voice came over the line, he was scrunched in a far corner of his bedroom.

"I miss you," he said.

"I miss you, too. I wish you were here. Christmas just isn't the same without you. We had so much fun picking out a tree last year."

"They don't worry too much about that here. My so-called father brought home a tree in a box last week. It's an aluminum stand with three legs and metal branches that fit into holes. There's a four-colored spotlight wheel that revolves on the floor and illuminates the ornaments."

"Well, at least you won't have to sweep up the zillions of needles as they fall off the tree."

"Different strokes for different folks, I guess. Ruby told me she loves it. She's thinking about buying some electrical thing that you plug into an outlet. It heats up scented water so that the room smells like a pine forest."

"Maybe there's one that smells like cheeseburgers. I'll bet you'd love that," she said, trying to make him feel better.

Nick chuckled but quickly returned to what was on his mind. "All kidding aside, I'm getting out of here soon. I'm hiring a lawyer now that I'm sixteen. And I'm buying a car so that I can go wherever I want whenever I want."

"And I want you right here," she said, her intimate tone leaving no room for doubt that she meant in her bed. "I'm so lonely."

Nick suddenly let his insecurities get the best of him. "What about Rocco? I thought he was keeping you company."

"I haven't talked to him in weeks. He seemed OK when he

first got here but these days he's acting strange. Some of the kids on the bus said he talks to himself. Like gibberish."

"I don't like thinking about you with him."

"There's nothing to think about. There is no me and Rocco. There never was."

"Isabella, I need to be with you. I can't stand this anymore. I want my old life back, the one where I see you every day, the one where I kiss you and hug you and do all sorts of things to you."

"Oh, god. Don't get me started. Just thinking about that makes it worse."

They both laughed simultaneously, but it was strained. Nick heard Isabella's father call her to the dinner table.

"I've got to go but we'll talk again soon."

Nick didn't reply.

"Nick?"

"I love you," he said, his voice cracking. "I just want this nightmare to be over."

30

THE WAITING IS THE HARDEST PART

January 1989
CIA Headquarters, Langley, Virginia

Bill Carrington's suspicions that higher-ups at Langley had become secretly involved in the Cuba situation were confirmed when he reluctantly reported having difficulty communicating with Decker.

"I can get messages to Decker if need be," Barlow said smugly with an air of condescension. "MI6 has a man inserted with the mercenaries who has access to a courier."

Carrington appeared both grateful and humble in Barlow's presence, but deep inside he disliked the man immensely. "So glad to hear it, sir. That's a relief," he said.

According to Barlow, a British Secret Intelligence Service operative assigned to Military Intelligence Section Six (MI6) and using the alias Trevor Rainsford, had infiltrated the mercenary force in Belize and later made his way to the Guatemala camp.

"Rainsford was able to send word back to London that the assassinations were delayed because the weapons shipment from

Boston was still en route," said Barlow. "MI6 shared that information with us."

The Deputy Director's words stung. Carrington understood
he had been left out of the intel loop, that the weapons shipment
paid for by Vinnie Merlino was actually made possible by the
CIA. He wondered whether Barlow had used one of the CIA's
many shell companies to provide the weapons at an affordable
price, or had simply dealt directly with Merlino. He doubted
Barlow would lower himself to speak directly with riffraff. In
either case, if the CIA was involved, Carrington felt he should
have been made aware of it before being dispatched to Cuba.

"May I ask how Rainsford was able to communicate with
London?"

"Turns out it was ingeniously simple. This Rainsford received
a seemingly benign personal package containing socks, cookies
and that sort of thing, along with a letter from relatives back in
England, inquiring about his health. The letter indicated a family
matter required his urgent attention. Rainsford replied with a
coded note, stating he was on a business trip and would likely be
back in contact before the end of January."

"If I may ask, sir, has Rainsford made his real identity known
to Decker?"

"Doubtful," said Barlow, adjusting his thick, black-framed
eyeglasses that make his owlish eyes seem even bigger. "I don't
believe he wants to jeopardize his cover in any way, especially
now that the assassination date is getting closer."

"So the weapons have reached Guatemala?"

"Yes, finally, but not without several headaches," said Barlow,
puffing deeply on his pipe in a way that seemed to reflect his
perplexed mood. "A problem erupted during the unloading from
the ship in Belize City. One of the skiffs capsized, dumping
several crates overboard. Fortunately the harbor is shallow and
the weapons were packed in grease. Once recovered, every piece
required cleaning and oiling. We also faced more demands for

cash from corrupt local officials. Those negotiations consumed a full day."

Barlow puffed methodically, sending plumes of blue smoke toward the ceiling as he continued his briefing. "Two different groups of bandits attempted to hijack weapons from the truck convoy along the road to the Guatemalan border. The Belize Defense Forces, whom we hired to provide security, were able to fend them off."

Carrington listened intently, seething over having been provided the information so belatedly. "Sir, if I may ask, without sounding insubordinate, why wasn't I informed immediately that you had received an update on Decker's status and new information about the weapons shipment?"

Barlow mumbled something with the pipe stem clamped in his teeth. "I don't like to micromanage my people," he said. "You're Decker's handler, so I presumed you had a way to reach him, and if not, you should have come to me immediately with a request for assistance."

Back in the Guatemalan rainforest, Decker and Rainsford were comparing submachine guns when the British spy decided the time was right to unveil his identity. "By the way, Mariel Becker is fine," said Rainsford, smiling sheepishly.

Decker was caught off guard. His mouth hung open, leaving him speechless.

Locking eyes with Decker, the spy said, "I'm with MI6. Apparently Mariel Becker was at Langley this week for more briefings. It was suggested by my superiors that I pass that information along to you. They indicated you would appreciate it."

Rainsford was obviously in the pipeline.

"Thanks. Haven't seen her in months," said Decker, "Anything else?"

"The Cuba plan is apparently set to roll sometime in January, at least that was the latest intel from a week ago. No specific date," he whispered. "What they don't have at my organization is a list of targets. I'm told you may be able to provide that. There's been some discussion in London and Washington of warning those people or somehow providing protection without their knowledge. You can imagine how that would impact the teams going ashore."

Decker didn't like the situation. If his orders from Carrington were to thwart the assassinations, he should know whether Fidel Castro, General Octavio Sanchez or any other influential member of the Cuban government was aware of the target list.

Decker looked directly at Rainsford. "Are you sure my people don't have the list?"

"I'm not sure of anything at his point," said the Brit. "If they've got it, they haven't shared it with MI6."

"Sometimes I hate all the game playing," said Decker. "Give me a job and let me do it."

"I agree. We're supposed to be allies," said Rainsford. "If there's any information you'd like to send back to your office, my courier who arrived with the gun shipment will be returning along the same route and can deliver it. I believe the convoy trucks will be staying here in case we need them, but he'll be departing in one of the Jeeps."

Decker had made a fine impression on Homer Duarte, who now included him and Selena in the strategy sessions. So at least he knew the basics of the plan. Forty mercenaries would be divided into ten teams of four, each assigned to assassinate one Cuban government official or businessman at the appointed hour, or as close to that time as possible."

"Do you have the target identities?"

"Not yet, only that there are ten, so that each team of four will take out one target. I was hoping to have the list before nightfall."

"Understood," said Rainsford. "That would be extremely

helpful. Right now, we don't even have a date for when this is supposed to happen."

"Date. Location. Time. We have none of that," said Decker. "And I'm still unclear on how these small teams are supposed to react if the Cuban military decides to stage an all-out assault. There doesn't seem to be any bailout plan in case that happens."

"That's where we are counting on Mariel Becker," Rainsford said wryly. "From what we've gathered, General Octavio Sanchez understandably does not trust the mobsters who are behind this attempted takeover. We don't know why, but despite those feelings, the general has agreed to do whatever he can to hold the Cuban military at bay as the assassinations get underway and are made public."

"Why would he agree to do that?"

"Presumably they have something on him. Whatever it is, it's enough to buy his loyalty, or at least his cooperation."

"And you're implying Mariel Becker is somehow involved in trying to make General Sanchez less loyal to his mob associates?"

"I'm suggesting Mariel Becker may be in the position to provide the general with options made available by the people you work for."

"Got it."

"So you'll try to get the target names and allow me to pass them along?"

"Consider it done," Decker said.

31

THEY POISON HORSES, DON'T THEY?

Isabella's voice was loaded with worry as she asked her father if he had fed Chance without her knowing.

"I depend on you to do that, Izzy, so I don't feed him unless someone tells me otherwise," he said matter-of-factly. "Why do you want to know? Is there something wrong?"

"He hasn't eaten any of the food I put out for him for the past three days. And he doesn't seem to want to leave his stall. It's weird."

"Want me to call the vet?"

"Not yet. Maybe he has a cold. He seems to be having trouble breathing. I guess he could be congested."

"I'll take a look at him, but you know Chance better than any of us. If you think it's something serious, we'll get Dr. Tomkins over here."

Rocco smiled knowingly when he overheard Isabella telling her friends on the school bus that her horse was sick. He regained his composure before turning around in his seat to address Isabella. "I'm so sorry to hear that. Is there anything I can do to help?"

"No. Thanks for asking," she said, giving him no more thought.

The following day, Chance was even more lethargic. He refused to eat apples, sugar cubes and other favorite snacks that were pressed against his lips. That's when Isabella noticed his gums were a pale, yellowish color, his heart rate unusually rapid, and his urine a dark red-brown.

The vet, a gruff young woman named Terry Tomkins who'd received her degree from nearby Cornell University, arrived later that evening, exhausted after visiting several farms where cows had ingested disagreeable substances, developed milk fever, and in one case retained her placenta after giving birth. She was familiar with Chance and immediately recognized the change in his mental status and vital signs. Firing off a litany of questions, the vet attempted to hone in on whatever had afflicted the previously-healthy Appaloosa.

"He seems dehydrated," said Tomkins. "Make sure he has plenty of water and keep an eye on him overnight. If his respiratory rate increases to a point where it seems like he's struggling to breathe, call me and I'll come over. I'm just not sure what the best course of action is right now. You're pretty certain his diet hasn't changed, and you haven't grazed him in any new pastures, given all the snow. It leads me to believe there must be another reason why he isn't feeling well."

Isabella slept in the stable next to Chance's stall. Her father brought her a sleeping bag, hot coffee and buttered toast, sitting beside her for a couple of hours before returning to the house and bed.

By morning, Chance was wobbly. The pale, yellowish gums had turned dark brown. His urine was nearly black. Isabella called the vet in a panic.

When Tomkins arrived, she wore a look of apprehension. Setting her medical bags just outside the stall, she cautiously approached the horse.

"His heart rate is through the roof," the vet said. "And he's still dehydrated. I'm starting to suspect it may be something he ingested that we didn't know about."

"But what could it be?"

"Did Chance have any access to automotive anti-freeze, something your father might have used for the tractor? It's sweet tasting. Small animals like cats and squirrels often succumb after drinking it."

Isabella brought her fingernails to her lips in dismay. "No. Nothing like that."

"What about motor oil, though I doubt a horse would drink that?"

"No. It's kept in the shed with the door closed. That's where we keep gas tanks for the power washer and other tools."

"Pesticides? Herbicides?"

"Also locked in the shed."

"Rat poison? Are there traps set in the barn? Have you sprayed the stable or barn with any chemicals?"

Isabella broke into tears. "I don't know. I'll have to ask my dad."

As though on cue, Chance shuddered and vomited into the hay that covered the floor of his stall.

Isabella shrieked. "Oh my god. He's getting sick."

"Let's get something to scoop it up so that we'll have a sample to take back to the lab."

Two hours later, the vet was on the phone with the Marceau family. "It seems Chance has eaten wilted red maple leaves. They're toxic, especially if he has ingested a lot of them. Do you think that's possible?"

The Marceaus were baffled. The horse was allowed to roam

the fenced pasture in all seasons, but the recent snowfall would have covered over most fallen leaves and brush.

"We may have to bring Chance to the veterinary clinic at Cornell, but I'm not certain he could withstand the road trip in his condition," said Tomkins. "Chance needs intravenous fluids and possibly blood transfusions."

Isabella pushed back her tears long enough to ask the vet a question. "Is he going to die?"

"I'm so sorry, Isabella. There's a chance that Chance will pull through, but the odds are not in his favor."

Chance collapsed in his stall the following day. Isabella rushed in to hug him, tears spilling down her cheeks and onto the warm horse. She held him and pressed her face against his muzzle. "Please don't die, Chance," she whispered in his ear. "Don't leave me alone."

For two days Isabella was too distraught to attend school. Sick from grief, she couldn't eat or sleep. It was a horrible way to start off the new year.

Hope Cooper stopped by the Marceau home to offer condolences and tell Isabella she was welcome to ride any of their three mounts. Isabella put her arms around Hope and sobbed, thanking her for reaching out. She might visit the Cooper stable once her emotions were under control. But right now, she needed to find out where Chance had encountered the fallen leaves that had caused his death.

At least a dozen species of tree leaves were scattered about the property. Some were drifted into piles against the house and barn, others in furrows along the fences. Thousands of leaves lay decomposing in the fields and often the wind blew them into the paddock and corral. The hillside overlooking the farmhouse was filled with red maple trees, *acer rubrum*, a deciduous species that every autumn went out in a fiery blaze of color. It was among Isabella's favorite images of the fall season and every year she waited for the show. Now she hated those trees, if it was true they killed her horse. She pictured herself with her father's chainsaw, cutting them down until there were none. Though in her heart, she knew such an act would not make her feel better. She tried to conjure the happiest moments with Chance, but that only made her cry. She missed him terribly. She just couldn't fathom how he had eaten so many of the toxic red leaves.

32

PREPARE FOR THE YANQUI INVASION

JANUARY 1989
CIA HEADQUARTERS, LANGLEY, VIRGINIA

Hannah's eyes were blurry from researching statistics on Cuban military strength, but she understood why Bill Carrington needed them. She also knew her report might, in some vague way, help keep Emmett Decker alive.

Carrington was responsible for determining not only the potential Cuban military response against a multiple-team assassination force, but also for keeping his operatives safe.

Perplexed by the lack of sound information from Belize and Guatemala and stressed by his inability to routinely communicate with Decker, he felt chained to his desk at Langley. It was an overwhelming sense of frustration that in some ways explained his need to clean and oil the weapons in the secured cabinet behind his desk.

Hannah's briefing to Carrington was flawless and to the point. It was Hannah at her best, providing just the facts and allowing the listener to draw their own conclusions.

"By 1980, Cuba had created a new militia to defend against the so-called *Yanqui invasion*," she said. "The Soviets sent them every piece of military hardware imaginable at a discount price – tanks, planes, armored personnel carriers, stockpiles of small arms. Castro divided the island into 1,300 defense zones and several hundred thousand citizens, male and female *milicianos*, were recruited to defend them."

Hannah noted troop strengths in the early 1980s consisted of 145,000 military regulars, mostly conscripted privates who served for three years.

Due to Soviet generosity, the Cuban military also possessed 300 T-62 and 650 T-54 battle tanks. The Cuban Navy boasted 12,000 sailors, three submarines, two guided-missile frigates, and dozens of patrol craft and mine sweepers.

"They own a lot of hardware, sir," she said. "They also have about 4,000 elite, KGB-style border guards. Add to that about 2,000 troops who work solely for government agencies and 15,000 more who are part of the country's secret police. Those are the guys who answer to the Department of State Security. Any and all of these can become an obstacle to an offensive force."

For a moment, Hannah felt like a bullshit artist, talking in numbers and vagaries. "I guess what I'm saying is, Cuba has a shitload of military and paramilitary troops, many of whom may know how to shoot a rifle or fire an artillery piece."

Carrington rested his elbows on the desk and cradled his chin in the palms of his hands. He seemed mesmerized by Hannah's voice, her ticker tape of statistics. He concentrated on her lush lips as she spoke.

"It actually gets worse," she said. "The number of armed troops, trained and partially-trained, is expanding rapidly. We've heard estimates Cuba now has upwards of 1.3 million men and women trained to fight an invasion. While that may be a some-what accurate number, it doesn't reflect their political sentiments."

"And what are those sentiments?"

"There's no fresh intel on whether these people will protest the loss of their key government and business leaders -- presuming those leaders are eliminated."

Carrington appreciated Hannah's briefing. The reported troop strength was significantly larger than he had imagined or anticipated. On the other hand, Cuba was the size of Pennsylvania, so those troops would likely be spread over the relatively large Caribbean island.

"I'm hoping you can relay this information to Decker," she said. "It might impact the sort of decisions he makes when the bullets start flying."

"Point taken," he said. "We have some communications channels open. They're only threads, but so far they have proved sufficient."

"Well, since that's the case, if I may be so bold, please tell Jared Malone in your next dispatch that I miss his ass and look forward his arrival home safe and sound."

Carrington smiled warmly. "Will do, Ms. Mariel Becker."

33

ROCCO'S REVENGE

JANUARY 1989

FINGER LAKES REGION, UPSTATE NEW YORK

On a whim, Isabella decided to get off the homebound school bus at the Cooper vineyard rather than at her home. She felt miserable about losing Chance and could think of little more than how her father had used the backhoe attachment on the tractor to dig a hole in the frozen ground and bury him. The ground was hard from the frost but after scraping through the top layers of soil the task became easier.

Together her parents and two sisters stood beside the grave as Isabella read a poem she had written for Chance. They each tossed a flower into the hole before it was covered over.

Isabella knew she needed to break out of the funk caused by her grief. Chance was gone, but she could still visit with the horses at the Cooper vineyard, especially Marvel, which had been Nick's favorite.

It was a sunny and cold late afternoon when the school bus stopped beside the roadside mailbox marking the entrance to the

Cooper property. Rocco lit a cigarette as soon as he stepped off the bus and caught up with Isabella who already had begun walking along the unpaved driveway.

"Those are gross," she said, referring to the cigarette. "Why do you smoke them?"

"I enjoy it. You want one?"

"Absolutely not. Doesn't it taste disgusting? I tried one when I was fourteen and coughed for about an hour. It was awful."

Rocco took an exaggerated puff off the Marlboro and blew the smoke out in a single exhale. "Ah," he said. "My mother, Angie, well, the woman who used to be my mother before I came here, smokes Virginia Slims. A pack a day, sometimes more. Vinnie didn't like her smoking but she didn't care. She hid them all over the house. Funny thing was, she'd complain if he lit up a cigar inside."

"Do you miss her?"

"Angie? Shit no. She means nothing to me."

"Hope told me Angie sent you a gift for Christmas. She said it was more like a care package."

"I guess you could say that. She made me a wool sweater, knitted it herself. That was nice of her, only the yarn colors she chose look like something from a Peruvian Indian tribe. She also sent some chocolate bars, as though we can't buy them around here. She probably thinks there's no chocolate for sale anywhere north of Albany."

"That's very sweet," said Isabella, picking up the pace of their walk, in part because she was eager to see the horses but also to limit conversation with Rocco.

"Angie thinks of everything. She actually stuck three packs of smokes, some scratch tickets and a box of rubbers in the box."

Isabella didn't respond. Rocco looked over at her with a menacing smile on his face. "Maybe I'll get lucky," he said, pausing purposefully before adding, "With the scratch tickets, I mean."

Hope and Gary were pulling out of the driveway in the Jeep Wagoneer. "We're headed to the supermarket. Do you kids need anything?"

Rocco flung the cigarette into the snow to the side of the driveway were the smoke continued to curl upward. "I'm all set," he said.

"Isabella it's so good to see you. Are you going to say hello to the horses?"

"I thought I would. Maybe just spend a little time in the stable. I don't think I'm up for riding yet."

"Do whatever feels right," said Hope.

Gary waved from the driver's seat. "You're always welcome here," he said sincerely. "We'll be back in a couple of hours if you'd like to stay for dinner."

"Oh, yes," said Hope. "Please do. I'll make homemade pizza. Or maybe I'll bring a couple of pizzas back from town. Do you like pepperoni?"

Isabella shrugged her shoulders, uncommitted, and marched straight for the stable. She set her winter coat and her backpack loaded with books just outside Marvel's stall and gently called to him. The horse murmured and neighed, twisting his head as though trying to get a look at Isabella.

"Did you miss me? I wish I had an apple to give you," she said, slipping inside the stall and running her hand along Marvel's muzzle. "I'll bet you miss Nick, too. He liked to ride you and I know he gave you all sorts of treats."

Rocco sneered. "I think Nick liked to ride you too," he said, his tone unmistakably contentious. "What is it about him that you like so much? He seems like such a loser. I'm sure my father, I mean Vinnie, has figured that out by now."

"You don't have to put down somebody you barely know."

"I'm not putting him down. Just stating the facts. He's a country bumpkin tossed in with some very sophisticated people. They're going to laugh at his shit kickers and flannel shirts."

Exasperated, hands on her hips, Isabella looked hard at Rocco. "Why are you here?"

"Where?"

"In the stable. Don't you have chores to do, or something? Homework?"

"Maybe I'll go do some yard work, rake some red maple leaves."

Isabella felt a chill rush through her body. Rocco stepped inside the stall and reached out to touch her hair.

"What are you doing? Get away from me!"

"You think you can just come in here like you own the place. Maybe that's what you did when your buddy Nick lived here, but things are different now. You want something, you gotta go through me."

"Oh, fuck off. Now you sound like a gangster."

Rocco grabbed Isabella's arm but she pulled away, backing farther into the stall. Marvel's ears were turned back sharply and pinned to the sides of his head. His tail swished as his head lowered slightly and snaked side to side.

"I think you like the attention," he said, pulling her into his arms. "I'll bet you haven't gotten laid for six months, so don't tell me you don't want it."

"Take your hands off me!"

Marvel snorted. His forelegs were stomping, coming down hard on the thin cover of hay in the stall.

Rocco pushed a hand beneath the back of Isabella's sweater and clumsily attempted to unclip her bra. When the clip didn't open he slid his hand around so that it was beneath one of the bra cups and began fondling her breast.

Isabella tried kneeing him in the groin but missed. She put both hands above her head and attempt to slip out of his clutches by lowering her body almost to the ground, as students had been taught in self-defense class, but Rocco was determined to hold onto her.

"Oh, we have a little tiger here," he said, nuzzling her ear. "Let's see what you've got down below."

Isabella dug her fingernails into his arms, causing him to momentarily release his grip. "You bitch," he said, staring at the claw marks before pressing her neck against the stall boards.

Marvel was stomping at a faster pace, his head waving back and forth, dipping lower until his muzzle nearly touched the hay-strewn floor.

Rocco stuffed his hand down the front of Isabella's bluejeans until he felt her warmth. Isabella twisted her neck out of his grip and bit down hard on his fingers.

"God dammit. You're going to pay for that," he shouted, pressing his full weight onto her so that she was pinned against the boards. He unzipped her jeans and tried to pull them down over her hips.

"Stop it, Rocco."

Rocco forced his tongue into her mouth. "You like that?"

"Let me go!"

Again he tugged on the jeans until they were at her knees. With Isabella still pinned against the boards, he undid his belt and yanked down his pants and underwear at the same time, exposing himself. "You know you want this," he said. "All women do."

Rocco was panting heavily as he maneuvered between her legs. Marvel was stomping and neighing. The other horses had picked up on the overall tension and were moving in their stalls. Isabella sunk her teeth into Rocco's cheek, drawing blood. Rocco pulled his face away but held tight, butting his forehead against hers so that the back of Isabella's head struck the stall boards. Again he tried to force himself inside her. Isabella screamed loudly as she made what she sensed might be her last attempt to fend him off. She grabbed his balls and squeezed with all her might. Rocco released his grip on her body, looking anguished, but his eyes were still filled with hatred and sexual rage. Isabella knew that in a few moments, Rocco would adjust to the pain and resume his assault. She needed to run.

The kick sent Rocco backward. He landed on his back outside the stall. The hoof had caught him squarely in the forehead so that he lay unconscious on the stable floor, his pants and underwear around his knees, blood gushing from his nose.

Isabella didn't bother to check Rocco's pulse. She didn't care if he was dead. She straightened her clothing, put her arms around Marvel's neck and kissed him a dozen times before she grabbed her coat and backpack and briskly walked home. She wanted to tell her parents what happened, but she was certain her father would go directly to the police and file a criminal complaint. The story would be all over the school and the small town. She'd have to deal with Rocco again in court if it came to that. It would also bring more trouble for Hope, who was genuinely a good person. Instead, she telephoned Nick.

34

NICKED OFF

Nick slammed down the phone receiver so hard Ruby jumped in the armchair where she was knitting a hat for Baby Carla. He stood in the middle of the small living room and growled like a wild animal, emitting a sound that was more a painful moan than a burst of aggression.

"What is it, Nick?"

Nick stormed off into his bedroom and slammed the door. Ruby could hear him punching the wall. Something made of glass shattered. Drawers were pulled open and slammed closed. When Nick emerged from the bedroom, his hair was disheveled, his eyes ablaze with a craziness and intent Ruby had only seen before in nightclub customers fueled by drink or drugs or lust as they attempted to climb onto the dance stage before the bouncers knocked them back.

"I've got to run," he said. "Isabella needs me."

Ruby was surprised Nick told her precisely where he was

headed. "Nick, it's cold outside. It's January. How you going to get all the way up there in New York without freezing to death? Whatever it is can wait."

"No, it can't, Ruby. Rocco just tried to rape Isabella. He's gone nuts. I'm the only one who can help her."

Ruby placed her right hand over her gaping mouth. "Oh, Nicky. I'm so sorry."

Nick slung the heavy backpack over one shoulder. "Please don't tell Vinnie, don't tell my father where I've gone. He'll be angry and he'll try to stop me."

Ruby looked fearful but promised to lie. She'd tell Vinnie she had fallen asleep with the baby and didn't hear Nick coming or going. When Nick failed to arrive at school the next morning, the attendance officer would undoubtedly notify the boy's father, kicking off a widespread search.

It was late afternoon and already dark when Nick bought a bus ticket to Boston. If Nick's luck held, his father would spend the night elsewhere, as he often did with a showgirl or stripper. As a result, Vinnie wouldn't find out Nick had skipped school until sometime before noon the following day.

The connecting Greyhound bus from Boston arrived in Ithaca, New York at 5:30 a.m. It was not yet sunrise. Nick knew he'd have to hitchhike the rest of the way. It was a school day so Isabella would likely be out of bed in about an hour, when he'd call her from a payphone.

Isabella's mother answered the call. She didn't ask Nick what he might need to talk about so early in the morning, but he could tell she wanted to know. Isabella whispered she intended to get a ride to school from her mother, who had an appointment in Ithaca. She'd wait just beyond the school grounds at the certain tree near the rear entrance road. She didn't want to take the bus for fear Rocco might be on it.

A junior-class boy driving a beat-up Mustang fastback spotted Nick walking along the road and gave him a ride.

"Are you coming back?"

"I'm trying to figure things out," Nick said.

"People were saying you moved to Rhode Island because a family there adopted you."

"Don't believe everything you hear."

"That would be weird."

"It certainly would."

Nick ran toward Isabella when she saw her pacing beneath the towering pin oak. It was their special place, somewhere to meet on warm days between classes and sit on the low branches. Isabella wrapped her arms around his neck and burst into tears.

"I'm so glad you're here. I know you're going to be in trouble, but I really needed to see you."

Nick kissed her repeatedly on both cheeks and forehead, holding her face in his hands. "I'm going to kill that fucker!"

"I thought Marvel already did," she said. "But Hope didn't call my house, so I'm presuming Rocco regained consciousness and made up some story about how he was injured."

"You're probably right. We should go somewhere warm where we can talk and then I'm going to find out if Rocco went to school today."

Rocco Merlino was absent from the regional high school. Hope had phoned the school to say he wasn't feeling well. She had found him in bed with a nosebleed and bodily bruises when she and Gary arrived home from shopping. Rocco claimed the injuries were his own fault and that they occurred while he was attempting to feed the horse and clean its stall.

Hope asked if Isabella had been present when Marvel suddenly kicked. According to Rocco, Isabella had spent a few minutes with Marvel and stopped to pet the other horses before leaving. The last time he saw her she was headed homeward.

35

A HARD NIGHT

Exotic dancer Delilah Deeply had riveted Vinnie Merlino's attention from the moment he first set eyes on her. She was a new hire at the Crystal V, one of the Rhode Island nightclubs from which he annually extorted ten-percent of the profits, making him in underworld terms a part owner.

Vinnie sat in the front row most of the evening and Delilah Deeply locked eyes with him whenever she wasn't forced to gaze out at the hungry audience. Her routine included placing a variety of objects in her mouth, including a policeman's baton and a stick of pepperoni, culminating with a short sword that disappeared down her throat until stopped by the hilt.

When her show was over Vinnie suggested they have a drink in the manager's office behind the stage where they could talk business. He assured her a promising future at the Crystal V. An hour later they were in the hot-sheets motel next door.

Delilah Deeply was naked and asleep when Vinnie awoke at

8 a.m. He didn't bother to say goodbye to the young woman but left two hundred dollars on her pillow. His head near bursting from a hangover, he drove straight to Ruby's apartment, not bothering to shower.

Vinnie leaned precariously on the wooden coat rack in the apartment entryway. It was just after 9 a.m. and daylight was streaming in through the living room windows. Vinnie heard Ruby rustling in the back bedroom.

"Ruby, my darling, I need some coffee."

"Hard night, Vinnie?"

"Had to work. Things came up."

Ruby knew that was the only explanation she would get. When Baby Carla began to cry she heard Vinnie say, "Jesus Christ, I wish to hell that kid would shut up. Fuckin' broads are all alike."

Ruby quieted Carla and went into the kitchen to make fresh coffee. When it had fully dripped she poured Vinnie a cup, spilling some over the rim.

"Sometimes I think clumsy is your middle name," he said, scowling and grabbing a dishcloth off the counter to swab the spill. "Not enough sleep? Maybe you should take something to knock you out."

"I can't do that, Vinnie. I have to be awake in case Carla needs me in the middle of the night."

"Speaking of sleeping, Nicholas's bedroom door is closed. Didn't he make it to school."

Ruby's pale complexion flushed and she looked away, as though she hadn't heard the question.

"Where's Nicholas?"

"At school."

"He better be, if he knows what's good for him."

Ruby took another coffee cup from the cupboard and set it on the counter. She poured herself a cup and purposefully made a ritual of adding the cream and sugar. It gave her something to do and a reason to avert her eyes from Vinnie's scowl.

"You're not telling me something. I can feel it."

Ruby stopped stirring the coffee.

"If you know something that I should know, you better spit it out."

"I've got to go check on Carla."

"Sit down," Vinnie said.

Ruby sat at the kitchen table and laced her fingers together.

"I'll try this again. Where's Nicholas?"

In a voice barely audible, her eyes cast down at the tabletop, she said. "He's gone."

"Gone where?"

"I don't know. I noticed some of his things are missing."

Vinnie pounded the table so hard the cups bounced and coffee spilled over their rims. "You're lying."

"I'm not. I was napping with Carla. She was awake most of the night. I was tired. I guess Nicky came in. I didn't hear him coming or going."

"Then how do you know he's gone?"

"I don't."

"You just told me he was gone."

"Maybe he is."

Vinnie cuffed Ruby across the face, hard enough to know she'd be sporting a raccoon eye by midday. "Where is he?"

"I told you, I don't know."

Another slap on the opposite side knocked Ruby off the chair and onto the floor. She screamed. "You bastard!"

Vinnie kicked her in the ribs. "Get up."

When she moaned, he kicked her again. Ruby got herself to a kneeling position. Vinnie grabbed her by the shoulders and slammed her down onto the chair. He gripped her wrists and squeezed them until tears spilled down her cheeks.

"You're hurting me."

"I've only just begun," he said. "Now where's my son?"

A third slap drew blood from Ruby's lips. She was no longer crying but blankly staring off into space.

"Did he go back to those pig farmers in upstate New York?"

Ruby didn't answer. She cried out when Vinnie gripped her hair and lifted her body from the chair.

"Yes."

"Yes, what?"

"He went to help his girlfriend, Isabella. He said Rocco attacked her."

"You mean Rocco raped her?"

Ruby's body was shivering from fear. "I think so."

Vinnie released Ruby's hair and she crumpled into the chair. He angrily stabbed his fingers at the keypad on the wall phone. Ruby heard him order Fingers and Alfredo to search for Nick and not to return to Providence until they'd succeeded in finding him.

FOLLOWING THE THREADS

JANUARY 1989
BOSTON, MASSACHUSETTS

Hannah brought up the police incident report on her computer monitor at the FBI field office in Boston's Government Center. The Federal Hill address in Providence, Rhode Island matched the apartment rented by Ruby Salerno.

"Look at this," she said to FBI Special Agent Sally Parker, pointing to the illuminated report. "The Providence police were called by neighbors because a woman was screaming at this address yesterday. It's where Vinnie Merlino shacks up with his girlfriend and their baby girl. Every name associated with the strike force investigation is flagged to come up."

Agent Parker sipped her coffee. "And you think this incident is somehow important? Sounds like a domestic."

"I don't know. It might be worth taking a ride to Providence and having a chat with Ruby."

Deputy Special Agent-in-Charge Jack McGuire rapped on the glass partition that surrounded the cluster of desks where the

Anti-Organized Crime Strike Force made its home, interrupting their discussion.

"I've got something here that may be of interest to you," he said to Agent Parker, holding what looked like the transcript of a conversation. "The name Isabella Marceau popped up in the data base. Apparently she lives in upstate New York and phoned our field office in Albany last night with a wild story about how her boyfriend is being chased by the mob."

Hannah and Agent Parker exchanged knowing glances. Parker asked, "Who's the boyfriend?"

"The name she gave was Nicholas Cooper. She hung up abruptly before she was able to finish telling her story. We have a trace on the phone so getting her address won't be difficult. We can have an agent from that field office pay her a visit."

"Did she happen to say why the mob is looking for Nicholas Cooper?"

"She did. She claims her boyfriend overheard his father plotting to kill several important people in Cuba on the same day. She said his father was bragging about it and showed him a list of names."

Agent Parker dropped the pen she was holding. "Oh my god! Nick knows the details of his father's assassination plan. No wonder they want him back under wraps in Providence."

"I assume this information is directly related to the strike force investigation?"

"It is, sir," said Agent Parker. "Nick Cooper's biological father is Vinnie Merlino. The boy didn't know that until last June. He was happily living in New York with a family he believed was his for fifteen years. But a DNA test and a court order changed all that."

The deputy SAC shook his head. "That's unfortunate for him, but potentially fortunate for us if we can get to him first," he said. "If you need additional resources, let me know."

Hannah and Agent Parker drove to Providence, Rhode Island

that afternoon. From their cruiser they watched the comings and goings at the apartment building. There wasn't much traffic. Ruby answered the door after about five knocks. She wore a pink two-piece tracksuit and was barefoot. She looked tired and bruised, blackish yellow rings around both eyes.

Parker flashed her credentials. "May we come in?"

"What's this all about?"

"We just want to talk to you."

Ruby backed away from the door, clearly frightened. "You've got to get out of here. If Vinnie knows the FBI was here and you talked to me he'll be really angry."

"It looks like he's already been angry," said Hannah, raising her eyebrows as she studied the woman's darkened eyes and cut lip. "We know the city police were here. When somebody gets beaten up, it's a crime against the state, not the victim. Besides, you apparently told the officers who responded that your boyfriend, Vinnie Merlino, also threatened your baby."

Ruby stepped behind the dining room table as though to put distance between her and the agents. "I want my lawyer," she said.

Agent Parker smiled warmly. "You're not under arrest. You're not a suspect in any crime. We were just hoping you might tell us where to find Nicholas Cooper."

"That's what Vinnie wanted to know. I'm going to tell you exactly what I told him. I don't know where Nick is. He's not here."

"But you may have an idea where he was headed," Parker said gently.

Ruby considered the question. She stepped out from behind the table. "You've got to leave, now. You don't know what Vinnie's temper is like when he's mad."

"I can just imagine," said Parker, turning to her partner. "Let's go, Hannah."

As they opened the apartment door to leave, Ruby stood in

the middle of the room, tears coursing down her cheeks. "Vinnie doesn't care about Carla, our baby. Only sons are important to him. He told me he was happy when Carla was born, but I knew he wasn't because she was a girl."

Hannah gently placed a hand on Ruby's shoulder. When she didn't flinch, Hannah wiped the tears from the woman's cheeks with the back of her fingers. "Girls can grow up to do great things. I'm sure Carla will be one of them," Hannah said. "Don't ever let anyone tell you otherwise."

Ruby closed her eyes, only partially convinced. "Nicky went to see his girlfriend in New York. Not the city. Up in the country," she said. "I don't know where, exactly. Her name is Isabella. Somebody tried to rape her and Nicky was going to find the guy."

Agent Parker handed Ruby a business card. "We have to go. But call me any time if you want to talk," she said.

Ruby looked at the card as if it was coated with bubonic plague. "I don't want any FBI card. Vinnie finds that, I'm dead."

Parker pocketed the business card and turned to leave. Hannah followed close behind.

Back in their cruiser, Agent Parker suggested stopping by Angie Merlino's apartment before heading back to Boston. It was only a few minutes away by car.

As soon as Angie saw the FBI shield in Agent Parker's hand, she tried to push the door closed. Hannah's foot was already inside.

"Please, Mrs. Merlino. We're not here to cause problems," said Hannah. "Your son, Nick, may be in danger. We need to find him. We thought he might be here or have contacted you."

"If you want information, talk to my husband," she said flatly. "Nobody tells me anything. I'm not even allowed to see Nick. Now please leave or I'll call the state cops and tell them you're harassing me."

Convinced they'd reached a dead end, the women backed out, apologizing for any interruption they may have caused.

"No matter what, that woman is always going to be loyal to Vinnie Merlino," said Agent Parker as she reapplied her lipstick in the car. "Believe me, I'm half Italian. It's a cultural thing."

"I'll take your word for it," said Hannah, sensing it might be true but wishing it wasn't.

At Agent Parker's insistence they stopped at Scialo Brothers Bakery on their way out of the city. She bought a dozen Pignoli almond cookies while Hannah sat in the car, trying to stick to her healthy foods diet. She prided herself on looking great in a bikini and wanted to keep it that way.

During the fifty-mile drive back to Boston the two women laughed and talked and finished the cookies. Both realized they could be friends.

37

THE HUNT

Nick knew he had to find somewhere to hide while he waited for the opportunity to beat Rocco Merlino to a bloody pulp. It was only a matter of hours before Vinnie found out he had run off and would send men to bring him back.

Isabella suggested the barn where Chance had been stabled. She'd bring him blankets and food but wouldn't tell her parents. He appreciated her willingness to help but rage at a magnitude he'd never before experienced welled up inside him. He needed to get closer to Rocco and, when the moment presented itself, make him pay for what he had done to Isabella. He would extract vengeance for her and, if he still felt the need, more punishment would be doled out for killing her horse.

"I know every nook and cranny at my old house. There are lots of places to hide on the property and I'll be closer to Rocco. I'll be ready for him when he goes outside at night to smoke a cigarette or drink the liquor he probably keeps stashed."

Nick and Isabella walked the horse trails until they reached the Marceau house. She went inside and quietly put fresh fruit, a ham sandwich, chocolate chip cookies and two cartons of orange juice in a paper bag.

"Take this with you. I'll get more tomorrow," she said, handing him a wool blanket as she longingly took in the sight of Chance's empty stall. "He was such a good horse. I can't believe that bastard killed him."

"Are you sure?"

"Right before he attacked me, I asked him if he shouldn't be doing some chores to help his mother and Gary. He laughed. He said he might go rake some red maple leaves. And he said it in a way that he wanted me to know he had fed them to Chance."

Nick approached his old home from the back acres where a row of trees divided the farmhouse and barns from the fields of grapevines. It provided adequate cover as he made his way past the barn to the stables, a spacious structure where Gary Schneider stored his supply of caskets until they were needed at the funeral home in town.

Nick climbed the loft ladder and squeezed through a narrow opening in the wallboards. It led to a quiet refuge he had discovered and claimed as his own when still in elementary school. He smiled with his eyes at the sight of two mostly-melted candles inside rusted tin cat food cans, a flashlight with long-dead batteries, a plastic soda bottle filled with water, a pack of playing cards, and a tattered copy of Playboy magazine.

When morning finally came, Nick was stiff from sleeping on the hard boards. The wool blanket had helped keep him from freezing, but his body was shivering.

Nick could see the farmyard from his perch in the barn loft. Hope, the woman he called Mom for fifteen years, was peering out the front door, her right hand locked around a mug of coffee.

It appeared as though she was talking, but she was not cradling a phone. Nick assumed Gary or Rocco was in the living room only steps away on the other end of Hope's conversation. Moments later, Gary sleepily stepped out onto the porch, kissed Hope on the cheek and slowly trudged across the farmyard to the barn. Nick watched as Gary counted the caskets and conducted some sort of quick equipment inventory related to his funeral business.

Still clutching her coffee cup, Hope headed for the stable to give the horses feed and fresh water. Their early-morning tasks completed, they met in the middle of the farmyard where Gary put an arm around Hope and pulled her in for another quick kiss on the cheek. From the years he had lived with this couple, Nick had never witnessed any extremes of passion. It seemed they got along and looked out for one another, but there was no sizzle, not the kind he imagined he might one day have if Isabella were his wife.

Nick watched Gary's covered pickup rumble down the frozen driveway, chugging toward town and what was undoubtedly another funeral service or meeting with a bereaved family. Hope followed him down the driveway minutes later, the brake lights of her Jeep Wagoneer glowing in the weak post-dawn light.

Nick made his way to the house and peered in the windows. The door to Rocco's bedroom, which had been Nick's bedroom until his life was turned upside down eight months earlier, was closed. The bedroom window was ajar. Rocco lay asleep.

38

THE CLASH

Nick rummaged in the tool shed where he found a spool of monofilament fishing line, pruning shears, a two-foot length of steel pipe, a burlap bag and a coil of heavy jute rope. He tossed the rope over a beam in the stable and tied a primitive hangman's noose at one end. The horses stirred but he quietly shushed them before reentering the farmhouse though the front door, which was never locked. He tied a length of the clear fishing line across the bedroom door about eight inches off the floor and sat down in one of the well-worn but comfortable living room chairs.

A half hour elapsed but there was no sign of Rocco. Nick became impatient. He twisted in the chair so that the legs made a rubbing noise on the floor. He tapped the steel pipe a few times. Muffled sounds came from inside the bedroom as Rocco stirred. Sleepy-eyed, Rocco opened the door and stepped forward, tripping on the fishing line. Sprawled across the floor in his polka-dot boxer shorts, he was stunned to see Nick sitting in the chair.

Nick struck him across the back with the steel pipe, knocking him so that he lay face down.

Rocco slowly got to his knees and cursed, vowing to have Nick killed. Nick struck him again with the pipe, this time aiming for the fingers on Rocco's left hand that were braced against the floor for balance. The pain caused Rocco to topple. Another pipe blow to the shoulder left him in a fetal position.

Nick pulled the burlap bag over Rocco's head and cinched it. Rocco was breathing but he no longer fought back as Nick dragged him by the arms across the frozen ground to the stable. The horses whinnied but Nick spoke to them in a gentle tone while he slipped the noose around Rocco's neck.

Marvel had turned in his stall, attracted by the commotion and the sound of Nick's voice. Nick petted the horse's muzzle and whispered in his ear as he backed Marvel out.

Rocco stirred where he lay on the concrete floor. Nick slipped the jute rope around Rocco's neck and tightened the hangman's knot. He tied the bitter end of the rope around Marvel and pulled the reins so that the horse would follow him farther into the stable. The rope went taut as the slack was eliminated and lifted Rocco to a sitting position. Rocco moaned, reaching for the burlap bag over his head.

Nick nudged Marvel forward until Rocco's body was upright, his feet barely touching the floor. Rocco cried out. "Why are you doing this?"

"You know why."

"I didn't fuck Isabella. That's what this is about."

"But you tried, against her wishes."

"It was a dumb move. I admit it."

"It's too late for confessions. You tried to rape my girlfriend and you would have if this horse right here hadn't kicked you in the head."

Rocco began to weep, the sound muffled by the burlap bag.

"My father will kill you."

"Did you forget already? Vinnie's not your father. Surely you don't mean Gary?"

Nick made a clucking sound with his tongue and Marvel took another two steps. Rocco pointed his toes, the only part of him in contact with the floor. His fingers were gripped around the rope to keep it from embedding in his neck.

"I'm sorry. Please. I don't want to die," he said, coughing in short bursts, his words barely decipherable. "I didn't mean to do it."

Nick pictured Rocco trying to push himself between Isabella's legs and the fury rekindled inside him. He clucked again and Marvel obeyed.

Dangling from the rope, Rocco gasped, his eyes bulging, legs scissoring the air. Nick swung the metal pipe into Rocco's groin. "You deserve to die," he said, tossing the pipe aside.

Nick backed up Marvel so that the rope relaxed, spilling Rocco onto the floor. Rocco groaned in pain. Nick kicked him in the head. "That's for Chance," he said, tossing the pruning shears next to Rocco's body.

"If you ever try to touch Isabella again, I won't be so merciful," he said. "I'll cut off your dick."

39

HAS ANYBODY SEEN NICK?

JANUARY 1989
FINGER LAKES REGION, NEW YORK

Gino "Fingers" Terranzetti and Alfredo "The Animal" Ponzi drove rapidly to upstate New York in a black Cadillac registered to a person whose name they'd didn't recognize. They assumed the car was borrowed or stolen but they didn't think much about it beyond that. It was business as usual. The trip should have taken six hours but Alfredo made it in just over four, pedal to the metal, keeping his fingers crossed that they wouldn't be stopped by the police for speeding. The unregistered guns in the trunk would have been hard to explain.

The Cooper vineyard on Cayuga Lake was their first stop. Fingers remained by the back door while Alfredo pounded on the front. Hope answered the door, startled by Alfredo's appearance in black -- pants, shirt, shoes and overcoat.

Alfredo didn't introduce himself. He assumed Hope Cooper might recognize him as the man who had dropped off Rocco at her door in June and handed her an envelope containing $5,000 in expense money.

"I'm here to collect Nicholas Cooper," he said, blowing cold breaths into his tight black leather gloves. "Is he here?"

Hope nervously shook her head, feeling her pulse quicken when she looked deeply into the man's emotionless eyes and realized they'd previously met. She saw a second man guarding the back door, which pushed her heartbeat faster.

"Can you tell me where I might find him? It seems he left home and became lost. We're here to help."

"And what's your interest?"

Alfredo's face was so serious and deadly it sent a chill through Hope's entire body. He stared directly into her eyes -- reminding Hope of a King Cobra rising from its wicker basket and puffing its hood. He waited at least fifteen long seconds before answering.

"I represent his father."

"Nick doesn't live here anymore."

"We're aware of that," said Alfredo.

"Well, I'm sorry I can't help you," said Hope.

Alfredo slowly adjusted the wrist straps on his black leather gloves, which always elicited a sinister effect.

"Sit," he said, guiding her by the arm to one of the club chairs in the living room. He alternated stretching his gloved fingers and making a fist, repeatedly opening and closing his hand as though he was loosening them for some undisclosed purpose. Hope watched out the corner of her eyes. She sensed he was toying with her. She assumed all would end peacefully if she simply remained quiet and polite. She realized her assessment was wrong when Alfredo punched her in the stomach, causing her to double over in pain. When she finally raised her head, Alfredo broke her lip with a quick jab.

Hope rolled back in the chair, protecting her face with her hands. "I told you I don't know where Nick is. He isn't here."

Fingers pushed through the back door and stepped into the house. "Little lady, please understand we have a job to do."

"Go to hell," Hope said in a moment of defiance. "Both of you. If you don't leave immediately, I'm going to call the sheriff."

Fingers swapped his smile for a snarl. He grabbed Hope's left hand and pushed a finger into the jaws of the compact bolt cutters he carried in his coat pocket. "If you no longer care about wearing rings, this shouldn't bother you," he said with a twisted grin.

Alfredo crossed his arms and stood back, as though preparing to watch a show. "We know Nick is here somewhere. When he hears about your fingers, he'll come straight to us," he said.

Hope knew what Alfredo said was probably true. Nick could be impulsive and on dozens of occasions over the years had stepped forward to help people in need, always seeking to right an injustice.

Fingers squeezed the bolt cutters onto Hope's ring finger where she wore a simple wedding band but no diamond. The pressure was too light to draw blood but Fingers wasn't in any hurry. He liked playing with his victims, something he had learned about himself as a boy when he slowly tortured a neighbor's cat. He had duct taped the animal's forelegs and rear legs so it was immobilized and helpless. For three hours he inserted hatpins into the cat's body, the ones he'd stolen from a drawer in his mother's bedroom. He cut off the cat's tail and whiskers with a dull pair of scissors, laughing as it moaned. The cat was bleeding from the punctures but refused to die. Fingers piled two cinderblocks atop its body and casually walked to the corner store to buy a Coke and a bag of potato chips. When he returned, the cat was dead. He tossed the carcass into a trashcan in the alley.

"Please stop," Hope cried out as the blades dug into her skin. "You're cutting me."

Alfredo's grin faded when he heard the sound of footsteps on the porch. "What was that? Did you hear something?"

Fingers slipped the bolt cutters into his coat pocket and rushed to the window. Alfredo was already aiming his Glock 17 at the ghostly figure that had staggered onto the farmer's porch.

"Holy Christ," said Alfredo, whipping open the front door. "Rocco. What the hell happened to you?"

Hope shrieked. "Get him inside," she said. "He's freezing to death."

Fingers put an arm around Rocco and led him to the couch. The rope was gone but the burlap bag, though no longer covering his head, dangled from his neck where a thick red furrow was cut into the skin. Rocco was shivering. His long blond hair was caked with blood.

Hope grabbed a plaid blanket that had been draped over the back of the couch and put it around Rocco's shoulders. "I'm going to call a doctor," she said, reaching for the phone.

Alfredo roughly gripped her wrist. "No. No doctors. No cops. This is a private matter."

"But he needs medical attention."

"We'll get him what he needs. He's breathing. He'll be fine. But first we got to find out what happened."

Rocco struggled to speak. "Nick," he said.

Fingers leaned an ear closer to Rocco. "Nick did this?"

Rocco curled into a fetal position.

"Is he still here? In the barn? In the stable with the horses?"

Rocco didn't reply. His crying had turned to sniffles.

"Stay here with them," said Alfredo, sliding back the action on his pistol to ensure a round was in the chamber. "I'll go check the other buildings."

Nick had returned to his hideout above the stable. He had enough food and water for about three days. He also had the hunting rifle he'd taken from the house. It had once belonged to the late Brent Cooper, the man he believed for fifteen years was his biological father. He wrapped himself in the wool blanket and thought about Isabella. She promised to meet him later that evening at a specific point along the horse trails. Two of the horses were gone, leaving only Marvel and two older mares in the stable. That meant Isabella would be waiting for him. But now their plan was seemingly off the table. Nick could hear Alfredo, frustrated by the turn of events, tossing equipment around in the barn.

Back inside the house, Fingers wasn't looking forward to calling Vinnie with the news, which was unpleasant for both boys. He also knew Vinnie was on edge because the Cuba operation was set to happen any moment. The organized crime families involved were going to meet in Miami the next day and not all of them were happy about the way Vinnie had divided up the potential spoils. If Cuba was going to be their country, several of the bosses wanted no interference in how they planned to run things.

40

HOLD ON, WE'RE COMING

Vinnie Merlino shouted into the pay phone for close to five minutes without pause after Fingers told him Nick was still missing and Rocco had been badly beaten up.

"We'll find him, boss. He can't be far, and it's winter. He's not going to stay outdoors. He's going to look for shelter," said Fingers. "This whole fuckin' place is ass-deep in snow and it's still coming down."

"I want you to get a dozen guys up there right away to help you. Make the calls," Vinnie said, still out of breath from his tirade. "It's my fucking son we're talking about here. He knows too much. I don't want the feds or anybody else pumping him."

"I understand, boss. Everything's contained. I'll get some muscle up here. What do you want me to do about Rocco?"

"Does he need a doctor?"

"I'm not sure. Nick did a number on him."

For a split second Vinnie felt secretly proud of Nick. "Rocco has always been a sissy when it comes to taking a punch," he said.

"He might have had his balls bashed in too, boss. He's doubled over on a bed in one of the bedrooms and he's got a lot of bruises and swelling."

"For Christ's sake, call Doc Rimsky and tell him to get his ass up there. Tell him there's two thousand bucks in it for him."

"Will do, boss. Anything else?"

"Just find my fucking son. Me and Nunzio are at the Miami airport waiting for LoScalzo to send a car. I'll let you know what room we're in when we get to the hotel so you can reach me. I'm going to be stuck at this sit down for a day or two with these bush league pricks.

Fingers used the Cooper farmhouse phone to call the Rhode Island doctor who could be trusted not to say a word about those he medically treated. Dr. Benjamin Rimsky promised he would be there as quickly as possible. Fingers informed him a car was already waiting out in front of his office.

After several more calls, a convoy of three black vehicles was assembled and on the move -- a Lincoln Town Car, a Buick Electra and a Chevrolet Suburban. Two men occupied each vehicle, all of which had a cooler of beer on ice and a variety of rifles, shotguns and pistols. Some were dressed in sporting wear, others in leather loafers, city trousers and pullover cashmere sweaters or cardigans. Once they arrived, they'd change into high-priced outdoor gear – mostly snow boots, hats, mittens and mountaineering jackets recently acquired from a hijacked tractor trailer.

Martino "Marty White" Bianco, clad in one of his two-piece tracksuits and sneakers, rode shotgun in the Town Car. He had been responsible for ensuring adequate manpower, stocking the firearms and ammunition, fueling the vehicles, prescribing the best highway routes, and making sure everyone had enough to eat and drink during the trip. He knew Vinnie would come down hard if any details were neglected.

41

MEET ME IN MIAMI

Vinnie Merlino was sweating profusely as he strolled into the Fountainebleau Miami Beach Hotel. The weather was hotter than usual for January in Miami.

Nunzio Carlucci was at this side, lugging both suitcases while Vinnie approached the reservation desk. Both men felt the many sets of eyes upon them. It was obvious their arrival was anticipated and the subject of much discussion in the underworld and the intelligence community.

"I smell G-men," Vinnie said aloud to Nunzio, laughing as though on holiday. "We'll have to call LoScalzo's housecleaners and get the room swept."

Vinnie would have preferred being accompanied by Fingers Terranzetti and Alfredo Ponzi, but the two trusted soldiers were busy searching for the elusive Nick.

Although Vinnie liked Nunzio Carlucci, he knew the man answered first and foremost to Garafalo, the Boston underboss who currently was giving orders from behind bars following his federal court conviction for racketeering.

Miami mob boss Patsy LoScalzo walked slowly toward his associates from New England, flanked by two burly young men with bulging biceps and unsmiling faces. He thrust out a hand so that he and Vinnie could shake.

"Welcome to Miami, my friend," said LoScalzo, patting Vinnie on the back.

Vinnie Merlino broke into a full smile, his one gold tooth gleaming. "*Amico*," he said. "So good to see you. We have to get together more often."

He introduced LoScalzo to his companion Nunzio Carlucci and the two men shook hands like old friends. LoScalzo didn't bother to introduce the bodyguards. He nonchalantly pointed his thumb over his shoulder. "When you've settled in, we'll see you at the bar. I'll show you some Miami hospitality."

"You're a saint," said Vinnie. "We could use a drink."

Vinnie phoned his Providence office but nobody answered. He called the number Fingers had given him to the Cooper house. Fingers picked up the receiver but didn't say a word.

"Is anybody there?"

Recognizing the boss' voice, Fingers immediately said hello and launched into an update about how the men he had requested were on their way and expected to arrive at the vineyard shortly. Alfredo was still out and about, searching the buildings and vehicles for any sign of Nick. The doctor was also en route. Not to worry. Rocco was breathing fine, and despite a pounding headache his overall body pain was lessening.

"I gave him three of my Percocets," Fingers said in a way most any caring father might when giving his son a Tylenol tablet. "He's on the couch."

"What about the mother?"

"She was pulling a nut job, completely *pazzo*, saying she was going to call a doctor, call the cops. We had to tie her up in the back bedroom."

"Well, don't hurt her. It's not her fault that she's Rocco's mother."

"Her husband hasn't come home yet. I guess we'll deal with that when the time comes."

"Use your best judgment," said Vinnie.

Twenty minutes later, the two New England mobsters were standing at the hotel bar with LoScalzo and two of his closest associates. There was plenty of joking and raucous laughter as they drank and swapped stories. While Carlucci pounded down several drinks in short order, Vinnie was far more reserved, choosing soda water every other round because he didn't want to be dull and hung over at the meeting of the families.

As planned, the sit down among the four crime family leaders got underway promptly the next morning in a spacious suite with panoramic ocean views that had been rented by LoScalzo.

"Welcome, gentlemen," said the host. "Be assured our room has been swept by the hotel's housecleaners and ours."

"A clean house is a happy house," said John Gotti, the so-called Dapper Don and head of the New York crime family. His words prompted a burst of muffled laughter. "That's the way we like it in New York."

"And in Chicago as well," said Sammy "Wings" Cardisi, head of the Chicago Outfit. "I'm grateful that we can all work together, see eye to eye."

"And in Providence," said Vinnie Merlino. "We're a good team. New York, Chicago, Miami, and Providence along with our associates in Boston."

Hours of debate followed, most of it concerning how the casinos and hotels would be operated once the Castro government was eliminated. Although no ironclad resolutions were reached, the men seemed in buoyant spirits as they left the room, planning to take up their discussions later in the evening during dinner.

Nunzio Carlucci was lounging near one of the swimming pools where dozens of young women in skimpy bikinis were sunbathing or frolicking in the water.

"We're free for the next several hours, thank Christ," said Vinnie, plopping down on a chaise lounge next to Carlucci. "You have a nice day so far?"

"It sucks being here," said Carlucci, gazing around at the bikinis.

"Any word on Nicholas?"

"I called the number Fingers left us an hour ago. There was no answer."

A white-jacketed waiter appeared with another beaded bottle of Budweiser and set it on the small table between the chaise lounges.

"Maker's Mark on the rocks," said Vinnie, looking exhausted as he slumped into a more comfortable position. "Not that I need it."

When the bourbon appeared, Carlucci raised his beer bottle. "Salute. To the families."

"To the families."

Vinnie closed his eyes. "After I have my drink, I'm going to walk the beach. Take a closer look at the local wildlife. It helps relieve tension. You're welcome to join me."

42

MARTY WHITE AND THE REINFORCEMENTS

Fingers Terranzetti breathed a sigh of relief when the Lincoln Town Car, Buick Electra and Chevrolet Suburban came barreling up the crushed-stone driveway to the Cooper vineyards.

Alfredo was still scouring the grounds, attempting to find Nick. Hope remained tied up in the back bedroom. Rocco was asleep in the smaller bedroom.

Fingers stepped out into the frigid late afternoon to greet Marty White and the five other reinforcements. "Head inside where it's warm," he said, patting his upper arms as though he'd just parachuted into Antarctica. "But don't go into the back bedrooms. They're occupied."

The six men clamored out of the vehicles, popping the trunks and hatchbacks to retrieve their weapons, winter clothing, food and drink. Soon they were gathered in the living room, dressed in boots, parkas and wool hats.

"We look like a goddam advertisement for L.L. Bean,"

quipped Marty White. "Whoever made this stuff had to kill a lot of flannels."

Giovanni Sacco, aka Breadsticks, was the largest man in the room and still struggling to put on his snow boots. His reddened face wore a look of confusion and frustration. "Marty, there ain't no such animal as a flannel."

"I know that, you shithead," said Marty White, astonished by the mere possibility one of his men was such a brickhead.

"You're both wrong. I've heard you can legally shoot a flannel," said Fingers. "But only when they're in season."

Marty White laughed. Breadsticks seemed even more confused. It was snowing and Marty White wasn't looking forward to a march through the woods. He surmised the men in his crew felt similarly. "We'll give the property a once over," he said. "Then we'll come back here, sit in front of the fire and have a few cocktails."

One of the men powerfisted the air and growled his approval. Others pounded the arms of the chairs or stomped with their feet. They liked the idea and were now motivated to do what they'd come to do and then have a few drinks in the warm farmhouse.

"Don't be surprised if you run into Alfredo," said Fingers. "He's been turning over stones for several hours. He's convinced the kid hasn't gone far."

Marty White divided the men into small teams and assigned them to search specific buildings. "When we're done with that, we'll fan out into the woods before it gets dark."

Shortly after the teams departed, a fourth vehicle pulled into the farmyard. Dr. Rimsky stepped out from the back seat clutching a medical bag to his chest and looking nervous. Fingers called to him from the porch and led him to the small bedroom where Rocco lay on the bed with eyes closed.

As Dr. Rimsky began taking the boy's vital signs, a covered-cab pickup rambled to a halt and parked amid the crowd of vehicles. Gary Schneider hoisted two grocery bags from the front seat of the pickup and trotted toward the house. He didn't like the sight of multiple Rhode Island license plates, and while his instincts told him to take it slow and, if necessary, call the 911 emergency number, he was propelled by the need to know if Hope was safe.

"Trouble," mumbled Fingers, but there was nobody else in the living room to hear.

Gary Schneider opened the front door. "Hope," he shouted. "Are you here? What's going on?"

Fingers stuck a gun in the man's back. "Shut your mouth! Any more noise and I'm going the put this gun to the back of your head and blow your brains out."

Digging the barrel deeper into Gary's spine, Fingers guided him toward the couch. "Sit down and shut up and don't make me tell you again."

Gary Schneider did as he was told, sitting quietly with his hands folded, forearms resting on his thighs, until he heard Hope moan. He instantly stood but before he could protest all went dark as Fingers slammed the pistol against the side of his head.

Dr. Rimsky heard a dull thud as a body collapsed on the braided rug. He peered out from the back bedroom but didn't say a word.

"When you finish with Rocco, you can look at this one," said Fingers, rolling Gary Schneider onto his back as blood gushed from the head wound. He pushed Schneider's head sideways with his foot so he wouldn't swallow his own blood and choke to death.

"I'll be right there," said Dr. Rimsky.

"Stay with Rocco. He's more important. I've got to take a look at our other guest."

Hope Cooper had wriggled off the bed and onto the floor, apparently in an attempt to reach the phone on the nightstand.

"You're being a bad girl," said Fingers. "We didn't come here to hurt you, but if you try to escape again, things might turn out differently."

Hope cursed, or at least that's what it sounded like through the adhesive tape pressed across her lips.

Fingers lifted the woman and tossed her on the bed, her body slightly bouncing as it landed on the mattress. He tightened the rope that held her wrists and ankles and put another strip of tape atop the first one across her mouth. "Be a good girl," he said. "As soon as we find Nick, we'll be gone."

Alfredo stomped his snowy boots on the front porch.

"Any luck?"

"I'm going to turn this place upside down and burn it to the ground if necessary," said Alfredo, tossing his snow-covered coat onto the nearest chair. "But first I need a cup of coffee. I'm freezing my ass off. I ran into Marty White and his crew. They're going over the same areas."

Alfredo was pacing near the large windows that looked out over the farmyard when Dr. Rimsky entered the living room and assessed Gary Schneider's medical condition. "You whacked him pretty hard," the physician." He might have a concussion."

"If you say so," said Fingers. "You're the doc."

"What I'm saying is, he might need a hospital. If you hadn't hit him so hard, he wouldn't."

"Fuck you, doc," said Fingers. "Your job is to fix sick people, not tell us how to do our jobs. So shut the fuck up and make sure that guy don't die."

Dr. Rimsky scowled as he tended to Gary Schneider. Rocco coughed blood in the back bedroom.

"Sounds like you're going to be busy," said Fingers. "The emergency room back in Providence is going to seem like a piece of cake after this."

"I don't work in the emergency room."

"Well, whatever it is you do, go do it."

Although it was still dusk, the search team members began

trickling into the farmhouse. Before long, they were gathered near the fireplace where they were having difficulty getting a small blaze started.

"You need kindling. Small dry stuff," Marty White said to the big man they called Dumbo, who was on his knees trying to entice a pile of twigs and paper towels to life with a match. "Keep blowing on it until it catches."

The fire still wasn't lit when Alfredo briefly disappeared and returned with a paper cup full of gasoline he'd siphoned from one of the vehicles. Without warning, he splashed the gasoline onto the twigs. A muffled explosion followed, causing Dumbo to lose his balance and topple to the floor with a loud grunt.

Alfredo snapped two dried boards across his knee and tossed them into the flames. He shook his head in disappointment as Dumbo struggled to his knees. "After you're done laying around, you can put some logs on the fire," he said.

43

FINGER LAKES FOLLIES

The Anti-Organized Crime Strike Force headquarters was a hive of activity as FBI Special Agent Sally Parker went over details of the mission on a whiteboard, her voice straining to stay above the shouting, clatter and ringing phones.

"We have a few stops on our list. We don't know what to expect when we get to the vineyard, but we can most likely assume there will be some opposition to our presence," she said, clicking the projector's remote control to show a bird's eye view of the property. "So we need to be on top of our game. Some of the people we're dealing with could care less about shooting a law enforcement officer, and I don't want that to happen."

Hannah Summers had faded toward the rear of the room and leaned against a wall, sensing FBI agents would prefer to hear the operations plan from one of their own. With Decker in Belize, Guatemala or somewhere else, she was the only CIA officer on the strike force.

"We'll take four vehicles," Parker said. "I'll be in the lead vehicle with Summers and two other agents. Twelve additional personnel will follow in the other vehicles. Special Agent Barba will give out your assignments. Everyone should wear body armor and take a radio. The tactical teams will carry tear gas, door-breaching explosives and the ram. All weapons should be double-checked to ensure they are functioning properly. Make sure you bring along extra magazines in case this thing turns into a shootout."

Agent Parker distributed color 8-by-10 photographs of Nicholas Cooper, Rocco Merlino, Hope Cooper and Isabella Marceau. "Our primary goal is to locate Nicholas Cooper, since he's the one with information about Vinnie Merlino's plan to assassinate government officials in Cuba," she said. "We currently have a team of agents in Miami where Vinnie Merlino has joined the heads of other organized crime families for what appears to be a high-level meeting. The surveillance team hasn't turned up a goldmine of information, but we can say for certain right now that Vinnie Merlino and Nunzio Carlucci are in Florida. That leaves us to speculate where Merlino's other top soldiers might be, especially Fingers Terranzetti and Alfredo Ponzi – both bad dudes."

Agent Parker held up another stack of photographs. "Two more pix for your photo albums," she said, trying to keep things light. "This is a rare one of Fingers Terranzetti smiling. Maybe he had just killed someone. The other, of Alfredo Ponzi, was taken by Agent Summers, who is currently holding up the wall at the back of the room."

The FBI agents craned their heads toward Hannah, who returned a two-finger salute.

"Let's hit the road and find Nick Cooper," said Parker. "We should be at our destination by midafternoon."

The Marceau farmhouse was the strike force's first stop. Tom and Sophie Marceau were arguing loudly in their kitchen when Hannah and Agent Parker knocked on the front door. The couple didn't hear the rapping or had chosen to ignore it as they continued the row. Hannah and Agent Parker used the opportunity to listen.

"Why didn't you keep an eye on her while I was out of town?"

"She's sixteen years old," said Sophie, cupping her hands over her face in frustration. "She doesn't listen to what I tell her."

"Do you know for sure that she's with Nick?"

"I don't know anything for certain, other than she's not in her room, the barn or the stable."

"God dammit, Sophie. I hope she didn't take off with Nick. These days, he's a magnet to trouble."

"She loves him and he loves her. Don't you remember what that feels like? There was a time when you would have done anything for me."

Hannah put her ear to the door while Agent Parker peered in through a front porch window.

"I know Isabella was scared, not for herself, but for Nick. He told her his father was planning to kill a lot of people in Cuba, and that there was a list with names on it. She asked me if she should call the police or the FBI to let them know."

"And what did you tell her?"

"I told her to stay out of it, not to get involved. That was the last time we talked."

"Do you think she called them anyway?"

Agent Parker glanced at Hannah. "Sounds like our cue," she said, giving a hand signal to the team of eager agents hunkered out of sight behind buildings, trees and fences. A return hand signal confirmed the team would remain in place and wait until provided with more instructions.

Without further delay, Agent Parker hammered the front door with her fist. "FBI," she shouted.

Sophie Marceau nearly fainted, her eyes wide with disbelief. Tom Marceau stormed toward the front door, filled with indignation. He yanked open the door and stared at Hannah and Agent Parker, both dressed in black fatigues and body armor, their handguns holstered.

"What the hell?"

Agent Parker pushed her way into the house and reflexively did a quick 180-degree surveillance.

"Do you have a warrant?"

"We're here to talk to your daughter, Isabella. She may have information that makes her a target for some very bad people."

"I don't know what you're talking about."

Hannah entered the house, gun drawn, quickly stepping right to get a better view of any rooms and stairways behind them. Sensing it was clear, she holstered her weapon and approached Tom Marceau.

"I think you know precisely what we're talking about, Mr. Marceau," she said. "Your daughter unfortunately knows about a grand plan to assassinate officials in Cuba."

"What a load of hogwash," he said, his thin lips formed into a deriding smile. "I don't know where you people come up with these stories."

"That knowledge could put her in jeopardy," said Hannah. "

Agent Parker puffed her cheeks and blew out an exasperated breath. "Two days ago, she called our office in Albany. The call was cut off, but it was obvious from the tone of her voice she thought it was important we know about this plan. She was very concerned that her boyfriend, Nick, might be harmed because he has refused to live with his biological father in Rhode Island. She indicated he was attempting to hide."

Tom Marceau's shoulders drooped in despair, his bravado gone, arms hung motionless at his sides. His wife began to cry, her head resting on arms folded on the table.

Hannah took a few steps toward the staircase leading to the second floor. "Do you mind if we look around?"

Tom Marceau shook his head, his mind in a daze. Hannah and Special Agent Parker checked the upstairs rooms and the cellar. There was no sign of Isabella. They sifted her belongings for notes, ticket stubs, anything that might offer a clue to where she was headed. But they came up empty.

"OK, she's not here. Can you help us find her?"

Tom Marceau flopped down on the couch. "I wish I could."

44

GETTING CROWDED AT THE VINEYARD

JANUARY 1989
FINGER LAKES REGION, NEW YORK

Special Agent Parker was brimming with frustration after meeting with Tom and Sophie Marceau. She radioed the SWAT teams to return to their vehicles, except for one officer who would stay behind with the Marceaus to ensure they didn't make any phone calls or do anything foolish that might endanger the operation.

"Our next stop is the Cooper vineyard, less than two miles from here," she said into the microphone fastened to her earpiece. "We'll establish a perimeter around the main house with teams One and Two. Everybody else will focus on the outbuildings. If we encounter any opposition, don't fire unless fired upon."

Parker keyed the microphone. "Respond by team if understood."

The teams acknowledged her orders as the vehicles barreled along the narrow country road. A few minutes later they were fanning out and surrounding the Cooper house. "Team Three. Give me license plate checks on all of those vehicles," she said into the microphone. "It might give us a better idea about just who's inside. Looks like some folks from Rhode Island got here before we did."

"Team Three, roger that," came the reply.

"Please bear in mind we're here to protect a potential federal witness in a case of suspected terrorism," said Agent Parker. "Keeping Nick Cooper safe is our primary objective."

Hannah gave Agent Parker an enthusiastic thumbs-up. "Let's do this," she said.

In the hidden compartment above the stable, painful cramps shot through Nick's legs, but he didn't dare move. He felt as though he hadn't breathed a full breath for hours.

The tiny room had seemed huge when he was ten years old, a secret space for three or four boys to get away from their parents and siblings and play cards, tell stories, look at girly magazines. But now it was just a hollow between the planks with only inches to spare if he stretched his entire length.

Isabella had given him two apples, a Hershey bar with almonds, a plastic bottle of water and a wool blanket. He felt grateful, but there was no time to eat or sleep. Once he became convinced the search party had given up and returned to the house, he'd make his way to Isabella. He wondered if she was waiting on the trail with two horses as they planned. Knowing Isabella, she'd be there, and they'd ride to the old cabin on the ridge and hope that Vinnie's men were not ambitious or competent enough to track them. And if they were, well, he had the hunting rifle and twenty rounds of ammunition.

45

A GOOD DAY FOR A SHOOTOUT

January 1989
Finger Lakes Region, New York

Fingers Terranzetti's sixth sense urged him to peer around the window curtains for a better view of the farmyard and the driveway approach. "Looks like we got company," he said.

"Two vehicles, maybe more. They're parked down on the road. Gotta be feds."

Fingers spotted Alfredo Ponzi standing near the side door to the stable, brazenly smoking a cigarette. Alfredo was also eying the vehicles.

"Everybody listen up. I need three of you at the upstairs windows. The others stay down here to cover the front and back doors," said Marty, clapping his hands for emphasis. "Let's go. Let's go."

The men lethargically headed to their assigned posts while cursing the government, the winter weather and in general the need to follow orders.

Dr. Rimsky poked his head out the door to the bedroom where Hope Cooper was bound and gagged. "Trouble?"

"No trouble. We haven't done anything wrong. We were invited here," said Fingers, stepping toward the couch where Gary Schneider sat with his hands folded in his lap. He grabbed the man by an ear and twisted it. Schneider cried out in pain.

"Ain't that so, Gary? We were invited."

The funeral director remained silent. The gash on his forehead from the pistol-whipping had dried into a crusty splotch. Fingers cuffed the side of his head. "Just in case anybody knocks on the door and asks, we came here looking for Nicholas Cooper and you invited us inside for coffee," said Finger. "You got that?"

Marty White grabbed Schneider by the forearm and escorted him to the kitchen sink. "Wash that blood off your head. Then we'll find you a Band-Aid."

Dr. Rimsky began pacing nervously in the living room. "What about the woman? Even if her husband cooperates, she's not going to stay quiet," he said. "I don't want to lose my license to practice medicine because you people decided to take hostages."

"Fuck you and your doctor's license," said Marty White. "You get paid generously in cash so just do your job. Can't you give her something? Don't you have a pill or a shot that will knock her out for a few hours?"

"Of course I do. But if the FBI is out there, they'll have questions about what happened to her, not to mention Rocco in the other bedroom. He's a mess."

Rocco groaned. He was leaning against bedroom doorframe. "Nick jumped me. When I get out of here, he's a dead man," he said. "I'm putting a hit out on him."

Marty White smiled pensively. "Rocco, you can't put a hit out on the boss's son."

Dr. Rimsky rolled his eyes and let out an exasperated snort. "The police are going to ask a lot of questions. They'll want to know who beat him up," he said.

"It's none of our concern. Rocco was like that when we arrived," said Fingers. "Maybe he can tell the feds what happened to him. We're only here because we're looking for Nick. There's no law against that."

Gary Schneider returned to the couch, the gash no longer bleeding but clearly visible beneath the small Band-Aid. "The police aren't stupid. They're going to know you busted your way in here and that you hurt Hope," he said. "There's a law against that."

Fingers braced a foot against the man's torso and pushed, knocking him to the braided carpet. "You just don't know when to shut up."

The phone rang six times before Fingers finally lifted the handset.

Tinny sounds emanated from the receiver. "Hello. Hello. Is anybody there?"

Fingers immediately recognized Vinnie's voice. "Right here, boss."

"Will somebody tell me what the fuck is going on? Do you have my son?"

A pause. "We're still working on it. Lots of places to hide around here."

"You still don't have him?"

"No boss. Not yet."

"What about the woman, Hope?"

"She's here. She's not going anywhere."

"What the fuck is that supposed to mean?"

"We're just holding on to her until we find the kid."

"Where's Alfredo?"

"He's still looking in the buildings."

"Fingers, I need you to find my son and bring him back to Rhode Island. We need to protect him. He's mixed up. We don't want him talking to the Feds until he has his facts straight."

"We'll find him, boss."

"I'm flying home tomorrow morning. I'd like to see Nicholas waiting at the airport with you when I arrive," said Vinnie, ending the call.

Rocco put on a winter coat and walked stiffly toward the front door as though in pain. Fingers blocked his path. "Where the fuck do you think you're going?"

"I'm going to find Nick and kill him."

One of the men guarding the front door to the house chuckled. "That's the spirit, kid," he said.

Fingers shot a glance at the man that warned him to keep his comments to himself.

"Nick is still in the stable. I know it," said Rocco.

"If he was, Alfredo would have found him," said Fingers.

"Nick knows this place better than anybody. If there's a place to hide, he knows where it is."

Rocco stepped out onto the front porch and shivered in the cold. He patted his forearms and studied his steamy breaths as they rose toward the ceiling. He was wearing only socks on his feet.

"Hey kid, at least put on some boots if you're going to stand outside," said Fingers.

Embarrassed, Rocco sat near the fireplace and tried on a pair of winter boots that were part of the hijacked goods. "I'll be right back," he said, again stepping out into the cold and heading for the stable.

Rocco fished the Dupont lighter from the front pocket of his pants. He also owned a vintage Zippo, but the Dupont was his favorite. He'd admired the weighty gold device since first discovering it years ago in Vinnie's nightstand drawer, intrigued by its sleek case, the sparking flint and the smell of flammable fluid. He liked the distinctive click it made when he flipped the cover closed.

Rocco guessed Vinnie wouldn't miss it, but he also understood that taking something without permission could have serious repercussions. The nightstand drawer was like a pirate's treasure chest, with knotted piles of gold chains, solid-gold religious medallions, and several Rolex wristwatches, some in their original display boxes, others just tossed into the mix. By comparison, a cigarette lighter was worth nearly nothing.

Once inside the stable, Rocco immediately noticed two of the five horses were missing. Marvel stirred as Rocco approached and climbed the stall planks, perching on the highest board. Marvel eyed him warily, moving side to side and tapping his hooves.

Rocco flicked the lighter. The sight of the flame made Marvel rear his head, his eyes bulging with fear.

"How do you like that, Marvel? You don't have to worry about going to the glue factory when you're old because you're going to be roasted horsemeat before the end of the day."

Rocco closed the lighter lid and then flicked it open, enjoying the precise pinging sound it made. He descended to the stable floor and again sparked a flame, extending it toward the horse.

"See if this feels warm," he said, igniting a clump of hay at the entrance to the stall. Marvel began snorting and stomping. A thin plume of smoke rose from the hay.

Rocco returned to the highest stall board from which he looked down at Marvel and laughed, clapping his hands. He was thrilled by the animal's look of fear.

"Going to get a lot toastier," he said, holding on tightly as the horse kicked the planks. Marvel bashed his hindquarters against the boards just as Rocco was sliding the Dupont into his front pocket. The lighter slipped from his fingers and fell into the stall.

"Fuck. Now look at what you did," he said to the horse.

The clump of burning hay had begun to smolder, threatening to spread to the loose fibers strewn across the cement floor. Rocco heard a cough. It came from somewhere inside the stable.

"Oh, Nicky. I know you're in here," he said, attempting to mimic the taunting voice of actor Jack Nicholson in the movie

The Shining. "Guess you're having trouble breathing with all this smoke."

Alfredo appeared in the stable entrance. "Jesus Christ, what the fuck is going on? Rocco, are you in here? Is that you?"

Another cough. Alfredo swung around toward the sound, his trigger finger twitching on the Mini Uzi machine pistol.

The smoke was getting thicker, rising into the rafters. The horses were snorting wildly. Rocco scampered down from the uppermost plank and tried to reach his arm through to recover the lighter. It was just beyond arm's length.

"Rocco? You in here?" Alfredo shouted.

Flames were dancing toward the stacks of hay bales and once they ignited the building would quickly become engulfed.

"Over here. I gotta get my lighter," he said, carefully opening the stall where Marvel was clomping his hooves. He dashed toward where the gold lighter sparkled in the hay, snatched it and began backing out of the stall when Marvel pinned him against the boards. Rocco flicked the lighter in the horse's face but the animal was already in full panic.

Alfredo swirled around at the sound of more coughing, his eyes wide as he watched the lid open on one of the dozen caskets stacked in the corner of the stable. Nick sat up, coughing and rubbing his eyes.

Alfredo pointed his machine pistol at Nick. "You've caused a lot of people a lot of problems today."

Nick was still coughing when a scream filled the stable. "Help! Back here. Help me!"

"Don't move a fuckin' muscle," said Alfredo, warning Nick to stay put. "Your father wants you back home so we'll be leaving here as soon as I find out what's happening with Rocco."

Alfredo backed toward the stalls from where Rocco's cry had come, the machine pistol still pointed at Nick. Another scream filled the air, louder and more urgent than the first, followed by a desperate moan.

Alfredo unlocked Marvel's stall, allowing the terrified horse to escape as it shrieked in terror. The other two horses kicked wildly in their stalls. Rocco lay sprawled in the smoldering hay, the glittering Dupont clutched in his right hand. His skull was deeply crushed, blood gushing from his ears, nose and mouth. It was obvious to Alfredo that Rocco was dead or would be shortly.

As Nick tried to climb out of the casket that was stacked atop two others, the wooden box teetered and crashed to the floor. Nick staggered as he got to his feet, halting momentarily at the sight of Alfredo pointing the machine pistol in his direction.

"This little game is over," said Alfredo.

"I'm never going back," said Nick, who turned and ran toward the stable doors.

Alfredo fired the machine pistol, the bullets ripping into and splintering the wood above the stable doors.

At the sound of gunfire, Special Agent Parker gave the command. "All teams move in," she said. "There may be hostages. I repeat. There may be hostages."

It was snowing as Nick raced into the farmyard. Alfredo sprayed the ground, kicking up chunks of frozen soil.

Two well-placed bullets struck Alfredo, one in each thigh. His finger continued to squeeze the trigger as he crumpled to the ground, unleashing a fusillade that forced Hannah to take cover. Alfredo writhed in the snow, still clutching the machine pistol. Another bullet slammed into his shoulder and the weapon skittered away.

Two FBI agents grabbed Nick as he ran toward the driveway. The other teams approached the farmhouse. Dr. Rimsky burst out the front door, hands raised above his head. "Don't shoot," he said. "Don't shoot. I'm a doctor."

In a moment of unbridled anger, Fingers picked up the hunting rifle leaning against the stuffed chair, aimed and fired. Dr. Rimsky fell forward to the ground, the bullet entering his back and opening a massive hole in his chest.

Special Agent Parker shouted into her microphone. "Hold fire. Hold fire. We don't know who's in the house."

Another radio transmission filled her earpiece. "Target acquired on the A side of building, upstairs east window. Requesting permission to fire."

"Hold fire," she said.

A second sniper radioed. "First floor target acquired. Subject is armed."

"Wait," she said.

Hannah kept in the shadows as she moved toward Alfredo. When she was out in the open, a bullet grazed her coat sleeve and she rolled toward the burning stable. The muzzle flash had come from the house.

Agent Parker's earpiece again chirped. It was Hannah whose voice was calm and clear. "First floor target has opened fire. I'm pinned down near the barn."

Parker edged the microphone close to her lips. "Second sniper, did you copy that message?"

"Message copied."

"Do you have the target in your sights?"

"That's a roger."

"Take him out."

A single bullet slammed into Fingers' forehead, bursting his skull into fragments.

The radio crackled. "Target is down."

The SWAT team medic accompanied by Special Agent Barba rushed to Alfredo's side to assess his wounds. Hannah didn't wait. She crawled into the burning stable, trying to stay below the layers of smoke. She could hear the two remaining horses snorting and kicking in their stalls. Keeping below the smoke, she unlatched the stall doors, but the horses refused to back out.

Hannah searched for a bridle but the smoke was dense. She found a bamboo stick tucked behind a hay bale and banged it against the stall boards. Still the two horses remained in place, turning in circles. She smacked the bamboo against the flanks of the first horse. The animal began to back away. She hit it harder the second time so that the horse reared up. A split second later she rolled into Marvel's stall to avoid the crashing hooves and 1,500 pounds of muscle. Her body came to a halt, obstructed by what she quickly realized was Rocco's body. The sight of him trampled and bloodied in the hay filled her with nausea but she still had another horse to save. Once again she resorted to the bamboo stick, striking the animal until it finally fled. Hannah got to her knees as the horse ran out of the stable.

With Fingers dead and Alfredo out of the fight, the others in the house looked to Marty White for leadership. "We're going to get out of here," he said. "We'll take these two with us for insurance."

Special Agent Parker raised her bullhorn. "This is the FBI. You are surrounded. Come out of the house with your hands over your head."

Four blinding spotlights illuminated the farmhouse from different angles. A helicopter hovered overhead.

Marty White gestured toward Hope Cooper, still bound and gagged in the bedroom, and Gary Schneider, seated on the couch where he remained incapacitated by fear.

"We're coming out with two hostages. If you do anything stupid, both of them will die," said Marty White, clad in a navy two-piece tracksuit. "So move your people back." He knew it was a dumb plan, but he was out of ideas. The FBI was less likely to open fire when two hostages might be harmed. That was a given. But even if they made to their vehicles, it was only a matter of time before they'd be forced to give up the hostages, or kill them. And it was bad enough already that they'd be charged with murdering Dr. Rimsky, unless they could prove Fingers did it without their approval or assistance.

Leaning against the wall nearest the door, Marty White

looked down sadly at the consigliere, blood puddles seeping across the floor, most of his head missing.

The phone began to ring. Marty White ignored it as he rubbed the gold crucifix around his neck with two fingers. He silently offered a prayer to St. Jude, saint of the impossible, asking for divine intervention.

Special Agent Parker waited patiently until the fiber-optic cable was snaked and provided a view of the interior, mostly the living room and adjacent doorways. Gary Schneider was on the couch. Hope Cooper was out of sight. One target was down on the floor, presumably dead. At least two others with weapons were in the immediate vicinity.

Special Agent Parker ordered the breach team to move closer to the front of the house but remain hidden. When she was certain all her agents were in place, she gave the go signal. Two agents wearing gas masks and armed with rams and shields burst through the flimsy rear door of the house as a tear gas grenade shattered a front window and began hissing on the floor, filling the living room with eye-stinging fumes.

Gary Schneider got up from the couch and charged toward Marty White, tucking a shoulder into the man's abdomen and momentarily pinning him against the wall. It was the first act of violence he had engaged in since returning from his deployment to Vietnam in 1968.

The breach team flattened the front door, powering into the living room followed closely by other heavily-armed agents in black helmets and gas masks. It was a chaotic scene punctuated by coughing, shouting and gunfire. Moments later, two of Marty White's men lay dead and two others – Dumbo and Breadsticks -- were suffering from non-fatal gunshot wounds. Marty White and Breadsticks were face down on the floor, handcuffed and spread eagle. An FBI medic attending to Alfredo radioed Parker that the patient had lost a lot of blood and was going into shock, but an air ambulance was en route.

Special Agent Parker untied Hope Cooper who hurried to her husband's side and burst into tears. She repeatedly asked whether Nick had been found and if he was unharmed.

"Nick is safe," said Agent Parker. "He's with our agents."

"I need to see him."

"That isn't possible right now."

"Why not? He's my son."

"I can't get into the details."

"Where's Rocco?"

"We'll talk about all of this later," said Parker. "You've had a very traumatic experience. You need to stay calm and try to relax."

Hannah appeared in the front door holding her right arm where a bullet had creased the skin. One of the SWAT team members dressed and bandaged the wound, which was superficial.

Hannah locked eyes with Agent Parker. "Time to talk to Nick."

46

DOUBLE-CROSSED

Most residents of Federal Hill likely heard the initial roar and the torrent of bitter invectives that emanated from Vinnie Merlino's mouth and out the window of his office.

Vinnie sensed not all was going well when instead of the usual driver a neighborhood kid he barely knew met him at Logan Airport.

"Where's Alfredo?"

"I don't know, sir."

"Where's Fingers? He was supposed to be here."

"I don't know that either, Mr. Merlino. I was just asked to pick you up and drive you back to Providence."

Vinnie went ballistic when he found out Fingers and Rocco were dead, Alfredo gunshot and hospitalized in Syracuse, and Marty White under arrest for kidnapping and murder. Dr. Rimsky and two of Vinnie's most-trusted associates were also headed to the cemetery. It was a bleak day.

But what most set him off was news that Nick was likely being interrogated by the FBI and spilling his guts about the Cuba takeover plan. If his suspicions proved correct, the Feds could now give all the targets a heads up that hit teams were coming their way. His mercenary force would be slaughtered.

For the first time in his life, Vinnie felt truly alone. But he was determined to push ahead, knowing the assassination squads were likely closing in on their targets. If he could keep his organization together during the coming weeks, everything would work out. He felt sick about Fingers but there was no time to mourn. He needed to get lawyers lined up for Alfredo and Marty White. Knowing the Feds, they would showboat those arrests and get plenty of media attention by arraigning Alfredo at his hospital bedside. Lights. Cameras. Stay tuned. News at five. A stand-up outside the hospital, a couple of pithy quotes from the prosecutor during the press conference, and best of all a long shot, framed from the hallway through a purposefully ajar room door, of the robed judge arraigning the patient. Zoom in. Get the underworld enforcer's face with oxygen mask, corrugated tubes and an IV bag hanging nearby.

Vinnie imagined the tabloid headlines: TOP MOB ENFORCER NABBED IN FBI SHOOTOUT, or maybe FEDS ARRAIGN GANGSTER IN HOSPITAL BED.

Vinnie needed to talk to General Sanchez, to make certain the man was still willing to hold back his army in trade for preserving his reputation. On their last visit to Puerto Rico, Alfredo and Fingers had made all the arrangements for the meeting with Sanchez aboard the yacht in San Juan. Now Fingers was dead, Alfredo in custody, and Vinnie felt stupid because he didn't have the general's phone number. He cursed Nick for having run away and causing this nightmare.

47

SADDLE UP

When the orders finally came to saddle up, the mercenary camp breathed a collective sigh of relief. The men were pent up, locked and loaded, ready for action. They'd been paid weekly in cash for their services, but there was nowhere in the rainforest to spend the money. A few had gambled it away in late-night card games, after which fights broke out in the camp, forcing Duarte to impose rules that few were happy about. It was late February and the men were scrapping to fight or get back to their families. Several complained they had other mercenary opportunities waiting for them that paid more and they were threatening to leave. It was time for action. They'd been anticipating this moment for nearly three months.

The assassination squads had been assigned their targets and provided details on where best to carry out their mission. Decker was given the premiere target – Fidel Castro.

Decker's squad included Selena and the two Colombian

mercenaries who claimed they normally worked for drug lord Pablo Escobar but had been instructed to join this operation as cartel representatives. The Colombians were brothers and snorted cocaine several times a day. Neither spoke English, which Decker and Selena viewed as a potential advantage in certain situations. Both Colombians toted sawed-off shotguns in the event of close-quarters combat.

The other nine targets included two of Fidel Castro's brothers – Ramon and Raul, the latter the country's Defense Minister and President of key government councils. Homer Duarte along with three of the Cuban ex-pats were slated to capture or kill Raul Castro who, nearly thirty years earlier, had stripped Duarte of his land, titles and bank account. Apparently Vinnie Merlino was undecided on whether Raul Castro would side with the new regime once the assassinations were over.

Also on the list was the First Vice President of the Council of State, First Vice President of the Council of Ministers, the Minister of Interior, anti-American members of the Secretariat and the Politburo, the President of the National Assembly of People's Power, and a pro-Castro private-sector entrepreneur from Moscow named Boris Sorokin who had amassed a fortune by circumventing the economic blockade imposed by the United States.

Four men were assigned the task of taking out the Russian -- the Australian soldier-of-fortune Chad Taylor who would serve as team leader, a South African mercenary known in camp only as Rhino, and two Latino thugs with long criminal records. Taylor was a demolition expert, but he wasn't quite sure how that particular skill would help them in this situation without the necessary explosive ingredients.

Trevor Rainsford was to target the Minister of Interior. His team included the rotund mercenary with an eye patch who jokingly identified himself as Che when the group first arrived in

Belize, and two Nicaraguan mercenaries, one in his teens and the other well past retirement age.

The method of attack would vary by target, as would the expertise of each assassination squad. Decker carried his Barrett M82 sniper rifle. Most of the squads packed Semtex, C4 and rocket-propelled grenades in addition to their automatic rifles.

As field commander, Homer Duarte planned to monitor the radios and direct the operation from inside Cuba, though his location would likely remain mobile until the situation stabilized and his team located Raul Castro.

The teams were slated to approach Cuba by different means. Sixteen mercenaries backtracked to Belize City aboard the deuce-and-a-half trucks and boarded a tramp steamer to a staging area just outside of Port-au-Prince, Haiti, a three-day journey by sea. From there, a Swiftships patrol vessel owned by the Dominican Navy and secretly leased by Preston Barlow on behalf of Vinnie Merlino, was to shuttle the sixteen mercenaries the final two hundred and fifty miles to the seaport city of Santiago de Cuba, ultimately depositing them ashore in two launches. The launches were to run without lights, doing everything possible to avoid Cuban Navy patrol boats and submarines.

Barlow had ordered his underling Jay Krutchner to take care of the prerequisite political details regarding the leased Dominican vessel. Krutchner was also tasked with convincing Vinnie Merlino that he had paid for the lease when, in fact, the price was much higher and the balance quietly assumed by the CIA.

Decker, Selena Delgado and the two Colombian henchmen entered the country via the Guantanamo Bay Navy Base, courtesy of their U.S. allies and Preston Barlow. Homer Duarte and the three Cuban ex-pats followed a similar route. Rainsford's team eventually made landfall on the island with help from two Navy SEALs in a rubber boat.

The mercenaries entering Cuba by commercial airliner or

cruise ship were to pose as workers or tourists, their luggage containing hotel brochures and sunblock cream or the tools of their trade. They were unable to carry weapons through Customs. A nighttime parachute drop was planned to rejoin them with their armaments, communications equipment and other field supplies.

48

A CALL FROM THE PRESIDENT

FEBRUARY 1989
WASHINGTON, D.C.

A ripple of fear ran through Barlow's body from head to toe when the private number for the President of the United States flash across his desk phone.

"Mr. President, sir."

"Preston, I want you to immediately call off this nonsense you've put into play."

"Sir?"

"Don't bullshit me, Preston. I know what you're doing in Cuba. I don't like Mr. Castro any more than you do, but this is not the time for a regime change there," said President Ronald Reagan, his tone grave and serious. "I've got enough problems in the Middle East with the Iraqis threatening to invade Kuwait."

"It may be too late to call back the mission, Mr. President," said Barlow. "It's already happening."

"God dammit, Preston, you're Deputy Director of Operations for the Central Intelligence Agency. I'm not going to allow a bunch of untrustworthy mobsters to take over that island. It could turn out they're worse than the communists. And once they're in place, it'll be difficult to oust them.

"But sir, the teams are in motion."

"You had no right to go ahead with something like this without my knowledge and approval. I hope you haven't gone and started a goddamn war with the Russians."

"I'm very sorry, sir. I thought I was doing the right thing for our country."

"Frankly I think you were doing this to get even for the thrashing you took at the Bay of Pigs. This was an act of personal vengeance and you've put a lot of lives on the line for no good reason. I want you to red light this mission immediately. I don't care how you do it, just do it. Understood?"

"Yes, Mr. President."

"Call me back in one hour and let me know what steps you've taken."

"Yes, sir."

49

WHERE THE HELL IS CARRINGTON?

FEBRUARY 1989
HAVANA, CUBA

Preston Barlow knew he had overstepped his bounds. He also understood that pulling the plug on his Cuba plans would likely require assistance from Bill Carrington, already in Havana with Hannah, who had been whisked from upstate New York by private jet.

But receiving help from the savvy field operative wasn't going to be easy, given that Barlow had often mistreated the agent by keeping him out of the intel loop and the larger plans at Langley. Barlow just didn't like the man, probably because so many field operatives admired Carrington for his courage, cunning and intelligence. Besides, women found Carrington charming, which was yet another reason for the aging and out-of-shape Barlow to feel contemptuous.

Barlow sent a coded message to several field operatives, including those in the British MI6 service, instructing them to locate Carrington and Rainsford as soon as possible, and inform them that at least sixteen and as many as twenty-eight of the original forty mercenaries had been pulled back from the mission or were incapacitated in some way.

If Carrington was able to contact Decker or Rainsford, the mission might get halted before any shots were fired -- unless, of course, something went wrong. Barlow's neck was on the line. He considered calling in a favor from a friend at the Pentagon but instantly scrapped the idea because it would undoubtedly raise a lot of unwanted questions.

Carrington was atop the roof of the hotel in Old Havana, uncharacteristically smoking a Cuban cigar and fiddling with the malfunctioning Sat-phone when Hannah, dressed in a sleeveless, knee-length tropical white dress, joined him on the parapet. It appeared someone at Langley had attempted to reach them, but the call had failed.

Carrington set down the bulky Sat-phone and raised his eyebrows at the sight of Hannah. "You look stunning."

Hannah smiled with lips closed, the tiny scar at the corner of her mouth twitching slightly. "Why thank you. Are you enjoying the afternoon sunshine?"

"Isn't that why we came?"

"Honestly, William. Some days I'm not exactly sure why we're here."

Carrington smiled knowingly. Hannah was the only person who addressed him as William and it thoroughly pleased him. To everyone else, he was Mr. Carrington, or Bill, or whatever alias he was going by at the time.

Hannah sat next to Carrington and leaned over the short masonry wall for a better look at the street below. She was glad he had helped her set up the weapons shipment from Argentina to General Sanchez. Carrington was among the best CIA officers in the business and he'd taught her plenty over the past two years. He was her boss, mentor, friend and, in moments when she dared consider it, perhaps something more.

"I couldn't stand being in that room a minute longer," she said. "I was chewing my fingernails and pacing."

"Mariel Becker would never do those things."

"I'm sure she wouldn't. She's far more cultured than me," said Hannah. "Remember, I'm just a simple girl from Kansas City, Missouri. Did you know our state animal is the mule? Am I stubborn? Did you know our state instrument is the fiddle and people actually square dance?"

Hannah could feel herself unspooling. She needed to stop talking. Carrington put an arm around her and she rested her head on his shoulder. "What are you worried about Hannah?"

"I can't help thinking about what Sanchez will do with those weapons if he suddenly decides to stop the mercenaries."

Hannah was concerned about Decker, but angry with him for trying to prevent her from taking on the undercover assignment in Cuba. She was also fuming because he hadn't stayed in touch since leaving for Belize, and for not saying he loved her often enough.

Hannah wondered whether Decker enjoyed being alone or was so emotionally damaged by post-traumatic stress that forced retreats were a matter of survival. Whichever it might be, she was left feeling lonely and unwanted. She wanted to be kissed and held. Simple as that.

Back in the hotel room, Hannah asked Carrington about the Cuban ex-pats that Vinnie Merlino had rounded up with help from Miami crime boss Patsy LoScalzo. She was curious about the people Decker was spending months with in Belize and Guatemala.

Carrington showed her a black-and-white photograph of Homer Duarte. The man certainly had good looks and some sort of magnetic quality in his smile.

"A handsome fellow. I presume he's the key to Merlino's ex-pat support from Miami?"

"Very astute of you," said Carrington, addressing her as

though she were a prize pupil, which in some ways, she was. "Duarte is a die-hard. His love for Cuba is all encompassing. He wants Castro out and is willing to take action rather than just blow out words like some windbag politician. The Cubans from Miami respect him."

"Is Decker with him?"

"That's what we've heard, but we've no way to confirm it. If the mercenaries are going to follow anybody, especially the ex-pats from Miami, it'll be Duarte."

"And what about her," said Hannah, picking up the black-and-white glossy of a beautiful Latina with long, shiny black hair, dark eyes and a fiery expression.

"Selena Delgado. Intellectual. Counter-revolutionary leader. Miami ex-pat. Beauty queen," said Carrington. "She hates Castro as much as Duarte does for what he did to her family."

"She's very beautiful. Is this woman in Miami now?"

"I don't have any reason to think so," he said, trying to guess why Hannah had asked the question so emphatically. "Last we heard, she was with the mercenaries in Guatemala."

Carrington saw the anxious look wash over Hannah's face. "Several of the ex-pats who joined up are women and some of them are better marksmen than the men," he said. "Besides, they typically eat less, complain less, have faster reflexes, and most often exhibit more common sense."

Hannah wasn't listening. She was lost in thought as she imagined Decker and Selena Delgado wrapped in a passionate embrace as bullets kicked up a storm of sand and smashed into brick walls all around them. She saw them groping, clawing and moaning wildly in a jungle tent, Selena Delgado naked and riding Decker horseback style, rivulets of sweat racing down past her nipples. She heard Selena Delgado cry out in Spanish, evidence of an orgasm like no other. And she heard Decker release in unison, pulling his Latina lover to his bare chest where the bullet scars were slightly raised.

50

WHAT YOU SEE ISN'T ALWAYS WHAT
YOU GET

FEBRUARY 1989
HAVANA, CUBA

Hannah didn't know whom to trust. In this new world of espionage she'd chosen, it seemed everyone she met operated on two channels. The public channel was a shell that included everything the operative wanted people to see and believe. But the private channel, far below the surface and guarded like a precious secret, was where the real motivations and loyalties could be found. It made her scoff at the acronym WYSIWYG often bantered about by the tech gurus at Langley: What You See Is What You Get.

When it came to spycraft, it seemed nothing could be further from the truth. The notion was maddening because a big part of her job was to know what certain people were thinking or planning.

Who was the real General Octavio Sanchez? On the outside, he was husband and father, the affable family man, middle-aged, chubby and pock-faced, who laughed loudly with his companions, drank piña coladas with a vengeance, and reigned over the country's Army. Many often remarked his facial features resembled those of Manuel Noriega, the brutal military dictator of Panama nicknamed Pineapple Face by his own people. Perhaps they were sensing something evil within the general. After all, Sanchez was a sadistic, blood-thirsty killer with a quest for power and an appetite for gruesome pedophilia.

Hannah asked herself if she really knew anybody? Who was the real Bill Carrington, someone she had trusted with her life on several occasions, a man who had escorted her through the secret door and down the rabbit hole to the world of clandestine service? The job had taken its toll on Carrington's marriage, but he seemed to accept the fact and not blame the CIA. He seldom talked about his wife and children, although Hannah knew he had a son and daughter and hadn't slept with his wife in nearly two years. He'd been a major part of her life ever since that fateful day in Ireland more than two years earlier when they'd crossed paths while working the Boston Butcher case.

And what about Preston Barlow? Was the pompous, obnoxious, owl-eyed Barlow loyal to the agency, or did the Deputy Director of Operations have his own agenda? If so, would it matter to him whether the lives of the forty mercenaries about to enter Cuba, including Decker and Rainsford, were carelessly spent? The man seemed to lack a soul.

Then there was Decker. Was he the man she thought she knew intimately, or somebody completely different, a stranger able to easily deceive her? She'd simply have to accept the notion that truth – the whole truth and nothing but the truth -- would always remain elusive.

Hannah attempted to discard her emotions and focus on the situation at hand. A few things seemed clear and she tried to list them in her mind. General Sanchez had his weapons, including the Chinese-made Red Arrow 8 missile launchers, and he had transferred payment to an offshore account as instructed.

The assassination squads were on the move, but as a result of security leaks and political chicanery, their targets might be expecting them.

Hannah wondered whether it was time to get out of Cuba before the fireworks began? She couldn't think of a single good reason to stay any longer, especially if Sanchez refused to reveal his intentions, although the frozen drinks at the El Floridita restaurant were sensational. Besides, the entire operation was giving her second thoughts. If Sanchez decided to use the weapons she sold him against the mercenaries, she would feel personally responsible should Decker be wounded or killed. She was forced to remind herself that first and foremost, Decker was an undercover operative just like her, a spy, and the fact he was her lover should not be part of her thought process. It was safer to remain disconnected.

Carrington had warned her about such feelings before she joined the CIA. It was what had worried him most – two agents with strong feelings for each other working the same assignment. The danger button had flashed inside his head. He had even gone as far as to clarify the phrase *strong feelings*, which he felt was a euphemism for romantic love, deep attachment, and what he imagined in this case were nightly sexcapades between two extremely attractive and healthy people. Hannah had laughed at the latter portion of his definition and said, "You make my love life sound a lot better than it is."

Carrington's voice jarred her back to the present, her complexion flushed pink from her private reverie.

"I assumed once General Sanchez got his weapons we'd be done here, but the situation has changed," he said, his tone serious and laden with disappointment. "We've got to find a way to stop the operation. Barlow knows he went too far."

"And how might we do that?"

"We need to know what Sanchez has in mind. If he's not going to pull the trigger on the mercenaries, maybe we can help him out when we get back home, find a way to keep Vinnie Merlino from releasing those films."

"Good luck with that. I get the feeling we won't know what the general is going to do until he does it. He plays his cards close to the vest."

"I didn't know you were a card player."

Hannah raised her eyebrows. "Only an occasional game of strip poker," she said flirtatiously. "I wouldn't know a full house from a flush."

"Well, I'd be glad to show you how to play poker, with chips, of course."

Enjoying the fresh banter, which had been rare with Decker for far too long, she said, "I'll keep that in mind."

During her earlier conversations with General Sanchez, while posing as arms merchant Mariel Becker, they'd danced around the man's well-known civil rights violations, the ones involving midnight executions of political opponents and detractors of the Castro government. Nor did she mention the tales she'd heard of small pickup trucks filled with bodies that were dumped into remote gullies after dark. But those previously off-limits subjects had come to the forefront after Carrington told her about the general's penchant for pedophilia and snuff films.

"Vinnie Merlino has copies of the films," Carrington had said. "That's why General Sanchez is being so cooperative. If he doesn't play along, the films go public and General Sanchez's wonderful life goes down the tubes."

After that revelation, conversations between Mariel Becker and the four-star general were strained, although Hannah did her best to disguise her contempt.

Hannah stepped onto the small balcony and Carrington joined her, leaning his back against the ornate wrought iron railing. She gazed out over his shoulder at Old Havana, quiet and lovely, all archways and narrow streets, the buildings painted in tropical colors. The night air was warm, lingering in the high seventies. She picked up the Sat-phone with its brick-like feel and foot-long antenna and fiddled with the buttons. "ET, phone home," she said into the speaker in a mock alien voice.

Carrington chuckled. He loved her sense of humor. Unlike many women, she wasn't afraid to act silly.

"When I was in college and had a problem, I'd call my mother and ask her what I should do. You think this phone can reach Kansas City, Missouri?"

"If you're convinced it'll help, give it a try," said Carrington, his reply clearly tongue-in-cheek. "Just don't mention the CIA, the hit squads, General Sanchez, me, Cuba, or anything about American gangsters."

Hannah laughed. "Well, that leaves recipes and neighborhood gossip."

Carrington sensed she was having difficulty keeping still. In traditional law enforcement, there most often had been an attainable objective, albeit a murky one. Person commits crime. Cops hunt down and arrest that person. There were good guys and bad guys, the issues black and white. But the world of clandestine service was nothing like that. It was mostly shades of gray. There were extenuating factors that played a role in almost every decision and every outcome. Hannah found the whole thing frustrating. She wanted Carrington to tell her whom to shoot.

What she wanted even more was to confront General Sanchez and tell him point blank if he were to use the weapons to successfully protect the mobsters, his alliance with them would not last long. She would remind him that mobsters often tolerate most any act of debauchery, but they are less forgiving when it comes to those who sexually molest children or, worse, kill them for sadistic sexual pleasure.

She imagined herself screaming into his startled, bloated face, "General, you are a sexual predator and once Vinnie Merlino and the other organized crime families are in power on this island, you won't be alive for very long. They'll have some fun with your death."

Both Hannah and Carrington knew if she met with the general while in such a mood and blurted out her true feelings, it might prompt the man to act out of spite and use his firepower to wipe out the assassination teams in an effort to keep his secret. Doing so would be a last-ditch attempt to save his personal reputation and his professional standing, but a man as intelligent as the general would also understand that such a betrayal would force Vinnie Merlino to release the sordid snuff films. So in the end, at least from the general's perspective, the outcome from either decision would be the same. Hannah suspected the general was conflicted.

"I think I should talk to the general again," she said with a burst of enthusiasm. "I'll make contact, saying I want to be sure he's satisfied with the weapons and that other purchases might be possible in the future."

"You think he might lower his guard and give you some indication about what he's thinking?"

"Maybe. Does he have some third option that we're not seeing? Can he call out his soldiers to stop the assassination squads and then bask in the limelight like he's some national hero, all the while preparing to deny any allegations about his sex life that might come to the surface?"

"Possible. But not likely."

"If he was recognized for saving the lives of Fidel and his top people, couldn't he then easily dismiss any complaints against him as sour-grape rumors planted by detractors or competitors?"

"We're still talking about torturing and killing children for sexual pleasure."

"As bad as that sounds, I still think it's worth a shot. And if it doesn't pay off, Mariel Becker will go back home to Argentina."

Carrington hadn't come right out and told Hannah, but he had hinted in the past there were those at the CIA who had no intention of allowing the assassins to accomplish their mission, despite the agency having bank-rolled a large portion of it.

Today he was more forthright. "There's a feeling among the key intelligence committees in Washington that Castro needs a good scare, a reminder that the United States is a stone's throw away in Florida and could easily take over the island," he said. "The U.S. can't send in the troops. That wouldn't play out very well on the world scene. Imagine the news footage of U.S. Marines hitting the beaches. We'd look like invaders. But it's always possible to use a proxy force, which is where Vinnie Merlino and his organized crime associates come into play. Only Vinnie Merlino doesn't know he's been set up for failure."

"By scare, you mean demonstrate to Castro how easy it would be to kill him?"

"Precisely," said Carrington. "But not everyone at Langley is on board with the scare plan, Deputy Director Barlow among them. Barlow wants blood. Or more specifically, Castro's blood, and I think he's lost sight of everything else."

According to Carrington, Decker and MI6 operative Trevor Rainsford would do their best to ensure the assassinations were not carried out. That was the overriding order they'd been given. If they were successful and nobody began shooting at the targets, General Sanchez would have no reason to use his weapons.

"But we have no idea how Decker or the British operative are going to attempt to do that, and no way to contact them directly."

"That's the odd thing about this business," said Carrington, running his fingers through his thick blond hair. "Sometimes, you just never know until it happens."

Hannah watched as Carrington set two stemmed glasses on the small table near the balcony and twisted the wire cage off the bottle of French champagne he'd purchased earlier in the day. Hannah giggled as Carrington popped the cork. The effervescence flowed down the neck but Hannah was quick to catch the spills in a stemmed glass.

"What's the occasion?"

"To foreign assignments."

Hannah smiled. "I've always loved the sound of that phrase."

"Well, here's to many more."

The moon bathed the balcony that overlooked the old city. After the first glass, Hannah and Carrington laughed loosely. When notes from a slow dance song wafted up from the outdoor café on the street, Carrington held out an inviting hand.

"Oh, William, I'm a terrible dancer," said Hannah, blushing.

"That makes two of us," he said, sipping the frothy wine that threatened to bubble out of his nose and mouth.

Hannah focused on the sheen the champagne had left on Carrington's lips. Although he was a dozen years older, she'd always found him attractive -- blond, handsome, fit, capable, funny and highly intelligent. She'd liked him since they first crossed paths in Ireland over two years ago. And she treasured the Nirvana T-shirt he'd bought her as a surprise when she and Decker were assigned to investigate a ring of eco-terrorists in the Pacific Northwest. The shirt was part of her undercover wardrobe while she posed as a timber-country waitress and bartender. It could have been any band T-shirt, but Carrington knew she liked Nirvana and had gone out of his way to find just the right one. He definitely had charm. He was also her boss, which put a different spin on things. But he wouldn't be the first older man she'd dated.

Before meeting Decker, she'd spent a year and a half in a relationship with renowned Boston surgeon Chandler Hughes, who also was a generation older and turned out to be a narcissistic dickhead. She'd always liked older men, though she didn't know why. When she'd mentioned that preference to her friends, they all immediately concluded she had a daddy complex, but Hannah knew that wasn't the case. Her father was strong and responsible, and filled with love for his family, but she'd never had the slightest thought of sleeping with him or anyone like him.

The romantic Cuban music filled the narrow street, mostly the sweet strumming of a guitar. Carrington set his glass on the small table and rested his right hand on Hannah's waist while the fingers of his left hand intertwined with hers. The song ended but was immediately followed by another that urged lovers to come together. Carrington pulled her close so that their lips were nearly touching. Hannah kicked off her sandals, lassoed her arms around Carrington's neck, pushed up on the tips of her toes and ground her lips onto his. They kissed without pause until Carrington swept Hannah into his arms and carried her to the bed.

"We can't," she said.

"We can do whatever we want. We all have one life to live. We could all be dead by tomorrow, especially in this business."

Hannah lay on her side, facing Carrington. She pushed his blond hair back from his forehead and kissed him, first slowly and methodically and then with abandon. Carrington slipped the white dress over her head and unclipped her bra, letting it fall from her shoulders, revealing her breasts in the moonlight.

Hannah unbuttoned his shirt and undid his belt, tugging at the zipper. Carrington tossed his shirt aside, slid out of his trousers and underwear and wrapped his arms around her. Hannah wriggled out of her underwear and closed her eyes as Carrington gently entered her. For the first time in months, she didn't feel lonely.

They were both asleep atop the sheets beneath the slowly whirling ceiling fan when the Sat-phone beeped in the middle of the night. It was Preston Barlow. He came right to the point. The assassination teams were moving toward their targets and expected to reach them within a matter of hours. They must be stopped at all costs. Find a way.

"We'll do what we can," said Carrington. "But first, you have to give me all your intel, everything you know about the operation. We need to know who we can trust."

51

WHEN PLANS UNRAVEL

MARCH 1989
PROVIDENCE, RHODE ISLAND

Vinnie Merlino sat down heavily in his office swivel chair and twirled it twice in a circle by paddling with his feet while he laughed aloud. He leaned into the edge of his executive-sized wooden desk and with one arm swept the stack of newspapers, two china plates laden with food, utensils, a full glass of orange juice and a dregs-laden coffee cup onto the floor. Nunzio Carlucci didn't flinch. He stood near the windows and gazed out at the street, a toothpick protruding from his mouth. He knew better than to intervene when Vinnie was in a foul mood.

Only the black, multi-line phone remained on the desk with its different-colored lights to show which lines were available or occupied. Vinnie vigorously jabbed the keypad. The call went through to the bogus company the CIA had used to sell him the weapons in Boston.

"Tarkington Enterprises. How may I direct your call?"

"This is Vinnie Merlino. I need to talk to Mr. Krutchner, immediately."

"Please hold. I'll see if he's available," said a pleasant female voice.

Vinnie squeezed the phone handle. He imagined his hands around Jay Krutchner's throat, his thumbs pushing deeply into the man's larynx until bulging eyes were accompanied by the absence of a pulse. This was the smug businessman in a tailored suit who'd sold him the weapons to equip his Cuba-bound mercenaries. The deal was carried out in cash in an East Boston warehouse. No written contracts. No signatures.

A few seconds later, Krutchner came on the line. "Mr. Merlino. What can I do for you?"

"Are you shitting me?"

"Pardon?"

"What happened to my weapons?"

"I can assure you any products you ordered from our company have been delivered."

"Well, last I heard, half the men I hired didn't even have a single gun. Now how is that?"

"I'd be glad to make some calls and check on the order. Can you be more specific regarding what products were not delivered?"

"Listen to me, you little prick. I paid you in greenbacks, lots of them, so I expect to receive what I paid for. Do you have a problem with that?"

"Absolutely not. Our records indicate your merchandise arrived in Belize and was offloaded from the ship by people working for you," he said.

"I know that, you asshole. I want to know why the weapons weren't given to everyone in the camp?"

Krutchner paused before answering. "I don't have any information about that."

"And what about the ship I rented from the Dominican Navy?

You took my money for that, too. One of my guys said the ship is back at the dock in Port-au-Prince instead of headed to Cuba and that sixteen of my men are still aboard."

"Again, I apologize. I can check into it. Perhaps the weather was bad and the boat couldn't go out."

"My guy says the sun is shining. It's a beach day on the island."

"Well, then perhaps there's another explanation. Let me see if I can reach the transportation company and get more information."

"Yeah, you do that, you prick. I paid those people on the ship to do a job and I paid your company to get them there on time. But neither of those things happened. That's the bottom line."

"I'll do my best to see why there may have been a delay or change in plans. As soon as I hear anything, I'll contact you."

"Why do I get the feeling you're pulling my chain?"

"I assure you, Mr. Merlino, there has been no attempt by me or anyone at Tarkington Enterprises to do any such thing."

Vinnie slammed the phone down. "Nunzio, you hear that shit? The Dominican boat isn't headed to Cuba. They're all sitting at the dock, playing cards, soaking up the sunshine on my fucking dime. This deal is squeezing my balls."

"Don't worry," said Carlucci. "Things will work out. And once we're established in Cuba, you won't need to think about anything but counting your money."

Vinnie did some quick arithmetic in his head. So far, he'd paid forty mercenaries each a hundred dollars a day. That translated to roughly $120,000 a month, and the group had been in the bush for over three months. That meant he was out a minimum of $360,000 plus transportation costs and food. Luckily most of them were satisfied with a diet of beans and rice, supplemented with whatever local edibles were available – scrawny chicken, muddy river fish, wild pig, corn, nuts.

To this ledger Vinnie added the amount he had paid for the

weapons and the tramp freighter from Boston to Belize, which pushed his overall investment to well over two million dollars. He knew that was a conservative estimate.

With the seven-digit number stuck in his head, Vinnie again called Tarkington Enterprises. He was told Mr. Krutchner had left for the day.

"I don't care if he's left for the day. You tell that motherfucker to call me within the hour or he'll regret it."

"We may not be able to contact him," said the pleasant voice.

"Listen to me. If you know where he is, you better tell him to contact me for his own good."

"Would you like to leave a voice message?"

"No! I would not like to leave a voice message. I want to talk to Krutchner!"

"I'll note that you called, Mr. Merlino, and we'll do our best to give Mr. Krutchner your message."

Vinnie was seething. He grabbed a full bottle of bourbon and hurled it across the room where it shattered in a far corner. "I want to kill that miserable prick," he said.

Nunzio Carlucci remained silent, sucking on his toothpick and staring out the window onto the Federal Hill neighborhood.

"Three times I met with Krutchner and three times he assured me everything would be delivered," said Vinnie, who was foraging through his desk drawers in an effort to find another bottle of bourbon. "He showed me the weapons, piles of them. We went aboard the freighter down on the East Boston docks. I even met the captain."

Carlucci opened the refrigerator and popped a can of Miller beer. "So where did it go off the tracks?"

"It went off the tracks when I didn't ask to talk to his boss. I should have stuck my gun in his balls and made him call whoever the guy is right then and there."

"Do you have any idea who Krutchner works for?"

Vinnie's face flushed with embarrassment. "No," he said, realizing for the first time that he may have been played. He didn't like the feeling and he was already envisioning the painful deaths that those who had wronged him would suffer.

"And the money that was transferred went though Krutchner?"

"It did."

"Cash?"

"All cash, no goods."

"Then you have no choice," said Carlucci, releasing a loud belch after finishing the can of beer. "We find Krutchner and we get what we need from him – information and a sizeable refund."

Vinnie grew solemn. "I'm going to walk over to the church. I need some quiet," he said. "Maybe the big guy has some answers."

"You want company?"

"That would be nice. We won't stay long."

52

CALLING OFF THE DOGS

MARCH 1989
HAVANA, CUBA

Two of the assassination teams landed on the island. They'd entered Cuba at the Guantanamo Bay Navy Base -- land protected and used by the U.S. military. They were proceeding toward their targets. A third team, led by Trevor Rainsford, had come ashore on a remote beach farther west on the island.

In an effort to save his own skin, Deputy Director Barlow had managed to divert the battered Dominican Navy ship that had departed Port-au-Prince for Cuba. As a result, sixteen mercenaries were pulled from the operation, but that still left twenty-four other assassins on the loose.

Barlow was also able to cancel the airdrop of weapons to the twelve mercenaries entering Cuba by cruise ship or commercial airliner. Even if those operatives made it to the drop zone, there would be no weapons to retrieve. In Barlow's mind, that effectively reduced the potential mercenary force to twelve.

Barlow eagerly relayed that information to the President of the United States. The President's response contained no praise.

Reagan's voice was terse. "Get in touch with the remaining operatives and pull them back. No ifs, ands or buts, Preston. Make it happen. The last thing this country needs right now is a war with one of its neighbors, especially one with ties to Moscow."

Barlow immediately contacted Carrington by Sat-phone to say he was no longer in communication with Decker, Rainsford or Homer Duarte. Carrington signaled Hannah to follow him to the hotel roof where the sketchy Sat-phone reception might be stronger. Carrington had little faith in the new telecommunications technology, but he had been forced by Barlow to bring along the device.

The city was bathed in a buttery morning light that Carrington would have preferred to enjoy with a cup of Cuban coffee and a newspaper. Instead he was forced to converse with a man he detested about a problem he didn't create.

"You and Agent Summers will have to intercede and make sure those last squads call off their mission," said Barlow in a tone that implied Carrington and Summers would somehow be responsible if the already ill-fated operation took a deeper nose dive.

The conversation was stymied by static and dead spots, and several sentences required repeating or clarification.

"Be wary of General Sanchez," said Barlow. "He has the list of the assassination targets in his pocket, so the teams won't have the benefit of surprise and nor will you. Sanchez can post a guard around every one of those targets or keep his men under cover until the teams approach. If the latter is what he decides, Decker, Rainsford and the others could easily be walking into a trap."

Hannah leaned her head toward the Sat-phone to better hear as Barlow spewed more orders at Carrington.

When the call ended they returned to the hotel room where

Hannah quickly slipped into the bathroom to change her clothes. She studied herself in the full-length mirror -- tight-fitting sleeveless red dress to the knee, low cut in front with a revealing slit up the side, black high heels and her string of lucky black pearls. Her blond hair was wrapped into an elegant chignon.

"You look absolutely stunning," said Carrington as she emerged, chin up, left arm poised on her hip as though posing for a fashion shoot.

"Thank you, William. Coming from a man of your impeccable taste, I'll take that as a high compliment."

Hannah gave Carrington a hug and a kiss on the cheek.

"Be careful," he said. "These people don't play nice, especially if they think you're deceiving them."

"I'm Mariel Becker, unrivalled merchant of death and international profit monger, just looking to solidify another sale before heading home to Argentina."

Hannah was feeling confident. She blew Carrington a kiss, closed the hotel door behind her and applied her scarlet lipstick as she strode toward the El Floridita restaurant to meet the general for a late breakfast.

As it turned out, their meeting over coffee, omelets, fresh croissants and mimosas was productive. Hannah had hoped to encourage the general's trust in her and get him to reveal his intention regarding the hit squads. She had shown him photographs of herself with heavily-armed soldiers in Argentina, Brazil and Paraguay, and others images in which she was meeting with heads of state or standing beside stockpiles of weapons. The CIA had doctored the black-and-white images to make them look authentic.

When she returned to the hotel, Carrington was studying maps of Cuba. "The general said he would consider the purchase of more weapons," she said. "He already tested out the RPGs and mortars. Everything was to his liking."

"That doesn't surprise me. He's like a kid in a candy store."

"I reminded him the price he paid for the weapons was so reasonable, he probably doesn't need to disclose the purchase to his superiors. He could maintain the stockpile separately. Deduct it from his budget as office supplies, for use only during an emergency."

"Did he like that suggestion?"

"It was like I was reading his mind."

"And what about his partnership with Vinnie Merlino and the other crime families?"

"We talked about how it can be dangerous to partner with rebel groups, criminals, or those not part of any official government."

"Did he agree?"

"At first he denied any partnership. He claimed he didn't know Vinnie Merlino or any other American gangsters."

"And?"

"I told him I was aware of his meeting with Vinnie Merlino aboard the yacht in Puerto Rico. He seemed surprised that I knew about it."

"Did he ask how you knew?"

"I lied. I told him a U.S. satellite was taking photos for a geologic survey and coincidentally captured images of the general, his bodyguards and certain underworld figures that were later recognized by the FBI. Some sort of advanced computer program had made it possible."

"Did he believe you?"

"I think so. I made up a story about how I'd sold the U.S. government some experimental software, which is why I was familiar with the satellite images."

"In the end, did Sanchez agree these partnerships with organized crime families can be dangerous and unproductive?"

"He agreed in part, but as he noted, it's not always easy to choose comfortable bedfellows."

"Did you talk specifically about Vinnie Merlino and what the man might be holding over him?"

"Yes. His demeanor totally changed when I brought up the films."

"I would have loved to have seen the expression on his face."

"He tried to play it cool, but I knew he was shaken. At first, he denied everything, saying he had no idea what I was talking about. But after a few minutes of what I can only describe as a weird and intense silence, he started asking questions. He really wanted to know how I'd found out about them."

"What did you say?"

"Only that I have many clients around the globe who are always looking for quality armaments, and sometimes during those negotiations information gets unveiled that probably shouldn't."

"Do you think he suspects you're more than an arms dealer?"

Hannah shrugged. "I don't know. He's got that poker face and it has more craters than the moon, so there's really no way to tell. Maybe he's already planning my death."

"Did he admit to anything?"

"God forbid, no. But I got his attention again when I mentioned that mobsters typically don't condone that sort of behavior, you know, when it comes to kids."

"He must have been squirming in his seat."

"If he was, he didn't show it. After that initial look of surprise, he remained unfazed, as though it was just another rumor in a country where rumors circulated freely and seldom held any truth."

"You think he'll use the weapons against the hit teams?"

"Only if the teams get caught in the act of trying to carry out an assassination. If we can contact Decker and Rainsford by tonight and tell them the whole shebang has been called off, maybe we can prevent that. They need to know that most of the other operatives have already been withdrawn. I'm mostly concerned about the Cuban ex-pats with Homer Duarte who are in the game emotionally, and that includes Selena Delgado. They want Castro and his pals in the grave. This isn't about money or power with them."

Carrington shot Hannah a smile that spoke to just how proud he was of her ability to wean information out of the toughest subjects without the need for pliers, scalpels, saws and electrodes. The woman was simply magical, like Scheherazade.

53

A VISIT TO FIDEL'S HOUSE

March 1989
Havana, Cuba

It was early evening when Decker, Selena and the two Colombians began following a circuitous trail toward the palm-shaded hacienda where intelligence reports told them Fidel Castro might be spending the night. In order to evade Cuban Army patrols, they'd kept off the roads and now they were exhausted from slashing and hacking their way through the bush.

Using his night-vision spotting scope, Decker aimed at what sounded like a rustling in the nearby trees. Seconds later, he spotted Homer Duarte and the three Cuban ex-pats scrambling toward them. He had hoped they'd gotten lost or delayed, but that obviously wasn't the case. Now he'd have to deal with them.

If necessary, Decker knew he could eliminate the two Colombians on his team with little trouble, but the thought of having to kill Homer or Selena was far more complicated and distasteful when he paused to think about it. During the months spent in the jungle, they'd become friends. They trusted him. How could he coldly eliminate them if the situation demanded? Firing his Barrett sniper rifle from thousands of yards away was a totally different kind of killing. It was detached. Removed. The target was just that, a target. Pulling the trigger was a job.

Decker tried to keep himself from thinking about it, but images of Selena slipped through his mind like ghosts. Together they had spent days foraging for food, field-stripping weapons and practicing combat tactics. They had talked and laughed long into the night around the campfires and in her tent. They shared their rations of rum and more than once gotten drunk and had fun despite being encamped in the bush amid dozens of trained killers.

Decker would never forget the sight of Selena washing her long dark hair in a bucket, squeezing out the water that spilled over her shoulders and drenched her T-shirt. He envisioned Selena cooking at the iron outdoor stove, a long line of hungry men savoring whatever she prepared. There was Selena smiling in her tent as she tossed her blouse aside and jokingly covered her bare breasts with two empty coconut halves, the same coconut Decker had sliced in two with his machete earlier in the day. Decker especially liked it when she was in a silly mood.

Feelings aside, Decker understood his job was to prevent the assassinations at all costs, which was a tall order, given that forty mercenaries were moving toward their targets. He was unaware the POTUS had ordered Barlow to immediately cease the operation. Nor did he know Barlow had already pulled back sixteen mercenaries who were aboard the Dominican Navy ship, and further hampered the effectiveness of several other soldiers-of-fortune by leaving them without weapons.

Two exterior lights, apparently wired to detect the loss of daylight, suddenly switched on and cast two cones of light, up and down, onto the walls of the hacienda. The sconces were more decorative than utilitarian, but their mild glow would be unwelcome by anyone trying to approach the house undetected. Duarte and the ex-pats flattened to the ground as soon as the lights came on. Decker watched them through his spotting scope as they slinked backward into thicker foliage.

A few minutes later, Duarte appeared on his knees, a Czech assault rifle slung across his back. He began brushing off his fatigues as though staying neat during a combat situation was somehow important. He flashed a perfect white smile and vigorously shook Decker's hand, clearly glad to combine their forces. He enveloped Selena in a hug, pressing his body against hers as though he'd not seen her in decades.

"Two blocks from here it looks like the staging area for a war zone," he said. "There are dozens of Russian tanks and armored personnel carriers parked side by side, but considering the amount of flaking paint and rust on the metal, they probably haven't rolled in quite some time."

"I'm surprised you didn't try to take one," said Decker.

"Believe me, my men thought about it. They're all former U.S. Army, two armored and one mechanized infantry. They wanted to drive one of those old tanks right through the hacienda's brick walls. But I told them it was more important we get together with you."

Duarte was yearning to approach the house to determine if getting a clean shot at Fidel Castro was possible. Decker was more concerned about setting off any security systems – heat sensors, sound or motion detectors -- or alerting guard dogs. So together the group crept quietly toward the shrubbery near the swimming pool that would provide the only dense cover.

Decker carried the Barrett M82 sniper rifle to eliminate suspicion about his role in the mission, though he had no intention of using the weapon for its intended purpose.

Duarte was armed with a Colt .45 handgun in addition to the Czech rifle. The two Colombians carried sawed-off shotguns, apparently anticipating close-up encounters with Castro's soldiers. They were hungry to get inside the home and blast away. Selena and the ex-pats toted AK-47s.

"I want to kill that fucker," Selena said, vengeance radiating from her dark piercing eyes. "And I want to kill his brother, Raul, as well. Then I'm going to shoot their balls off, or maybe I'll cut them off and make soup."

The three Cuban expats smiled proudly and elbowed each other as a sign they approved of Selena's fighting words. Somewhere in the distance a dog barked, setting the group on edge. It was more howl than insistent bark, suggesting it wasn't a guard dog. But it made the group pay closer attention to their surroundings.

Duarte scanned the hacienda with his binoculars, hoping for a glimpse of Fidel Castro and perhaps his brother, Raul, the defense minister. General Sanchez had mentioned to Vinnie Merlino that the two Castro brothers often got together at the hacienda on the first day of each month for lengthy discussions that tended to last far into the night. Decker looked at his chronograph diver's watch. It was the first day of March. Duarte hoped the information about the Castro brothers' habits was accurate. Killing both brothers in the same place on the same day at the same time would be a miracle, he told himself. It would be a day marked on the calendar of every Cuban ex-pat and many residents of the island who had struggled under the regime for the past thirty years.

Decker suggested he and Selena watch the front entrance that faced north while the two Colombians monitor the east facade. Duarte positioned himself at the rear, which left the three Cuban ex-pats covering the west and final exposure.

Decker hailed Rainsford on his radio and gave him their coordinates. Rainsford's squad was assigned to kill the Minister of the Interior, whose home was less than three miles from Fidel Castro's hacienda. Rainsford's task for MI6 was to make sure that didn't happen.

The British spy gave Decker a brief rundown of their situation, adding he would hike in their direction but couldn't say for certain how long that might take.

Rainsford had encountered his first obstacle during the nighttime beach landing, when the rubber boat overturned in the waves and hurled them into the dark water. Only three made it ashore. The affable *Che* squeezed seawater from his eye patch as he explained to Rainsford that the older Nicaraguan could not swim. The man had desperately waved his hands over his head but seconds later he vanished beneath the surface. The waves soon tossed his limp body onto the sand. Nothing more could be done. It was an act of God.

The three men standing on the beach were soaked and all had swallowed seawater. Some of their gear had been lost and their weapons, although wrapped for a wet ride, would require stripping and oiling.

At dawn, still wet from their ocean immersion, the chilled trio came across a Cuban Army patrol and was forced to hide for two hours in the thick brush. Just before noon, they encountered peasants cutting sugar cane. The peasants eyed them suspiciously but there was no time to wonder whether any had the desire or the means to report foreign soldiers wandering through their plantation.

Rainsford suggested they leave the field and make their way through the rainforest. The three men walked for miles, cursing the trees and vines and the iguanas that leaped from branch to branch high above, threatening to loosen head-busting coconuts. To keep them entertained, Che told the story of a village man who'd been struck by a falling coconut and suffered serious brain damage. The villagers nicknamed him Coco Loco because he began acting weirdly. The man spent the rest of his days climbing the tallest of coconut palms and knocking the fruit to the ground so that other villagers might not befall the same fate.

The wide-eyed Nicaraguan appeared confused. "What happened to him?"

"He grew old and fat and died."

"But what is the point of the story?"

"There is no point. Only that the villagers appreciated what he had done and named their favorite rum drink in his honor."

"And what was that?"

"Coco Loco. Now don't you wish you had one in your hand right now?"

Rainsford knew Che's story was lacking but if it helped boost the Nicaraguan's sagging morale even the slightest, then it had some value. The man was distraught at the loss of his friend in the surf and had begun talking incessantly about wanting to empty his rifle into his enemies simply for the sake of killing.

It was tough going in the rainforest, but Rainsford kept them moving with the goal of tiring them out. *Che* and the younger Nicaraguan believed they were getting closer to the interior minister's home with every step, when in truth Rainsford had abandoned that mission and, doing as pre-instructed by MI6, was pointing his compass at the coastal rendezvous site.

Rainsford estimated he was four miles from the coast when he radioed Decker to say his mission had been scrapped.

"We stripped off the Nicaraguan's uniform and personal belongings and got rid of them, but we didn't have time to bury him," Rainsford said apologetically. "I doubt if anyone will be able to identify him."

Decker understood Rainsford's team was out of the game.

It was well after 9 p.m. when Selena Delgado scurried alongside Decker to say Fidel Castro was sitting alone at a large desk visible through the floor-to-ceiling windows. She reached out and caressed his Barrett sniper rifle, giving Decker a seductive smile.

"Do you think you can kill him from here?"

"It's not just the distance," he said. "Lots of other factors. But if the chance for a clean shot opens up, I'll take it."

"I'd like to kiss the round that penetrates his communist skull," she said. "I'm hoping that Raul shows up soon. In the meantime, what can I do to help?"

"Rainsford will be my spotter and calculate the range," he said. "I gave him our coordinates. He should be here in a few hours. Maybe you should see if Homer needs assistance. Your eyes may be better than his in the dark."

Dissatisfied with Decker's answer, Selena sulked. She wanted Decker to shoot Fidel Castro and if he wouldn't do it, she would.

Less than a half hour later, a sedan pulled into the long gravel drive. Defense Minister Raul Castro stepped out of the back seat and was quickly flanked by two bodyguards. Together they entered the house where the brothers embraced.

Selena flopped down next to Decker. "Where's Rainsford?"

"I told you, he's on his way. They ran into trouble."

"Like what?"

"Like patrols and curious peasants. One of his men drowned during the beach landing."

"Mierda! Well, God bless his soul. But we still have a job to do."

"And I'm doing it by waiting here for Rainsford."

"I can be your spotter."

"I doubt you know how to make those calculations. Rainsford is a trained sniper."

"We know Castro and his brother Raul are in the house. Why can't you just point your big, macho rifle and shoot them from here? I've heard so much about the Barrett and its .50-caliber bullets. I knew a man who fought in Beirut and he told me a sniper with this rifle shot a man dead from more than a mile away."

"That may very well be true."

"So why can't you do it? It's probably only two hundred meters to the house."

"We don't know whether the window glass can deflect a bullet, or slow it down and throw it off course. There are a lot of factors involved. The shots have to be perfect. For all we know, the window glass could be bulletproof."

"Let me see that gun," she said, attempting to pry the heavy Barrett sniper rifle from Decker's grip. "I'll shoot them if you won't."

"You need to chill out, Selena," he said, clasping his hands over hers. "If the opportunity arises and the outcome looks promising, we'll take it. If not, we won't."

"Is that what you thought when you were in my tent? You saw an opportunity and you took it because the outcome looked promising," she said bitterly, pulling her hands out from under his. "One perfect shot at Selena."

"Selena, please. You know it wasn't like that. I care about you. You're an amazing woman. I admire your strength and courage. Everyone does. You're like a goddess around here. And from everything you've told me, I think I understand the hardship you went through as a kid because of the revolution."

"Then forget what my heart says and listen to what comes from my head," she said, her eyes afire with vengeance. "We need to kill Fidel Castro and we need to do it now while we have the chance! Maybe you would understand if it had been your family he drove to ruin. Or maybe it's just that you don't have the nerve. Your words are machismo but your actions are those of a scared child. You want to stay here, hiding behind these bushes."

Selena scowled at Decker. "You obviously left your balls back at the camp. Maybe Homer brought his. I sure as hell hope so."

Selena made her way to the side of the house where Duarte lay in the tall grass with his binoculars. She tucked her olive green beater T-shirt snuggly into her pants so that it showed the outline of her nipples. "We need to act while we have the chance," she said, crawling on her elbows until they were shoulder to shoulder, their faces inches apart.

Duarte allowed his eyes to roam over her breasts and felt a pang of desire in his groin. For a moment it seemed difficult to breath, as though his lungs were unable to fill. Most women of such beauty were not found on the front lines of a guerilla war. Yet here was this wild creature nestled against him in the dark. It was a magical moment for him, though he wished the circumstances were different, a sunny beach or a fluffy hotel bed.

"Decker is being a pussy," she said, her tone condescending. "He could easily shoot Fidel from where he is positioned. Instead, he talks non-stop about ranges and trajectories and probabilities. He lists all the ways it cannot work instead of believing in the ways it can."

Duarte saw the intensity in her eyes and knew he needed to find the right words to calm her before she did something everyone would regret.

"Let's give Rainsford a few more minutes. If he comes and they can't make a decision, I'll convince them to take the shots. And if it turns out that I can't, that my words fall on deaf ears, we'll take action ourselves."

Lying on her back so that she could look up at Duarte, she stroked his face with her delicate fingers and said, "Homer, my brave and honorable friend, my Don Quixote. Do you promise?"

Duarte didn't answer immediately. His throat had suddenly closed up, making it hard to swallow. When he finally regained his composure, he said, "I promise, Selena."

"I don't believe you," she said, pushing him away with an expression of disgust on her face. "You're just trying to stall until the opportunity has passed." Duarte looked stunned.

Impatient and impulsive, Selena moved off into the night cradling her AK-47, filled with a brazen sense of invincibility. She was convinced Decker lacked an appropriate amount of aggression. She added Duarte to that list. Where was their testosterone?

She decided to take a closer look at the target and, if possible, complete the assassination of the Castro brothers herself, even if it meant blazing away with her assault rifle like some pray-and-spray Jihadi.

The first searchlight lit up Selena Delgado's silhouette on the manicured lawn and the distinctive AK-47 she had strapped over her shoulders. Another powerful beam crisscrossed with the first. A klaxon alarm sounded and the bodyguards inside the house began rushing toward the nearest exits.

General Octavio Sanchez stepped out of the darkness near the house where he had been standing.

"Good evening, señorita," he said as at least five soldiers aimed their rifles in the lone woman's direction. "Please put down your rifle and kindly place your hands over your head."

54

HAS ANYBODY SEEN OUR GUNS?

MARCH 1989
CUBA

Chad Taylor the Australian was first to arrive at the drop site. He doubled-checked his map and compass, surprised to find no rumpled parachutes or padded crates filled with weapons, field rations and communications equipment.

Taylor radioed the two other teams that had made it into the country by commercial flight or ship. They, too, had posed as tourists and workers and carried only their suitcases filled with carpenter's tools or beach toys.

For a moment he imagined the other teams had gotten to the drop site ahead of him and made off with the entire cargo. It was doubtful. His team had moved rapidly and efficiently. Besides, the others would have radioed to say they had found the equipment and were relocating with it. He wondered what had gone wrong.

Taylor's radio crackled. The two other teams were still en route to the drop site. He told them not to rush because there were no weapons in the clearing or in the surrounding copse of palm trees. He assumed the plane had been delayed. They could keep out of sight and wait for several hours, since if the aircraft was still on its way, the drop wouldn't happen until after dark. It was also possible the plane had dropped the weapons in the wrong location.

Taylor wasn't the type to despair, nor was Rhino, the South African. "If the weapons don't come, we'll find others," Taylor said. "We've got to be resourceful."

The two Latino mercenaries whose prison gang tattoos embellished their arms from wrist to shoulder were thinking along those same lines. "We can steal weapons," the taller one said. "The haciendas will have guns. Locked doors are no problem."

"I was hoping for something with a bigger bang than an AK-47 or a hunting rifle," said Taylor, a demolition expert who'd blown plenty of bridges and buildings to smithereens during his career. "If we know for certain our Russian friend is home, we can bring the walls tumbling down on his head. Just a matter of finding the right ingredients for the blast."

"You tell us what you need, Señor Chad, and we will get it."

Taylor rattled off a list of items used to make an explosive device powerful enough to blow up a modest-sized dwelling. The men assured him the ammonia and fertilizer could be found on one of the nearby farms. A construction company they passed en route to the drop site would mostly likely have Thermite, maybe some fine power aluminum and a magnesium strip. There was also the possibility the yard might have a secured building for storing dynamite and other explosives. The tattooed mercenaries grinned with excitement as they departed on their search mission.

When the two other teams arrived, all retreated into the bush and shared snacks purchased at the airport and dock terminal -- Almond Joy and Hershey chocolate bars, Lays potato chips, peanuts, licorice sticks and coconut macaroons. It wasn't much food for twelve men, but better than none. They presumed the airdrop would include MREs, the pre-packaged military meals they were fond of mocking.

Taylor spread his map on the grass. "We have three different targets among us. Let's take a look at the best exit strategies for everyone because there won't be time to do that once things start heating up. Make sure you're clear about the two rendezvous points as you head for the coast. I'm not sure how long your rides will wait. There may be more Cuban Navy patrol boats on the water because of our activities. We don't know what the other teams are doing. If they've attracted attention, we're all going to have to move quickly."

55

TEMPER TANTRUMS GET YOU NOWHERE

MARCH 1989
CUBA

Hannah and Carrington, clad in black boots, watch caps, trousers and long-sleeve pullovers crouched in the shadows about one hundred feet from where Cuban Army soldiers were pointing their rifles at Selena Delgado.

The searchlights had attracted the attention of those inside the hacienda and more lights had been switched on near the swimming pool and cabana. Four bodyguards were ushering Fidel and his brother Raul away from the tall, plate-glass windows but it appeared the brothers were attempting to maintain their view of the action. Other bodyguards were running toward the assailant.

General Sanchez boldly approached the gun-toting woman dressed in jungle camouflage fatigues, stopping when he was no more than ten feet away. "Please put down your rifle, señorita. You are obviously outgunned here and there's no reason for this

beautiful evening to have a tragic conclusion," the general
suavely said.

Selena realized her temper had gotten the best of her and
now she was mired in a large heap of trouble. She imagined
Duarte, Decker, Rainsford and some others peering through their
riflescopes and binoculars at the drama unfolding before them.

"Can you please tell me what a beautiful woman as yourself is
doing here outside the President's house after dark and carrying a
rifle? If this is some sort of mistake, please explain," the general
said.

"I came here to kill him for what he did to my family," she
said, still clutching the AK-47 with the barrel pointing toward
Sanchez.

"Is that so? Well, it seems tonight is not an opportune
moment," the general said. "So I'll ask you again, to please set
your rifle on the ground. Otherwise, I will have to ask my men to
seize it from you."

Selena twisted her neck left and right, as though expecting
something to happen. She let the AK-47 fall to the ground.
Sanchez barked an order in Spanish and the soldiers ran toward
the woman, pointing their rifles in her face and ordering her to
lay down on the grass, arms and legs spread.

The general ordered his men to take the woman to the pool
cabana. Selena struggled to free herself from their firm grip but
the soldiers dragged her along by the arms, her boots bumping
on the ground.

The bodyguards were shouting and running back and forth
with their machine pistols. Sanchez suggested they simmer
down. With the exception of the four guarding Selena, the
general ordered his soldiers to return to their posts. A single
woman with a rifle was not much of a threat.

"This may be an isolated incident," he said. "Nothing to fear."

When Sanchez entered the cabana, Selena was duct-taped to
a straight-back chair, just as the general had instructed. Her

calves were taped to the chair legs, her wrists and forearms to the chair arms. She spewed curses at the general who stood silently in a corner, smoking a cigar and observing her. He considered slapping a piece of duct tape over her mouth, but decided without it she might actually say something useful.

Hannah and Carrington were well hidden in the foliage but able to see the hacienda and cabana. "I can't believe she just did that. It accomplished nothing. So fucking dumb," said Hannah, shaking her head in disapproval. The distain in her voice reflected her dislike of Selena Delgado.

Carrington silently peered through his spotting scope. "Certainly not the smartest move," he said. "Too many people thinking with their hearts instead of their heads."

"I guess so."

"Looks like we might have another one."

"What do you mean?"

"Homer Duarte. He's inside the flower garden and moving toward the cabana."

"Oh, Jesus."

"Decker's right behind him."

Hannah squinted into the night-vision scope. "What do those assholes think they're doing? This is turning into such a clusterfuck."

"Have to agree with you there."

"Any ideas?"

"Not yet. We'll just stay right here for now and see how this thing plays out."

"I hate sitting still."

"Apparently so does Selena Delgado and look where it got her."

"Touche."

56

GOOD EVENING, SELENA

General Sanchez shouted at the four soldiers in the cabana, ordering them to stay in place and guard the prisoner. The soldiers seemed panicked but did as they were told. More soldiers were arriving in a deuce-and-a-half truck and an armored personnel carrier, clamoring out the backs of the vehicles and running full bore toward the hacienda. Part of the general's rapid-response force, they moved with precision and purpose. The general had activated them as insurance in case the lone gunwoman was accompanied by a much larger group of mercenaries.

The bodyguards were fanning out on the property, their probing flashlights like fireflies in the night.

Homer Duarte slowed to a crawl about fifty feet from the cabana and wedged his body out of sight between the tall hedges and the flowerbeds. Decker reached out and grabbed Duarte's boot, tugging lightly as a signal to stop.

"I'm going to get her," he said, yanking his foot loose.

"No. I'm going," said Decker. "But first we need to find out how many guards are inside."

Decker peered through a crack in the cabana wall. Selena was duct taped to the chair, legs and arms, another strip of tape across her mouth. The four soldiers were gathered at one end of the room, taking in the view of the feisty, beautiful woman who repeatedly rocked the chair in an effort to tip it over and free herself. Two of the soldiers were smoking.

Duarte once again tried to take the lead but Decker had already made up his mind.

"I already told you, no. I'll go first. I'm younger, faster, and I've had lot more practice shooting people than you have. Just stay nearby and provide cover if things get hot," he said, not giving Duarte time to refuse as he charged through the cabana door firing his Beretta 92FS pistol with silencer. Decker shot three of the four soldiers in the head and would have killed the fourth the same way if a rifle butt had not caught him squarely on the side of his skull.

When Decker regained consciousness, with help from a bucket of water someone splashed in his face, he realized that like Selena, he was duct taped to a wooden chair in the middle of the room. His right eye twitched in pain and drops of blood from a head wound were creating dark spots on the front of his shirt.

"That was very courageous of you, but unfortunately not very successful," said General Sanchez, a wry smile on his face.

Sanchez, hands clasped behind his back, walked a circle around both chairs like an anthropologist studying newly-acquired specimens. The bodies of those Decker shot dead had been taken away, replaced by other soldiers who no longer smiled or talked.

Sanchez lifted Decker's chin with two fingers. "I don't think we've had the pleasure of being introduced. Would you mind telling me your name, since you have arrived here uninvited?"

Decker knew the man was screwing with him and once the game had lost its luster would undoubtedly put a bullet through his prisoner's head. "I didn't like the way you were treating this lovely woman, so I thought I'd take her away from the party," Decker said.

Sanchez chuckled and lit a cigar, puffing the smoke in Decker's face. Selena began rocking her chair, which put the new group of soldiers into a trigger-happy alert mode. With tape across her mouth, it was near impossible to understand what she was saying.

"Are you angry because I didn't offer you a cigar, señorita? If that's the case, I'll remove the tape and allow you to enjoy Cuban tobacco, one of the wonders of the world," said Sanchez.

A sudden, massive explosion in the distance was loud enough so that even the less-experienced soldiers knew it was a blast powerful enough to knock down a building or destroy an ammunition depot.

Decker smiled. He liked Chad Taylor and respected his ability to make things go boom. From the sound if it, Taylor's team had reached their target and successfully eliminated it. Decker knew there was nothing he could have done to stop it. He looked at Sanchez's face but it gave no indication of what the general was thinking as he tossed his cigar to the tile floor and crushed it with his boot.

Decker envisioned the Russian businessman preparing his guests for a lovely evening when the magnificent home burst into thousands of pieces without warning. That would send a message to other entrepreneurs hoping to circumvent the American blockade on certain goods entering and exiting Cuba.

General Sanchez was on the phone, barking orders and asking questions.

Decker looked over at the general and grinned. "Could you ask them to keep the noise down? I thought this was a quiet neighborhood."

The comment earned Decker a full slap to the side of his head from the general's thick hands. The blow knocked over the chair, so that Decker struck his head on the tiles. Sanchez motioned to his soldiers to right the chair.

Sanchez stomped out of the cabana and headed toward the hacienda. The Castro brothers were unhappily pacing, sequestered in an interior room and surrounded by bodyguards.

Sanchez soon learned more about the explosion. The blast had leveled a large home, killing Russian businesswoman Lena Sorokin, who was a personal friend of the general's, and three of her guests. Rescue crews were still on the scene, but the prospect of finding additional survivors was unlikely.

Ten minutes after he had left the cabana, General Sanchez marched back through the door with a determined expression on his face.

Sanchez slapped Decker on the shoulder like they were old pals. "Was the Russian woman one of your targets?"

"I don't know what you're talking about."

"Oh, I'm sure you do. I know about the list. And Boris Sorokin was one of the ten people on it. Apparently he wasn't at home, but his wife was there along with his daughter."

Decker lifted his head. "You're really confusing me, general."

"Your CIA has just killed a close friend of mine. Perhaps you have noticed I am not smiling," he said.

Selena began rocking her chair with such force it toppled to the floor. Two soldiers quickly moved to upright her but Sanchez intervened. "Leave her," he said. "She's nothing but scum. She can lick the floor."

Sanchez returned his attention to Decker. "Lena was a lovely woman. She never harmed anyone. There was no reason to put her on your list."

More commotion erupted near the hacienda. A young soldier entered the cabana, saluted the general and in a voice simultaneously excited and frightened said a T-54 tank had smashed through the wrought-iron perimeter fence and was moving toward them.

The tank's engine roared as the treads clanked over the grass, squeaking and rumbling. Homer Duarte was in the commander's seat, his head and torso visible behind the turret hatch. One of the ex-pats was driving while the other two manned the gun. The tank was an aging model built in the 1970s and one of nearly 1,000 given to Cuba by Russia.

Carrington, Hannah and the two Colombians watched the drama unfold. "We need to get closer," Carrington said. "I'm not sure what Duarte has planned, but we've got to be ready to take advantage of the situation."

Several soldiers opened fire on the tank, forcing Duarte to duck into the turret as the driver closed his hatch. General Sanchez was shouting emphatically into his radio. "Flecha roja! Flecha roja!"

"He's calling for the Red Arrow," said Carrington.

The clanking tank was less than one hundred feet from the hacienda. Before Hannah could reply, a swooshing sound preceded by a fast-moving projectile struck the tank with great force and set it ablaze. Flames scorched the tank from all sides.

"I sold Sanchez that weapon," said Hannah. "I just didn't think he'd have opportunity to use it." She was stunned by the sight of Duarte and the others burning to death inside a mound of superheated steel.

"Let's see if we can get to Decker," said Carrington, unstrapping his Beretta from its thigh holster. He signaled Hannah and the Colombians to follow.

Sanchez had returned to the cabana. "Too bad about your friends," the general said. "Apparently they were going for, what is it you Americans call it, a joyride? But that is no longer possible."

Selena was screaming, but the duct tape over her mouth kept down the volume. Her arms and legs were still taped to the chair, which lay sideways on the floor. Carrington and the others could hear the conversation in the cabana.

"Well, I've had enough disturbances for one day. We must conclude our business here," General Sanchez said to Decker. "I will give you one final chance to tell me who you are and who sent you?"

When he received no reply, the general scrunched his face in anger. He pulled a revolver from the leather holster on his belt and pressed the black barrel against Decker's head. The four soldiers in the cabana locked their wide eyes on Decker and the general, awaiting the execution.

"On three, I pull the trigger," he said. "One, two..."

The bullet struck General Sanchez in the forehead. Hannah then pivoted her Heckler and Koch MP5 and quickly shot two of the four soldiers, the high-powered rounds piercing their targets and then dangerously ricocheting inside the small building. Before the remaining two could react, Carrington was inside the cabana. Hannah saw the glint of metal as Carrington's knife slashed one soldier's jugular and drove the blade into the second one's kidney, savagely twisting it.

Hannah cut Decker free of the duct tape. Carrington did the same for Selena, gently removing the strip across her mouth. "We need to get out of here, right now," he said.

"I'm not going," she said. "This is our chance."

Decker grabbed Selena by the wrist. "We have no chance here and there's nothing we can do for Homer and the others."

The two Colombians blasted away with their sawed-off shotguns at a group of soldiers who had approached the cabana and were now scurrying for cover. The short-barrel shotguns were devastating at close range but relatively useless outside of twenty feet. Nonetheless, the blast and muzzle flash was enough to discourage their pursuers.

The six zigzagged across the lawn, gunfire kicking up divots near their feet. They ducked behind a thick hedgerow from where Selena turned to look back at the hacienda. Bodyguards were escorting Fidel and Raul Castro to a waiting car. The brothers were no longer behind the thick glass.

"They're out of the house. This is what we've been waiting for," she said, snatching Hannah's Heckler and Koch MP5 and breaking into a full run.

One of the searchlights found Selena. She was aiming the machine gun toward the Castros and firing on full automatic. The soldiers returned fire, their bullets striking Selena's body and making it do a macabre dance like a stage performer under a spotlight until it collapsed to the ground.

Decker stood but Carrington pulled him back by the belt. "You're not going anywhere."

Decker struggled to free himself but Carrington persisted by forcing him to the ground with an arm lock and a knee in his back.

"She's dead. Let it go."

"They're coming," said one of the Colombians, who again fired his shotgun into the night. "Keep to the same path that brought us here. We'll slow them down where it narrows."

Hannah looked at Decker who was rubbing his eyes. "I'm sorry, Decker."

Decker took a deep breath and held it to keep his eyes from tearing up. "She was a good soldier."

"No time for mourning," said Carrington. "Unless you want to end up like the others."

Carrington glanced at Hannah, wondering what was going through her mind. "I've still got my MP5," he said, handing Decker his Beretta pistol. "We've got to move quickly if we're going to make the rendezvous."

As they hustled along the trail, several shotgun blasts echoed through the trees. The Colombians were slowing the soldiers who seemed in disarray following the death of the general.

Two Navy SEALs were hiding in the brush near the beach

when Carrington charged onto the open sand. Clad in wetsuits, their faces blackened, they pointed their stubby rifles at the blond man with the wild look in his eyes. Carrington raised the rifle above his head. "Friendly," he called.

The taller SEAL stepped forward until he was nose-to-nose with Carrington. "How many of you?"

"Six."

"That's too many. We don't have room. We were told two to four."

More shotgun blasts were heard, answered by a torrent of small arms fire, mostly likely the rifles of Cuban soldiers.

"Two of our boys are guarding the rear," Carrington told the SEALs as Hannah and Decker reached the beach and kneeled in the sand to catch their breath.

The distant gunfire increased in intensity, followed by the *whump whump* of two grenades. Then all went silent.

The taller SEAL checked his wristwatch and stared authoritatively at Carrington. "Two more minutes, then we go. We're already pushing it. I'm sure the sub has already surfaced but it's not going to sit there for long."

"Understood. Two minutes," said Carrington, looking at his own chronograph to show he expected them to wait the entire time and not a second less. "I'll stand by at the end of the trail to discourage anybody who isn't a friendly from trying to reach the beach while you load up."

"Fair enough," said the SEAL.

Exactly two minutes later, Hannah and Decker were in the bobbing rubber boat. Decker was in a daze, possibly due to striking his head on the tile when his chair was tipped in the cabana. Carrington was nowhere in sight. The SEAL took a deep, exasperated breath. "Last call," he said, loud enough for anyone within twenty feet to hear. The two SEALS nudged the inflatable boat into the surf and hopped inside.

"Wait," said Hannah. "You can't leave without him."

"Time's up, lady."

Hannah pointed her Beretta at the taller SEAL who was startled to see the barrel aimed at his head. "He'll be here. He just needs a few more seconds."

"You fucking spooks just don't know when to quit."

"Take your hand off your knife," said Hannah.

The SEAL was quietly impressed that the half-crazed woman with the pistol pointed his way had noticed his hand attempting to free his dive knife. He released his grip on the sheath and waited, resting his back against the inflated tube. The second SEAL shifted his position in the boat.

"Sit still, or I'll put a bullet between your eyes," said Hannah. "And it won't be the first time I've done it today. Believe me, I'm not fucking around."

The SEAL stopped moving. "Maybe your friend's not coming," he said. "He might be a casualty. You heard the grenades."

Just as the word casualty flowed off the SEAL's tongue, Carrington burst out of the foliage and raced toward the water's edge, a wild mop of blond hair hiding his reddened his face, his heart pounding so hard he thought it might explode inside his chest. "Sorry for the delay," he said, hurling himself in the boat. "There are no more passengers."

57

WHAT WENT WRONG?

Vinnie Merlino and Nunzio Carlucci stretched out in the first-class section of the aircraft as it soared from Boston to Miami. The flight attendant gave them plenty of attention, bourbon for Vinnie, beer for his companion, and even endured harassing pinches on her butt cheeks because each round of drinks resulted in a fifty-dollar tip.

"When we meet with the family in Miami, I want to make it clear we were not responsible for the failure of the mercenaries to reach the island," said Vinnie. "I paid that fuck Jay Krutchner loads of greenbacks to get everybody in place by a specific date and with guns in their hands."

Upon arrival, the two men checked into a Miami hotel and Vinnie began making phone calls from the room. The first call was to General Sanchez, who didn't answer. The second was to Krutchner, who picked up after ten rings.

"Listen, you punk. I gave you money to arm and equip forty

mercenaries, but that's not what you delivered. Now I want my money back."

"Mr. Merlino, I hope you're aware that some of your people did make it onto the island."

"I'm aware. But sixteen of them are stuck aboard a ship in the harbor in fucking Haiti that appears to be going nowhere. What about that? I also paid for their rifles, ammunition and other supplies. And if what I've been told is true, another twelve of my soldiers landed on the island but when they got to the spot where their weapons were supposed to be dropped, there were no weapons. You can imagine their surprise. So, Mr. Jay Krutchner, that makes twenty-eight of forty out of the game. If I was a betting man, I wouldn't consider those good odds."

Krutchner didn't reply immediately. After a long pause, he said, "I'll see what I can do about getting the weapons returned to you, at least the ones handed out to those twenty-eight operatives."

Vinnie hurled a glass of bourbon across the hotel room where it shattered against the patio doors overlooking the waterway.

"Listen to me, you little cocksucker. Unless you make this right, if you've got a wife, she'd dead. If you've got a girlfriend, first she'll be gang-fucked by twenty guys with dirty dicks and then she'll be dead. If you've got kids, say good-bye to them now because some day they won't make it home from school."

"Every business plan is susceptible to not succeeding, Mr. Merlino. Your plan had a lot of moving parts, and some of them didn't move when they should have."

"Don't lecture me about business. I know how to do business. Somebody fucked with my plan, you or somebody you work for, and when I find out who that was, they'll wish they'd never been born."

Vinnie slammed down the receiver and as quickly plucked it from its cradle as he punched in the private number of Miami's underworld boss, Patsy LoScalzo. He wasn't looking forward to making the call, but he knew by now LoScalzo would have talked to the other crime families about the loss of their investment and, more importantly, the dissolution of their dreams for taking over Cuba.

Vinnie suspected Sammy Wings of the Chicago Outfit would be livid and demanding while John Gotti in New York would probably do something publicly to make a point that Vinnie Merlino was a loser, an amateur who couldn't be trusted with their money. Gotti would surely emphasize to the other crime bosses that none of the ten assassination targets were actually hit, unless they counted the Russian businessman's wife, which makes Vinnie Merlino a zero-percenter.

"I don't know why I ever got involved with these Cubans. Nothing but trouble. All that money spent and now I've got to find a way to pay back the other families, including Jerry the Joker."

Carlucci popped the cap on a bottle of Heineken beer and poured two fingers of bourbon for Vinnie. "Let's wait and see how this all plays out," he said, taking a long pull from his beer.

"It looks like everything has already played out."

Quoting famed New York Yankees catcher Yogi Berra, Carlucci said, "It ain't over till it's over."

Vinnie sipped his bourbon. "They're all going to want a refund. They won't want to hear some song and dance about how it was a risky plan from the start. They're going to ask me what went wrong and I don't have all the answers."

"You tell them the truth. You hired the guys with Ray Junior's blessing. You bought the guns, also with Ray's blessing. You did your best to put everything in play."

"I'm going to kill Krutchner."

"Let's see if he gets you the guns. Once they're returned you can at least sell them on the black market, probably to the same people in East Boston where you bought them in the first place."

"I'll still be out all the money I paid to keep those fucking mercenaries happy and fed in the bush for three months."

"That may be true," said Carlucci. "Too bad we're not legitimate. You could take that as a business loss on your taxes."

Vinnie smiled. "Hey Nunzio, did I ever tell you I hate fucking Miami?"

"I think you might have mentioned it once or twice."

58

TAKING A BOW AFTER THE SHOW

MARCH 1989
SYRACUSE, NEW YORK

Jack McGuire, deputy Special Agent-in-Charge of the FBI field office in Boston and head of the Anti-Organized Crime Strike Force, took special pleasure in attending the hospital bedside arraignment of Alfredo "The Animal" Ponzi in Syracuse, New York.

During the televised press conference, McGuire also focused on the arrest on homicide charges of mob associate Martino "Marty White" Bianco. Although Bianco was well known in federal law-enforcement circles, his biography was less colorful than that of Vinnie Merlino's longtime consigliere, the late Gino "Fingers" Terranzetti.

McGuire repeatedly emphasized during the press conference that Terranzetti had been fatally shot by an FBI SWAT team while resisting arrest. "Taking a guy like Fingers Terranzetti out of the mix is like cleaning the streets. Things look a lot better when you get rid of the garbage."

The news media relished McGuire's comments, which were broadcast and published for two news cycles.

Asked whether any criminal charges would be brought against Vinnie Merlino because of his association with the men under arrest, McGuire said, "We plan on talking at great lengths to Mr. Merlino and his attorneys. I have a feeling we'll be spending a lot of time together in the coming months."

Vinnie watched the press conference on the TV in his hotel room. "Nunzio. Come look at this. McGuire never even left his desk in Boston, but now he's taking credit for everything like he's the big man."

Nunzio laughed. "He's bucking for a promotion."

"I'd like to make him a cocktail that would burn out his tongue."

"Let it go."

"How can I let it go? Right now, he's basking in the glory, but once the applause stops, he'll be looking for more. He'll be coming after me."

59

IN PRAISE OF FOSTER FATHERS

MARCH 1989
PROVIDENCE, RHODE ISLAND

Vinnie was arguing loudly with Ruby when federal agents surrounded the apartment building and began moving cautiously up the stairwell.

"I don't care what I said when Carla was born. You can't keep buying things for her like I'm made of money. I'm broke, Ruby. Do you hear me? I'm out of cash."

"I only bought a stroller and some dresses," she said.

"And a diamond necklace. Babies don't need diamonds. They need milk from your tits."

"I'm sorry, Vinnie. I'll return the necklace and the stroller. I'm not sure whether they'll take back the dresses."

Vinnie leaned heavily on the kitchen counter. "Did you get the necklace from the pawn shop on the corner?"

Ruby began sniffling, but offered no answer.

"The Greek fronted it to you?"

More sniffling.

"For Christ's sake, Ruby, bring back the necklace. Tell The Greek it was a misunderstanding. But keep the fucking stroller and the dresses."

Four heavily-armed FBI agents pounded on the apartment door. Vinnie's heart sank. He knew they'd come for him sooner or later, only he had been hoping it would be later.

"FBI. Open the door or we'll break it down."

Vinnie shuffled toward the door. "Don't break the door. I'll open it."

As soon as the doorknob moved a fraction of an inch, the agents stormed inside and pushed Vinnie up against the wall. "Vincent Merlino, you're under arrest for racketeering," said Agent Sally Parker who read Vinnie his Miranda rights while FBI Special Agent Pete Barba slapped on the handcuffs.

Ruby burst into tears, looking to Agent Parker for an explanation. "Where are you taking him?"

None of the agents replied as they ushered Vinnie out the door. Ruby wanted to cry, but Carla beat her to it. The baby was still wailing, the cries escaping from the bedroom window as a gaggle of neighbors formed on the sidewalk below to watch the action. Agent Parker felt sorry for Ruby, but there was really nothing more to say.

"This is all a lot of bullshit. They're just putting on a show for the television people," said Vinnie, staring at the street crowd and cocking his head toward the two news vans parked across the street, their satellite dishes extended and ready for a remote broadcast.

One of the TV reporters and his cameraman quickly jogged alongside Vinnie and the FBI agents, thrusting a microphone toward his face. The reporter could barely contain his enthusiasm. "Mr. Merlino, what do you have to say about all of this?"

Vinnie put on a courageous smile. "I'll be home for dinner," he said. "We're having lasagna with lots of ricotta."

It was Sunday, March 19, which in Providence, Rhode Island

marked the Feast of St. Joseph, a religious holiday celebrating the foster father of Jesus Christ. When a staffer at the FBI field office in Boston mentioned the feast to McGuire earlier in the week, the Special-Agent-in-Charge decided it would be an appropriate occasion to arrest Vinnie Merlino.

The celebration that annually clogged the streets of Federal Hill was under way as the agents jostled Vinnie into one of four dark sedans and SUVs parked along the curb. A procession of Italian residents, nearly all of them wearing at least one bright red garment, marched past the FBI convoy. Vinnie looked through the rear window at the celebrants and he was overcome by sadness and despair. It showed on his face and the way his shoulders drooped.

"The Feast of St. Joseph," he said to Agent Parker and the other two agents in the sedan. "No shamrocks. Those are for St. Patrick. The Irish had their fun two days ago. Today it's fava beans. These people are headed for the church to put their offerings on the altar -- flowers, limes, cakes and the best zeppole you ever tasted. The women around here have been baking for days. The priests say the bread crumbs in the baskets represent sawdust because St. Joseph was a carpenter."

Vinnie knew he was talking too much and an awkward silence followed his monologue.

"It's nice to have such traditions," said Agent Parker, her response more out of kindness than interest.

"Maybe we can buy some pastries before we leave," said Vinnie, suddenly seeming hopeful. "My treat."

Agent Parker smiled warmly. "I don't think we're going to have time for that."

Agent Barba in the driver's seat caught Parker's eyes in the rearview mirror. Parker signaled for the convoy to head for the interstate highway and the drive north to Boston, blue lights flashing all the way.

60

JUDGMENT DAYS

Eight months had gone by since Vinnie Merlino announced to his neighbors he would be home for lasagna dinner. Since then he'd eaten mostly jailhouse food. He'd spent the entire time in federal custody, awaiting trial in U.S. District Court on racketeering charges.

The federal prosecutors had lumped the death of Doc Rimsky into the indictment, although Vinnie was not present at the upstate New York vineyard when the physician was allegedly shot to death by Mafia consigliere Gino "Fingers" Terranzetti. In the minds of the government, it was guilt by association.

The racketeering case was mostly founded upon FBI surveillance videos and witness statements. FBI Special Agent Sally Parker showed the jury disturbing video footage of average people in all shapes and sizes, old and young, being savagely beaten by Mafia enforcers purportedly working for Vinnie Merlino. In almost every instance, the beatings were related to overdue loans made at exorbitant interest rates, leaving the borrower with no way to ever pay back the money. A gaggle of experts testified on behalf of the prosecution about the mob's involvement in prostitution, sports betting, loan sharking, hijacking and the drug trade.

Prosecutors were excited to play the audiotape from the Mafia blood oath ceremony secretly recorded by Hannah and Decker near Boston in June 1988 – eighteen months earlier. Vinnie Merlino's conspiratorial tone helped convinced the jury of his guilt. It was the sort of juicy evidence that news reporters went wild for when covering a criminal trial.

Martino "Marty White" Bianco and Alfredo "The Animal" Ponzi were listed in the indictment as co-conspirators and were part of the federal court proceedings. The news reporters also appreciated these defendants had nicknames because it made for more colorful stories. Both men had been in federal custody since the vineyard shootout. Alfredo Ponzi, despite having been shot in both legs and the shoulder by CIA agent Hannah Summers, was up and walking by the time his court date arrived. Although the prosecutor mentioned Ponzi's wounds to the jury, it was never stated that a CIA agent had done the shooting because Carrington wanted to keep the agency's involvement to a minimum. The FBI had no problem withholding that information since it would appear to the public that one of its own specialty teams had taken out the bad guy. It was another lesson for Hannah – the CIA wasn't interested in headlines or taking credit. Most often the job was to be a helpful ghost.

As the trial progressed, Hope Cooper and Gary Schneider were ordered to testify about the day they were held hostage. Isabella Marceau and her parents were also called to the witness stand, though they had less information to offer. Isabella's testimony was important because she had notified the FBI about the hit list and the possibility Nick was in danger.

No charges were brought against Nick for the beating of

Rocco Merlino. After all, as the prosecutor pointed out, Marvel the horse had finished the job so any autopsy would be inconclusive. The news reporters were joyous to learn of a horse-hero angle to the story and Marvel's face appeared on TV broadcasts and in newspapers and magazines for weeks.

The FBI, at the urging of the State Department, made an effort to avoid an international conflict with Cuba and her allies by playing down the significance of the assassination and takeover plan. Deputy Special Agent-in-Charge Jack McGuire described it to the court as "a pie-in-the-sky dream by a washed-up wiseguy named Vinnie Merlino."

According to McGuire, the two-bit Mafioso was able to convince some of his associates around the country to front him money to support his ill-begotten venture.

"There was never any reason to believe Mr. Merlino's plan posed a threat by the United States to Cuba or her allies," he said. "Whatever was going through Mr. Merlino's mind as he concocted this plan has nothing to do with the stable mutual relationship enjoyed by the United States and Cuba."

As for the deaths of Homer Duarte, Selena Delgado and three other Cuban ex-pats from Miami, federal investigators summed up their actions as "an isolated incident" that spread no further than the five individuals involved. The matter was still under scrutiny by Cuban authorities due to the theft and destruction of military hardware, namely a Russian T-54 tank.

Fidel Castro used the situation to praise the late General Octavio Sanchez for his bravery. He posthumously commended the general for using a portable Red Arrow 8 missile to knock out the stolen T-54 tank before it could do damage and "for killing the Yanqui invaders at the cost of his own life."

In another attempt to smooth over the situation, two State Department representatives met privately with attorneys for Fidel and Raul Castro in April, a month after the mercenary attacks, and all agreed the "isolated incident" description was the most palatable way to unveil what had occurred at the hacienda to the media and the public.

The State Department officials noted in their reports that Fidel Castro "seemed rattled and unnerved" by the botched attempt on his life by American citizens. The Cuban leader might have further praised General Sanchez's heroics but the State Department had subtly suggested he keep it to a minimum, otherwise the man's snuff film collection might not remain under wraps.

Although Homer Duarte and Selena Delgado were briefly celebrated as the "Martyrs of Miami" in their Cuban enclave and in newspapers and television reports in most major U.S. cities, their story soon faded from the headlines. Had they assassinated one or both of the Castro brothers, their fame undoubtedly would have lasted longer than two news cycles.

The deaths of Russian businesswoman Lena Sorokin, her daughter and several guests in Cuba were attributed to an explosion in their home caused by a faulty natural gas pipe. Cuban authorities were satisfied to announce the explosion was another isolated incident. An account of the blast, released by Fidel Castro's press office, noted the street upon which the Sorokin home was located had undergone recent repairs, which investigators believe ignited the gas line.

Preston Barlow was forced to resign after the failed assassination plan. Cuban operatives, who showed up a few days later and threatened to go public with the story, had demanded it. By midsummer, Barlow was back in action, privately consulting for a well-established public relations firm within the Washington, D.C. beltway. Hill & Knowlton had been hired to convince Americans that Iraqi soldiers were snatching sick infants from their incubators in a Kuwait hospital and burying them alive.

Barlow was eager to spread the rumor that Iraq's dictator, Saddam Hussein, had ordered the slaughter and must be overthrown. It was just the sort of assignment he relished and he had

no trouble pursuing it even though he knew there was no truth to
the story.

Following the shootout at the Cooper vineyard, Nick returned
to upstate New York where he settled into his old digs. Gary
Schneider lawfully adopted Nick, although the boy kept his original surname, which made Hope happy.

Rocco Merlino's body was autopsied in upstate New York to
ensure his death had been caused by traumatic injuries sustained
as a result of being trampled by a horse.

Hope and Gary had offered to bury him and pay all expenses.
After all, he was Hope's biological son. But Angie pleaded that
Rocco be buried in a cemetery in Providence, where she could
visit his grave every day or as often as possible. Vinnie didn't get
involved in the negotiations between the two mothers. He didn't
care one way or the other. He had his own problems to deal with.

Ruby had convinced Angie to let her dye and style her hair
for the wake and funeral. It was Ruby's way of making amends
because their fates were tethered, both stuck with a second-rate
Mafia boss named Vinnie Merlino who was behind bars until
maybe forever.

Vinnie attended the small funeral, flanked by two U.S.
Marshals who were supported by three FBI agents outside the
church. Ruby, holding Carla in her arms, had stood next to Angie
one pew behind Vinnie and the federal marshals. At one point
during the service, Angie put her hand atop Ruby's and smiled
sadly. Tears were racing down Ruby's cheeks and onto baby Carla
but nobody seemed to notice.

Hope and Gary had also attended the funeral, sitting in the
back pew and feeling out of place. Despite the awkwardness,
Hope wanted to be present as Rocco left the world. She was still
having difficulty believing this young man had come from
her womb.

The priest kept his message simple: It was a tragedy whenever
a young person died, for whatever reason.

It seemed everyone in the church had breathed a sigh of relief when the sermon ended quickly. The church was filled with a palpable tension that nobody wanted to witness in the event it sprang loose.

When September arrived, Nick began his sophomore year of high school. The students continued to refer to him and Isabella collectively as Nikabella because they were inseparable.

It was grape harvesting season and when not in school, Nick spent his time in the fields, side-by-side with the other workers, or riding horses with Isabella. They seldom mentioned Rocco and Nick was personally pleased the boy was not buried on the vineyard or in a nearby cemetery. Rocco was not his blood brother and never had been. He owed him no allegiance, even in death, and felt no remorse for any pain he might have caused.

Nick occasionally wondered if the experience had changed him, made him capable of acts previously unimagined. Most days he tried not to think about it.

61

FULL CIRCLE

JANUARY 1990
FEDERAL PRISON, FORT LEAVENWORTH, KANSAS

Vinnie Merlino opened his arms wide as Angie and Ruby entered the visitors' room accompanied by a prison guard. He draped an arm around each of their shoulders and pulled them to his chest.

"I'm glad you both came," he said. "How was the flight?'

Angie burst into tears and wiped her eyes on the sleeve of her dress. Ruby smiled, though it wasn't filled with warmth or acceptance.

"We would have been here sooner, but the airline lost Angie's bag. We had to wait around at the Kansas City airport until they found it," she said.

Vinnie shook his head. "Angie, why didn't you just bring a carry-on?"

"I didn't know what to wear. I had to bring things," she said.

Vinnie chuckled. "Nobody's dressing formal around here. That's for sure," he said, tugging up his pants so they could see his ankles. "Look, they make us wear white socks. I always wore black. All that time I never knew how much dirt was on the floors."

Angie shook her head, confused and offended, unappreciative of Vinnie's wry humor. "Maybe it was dirty some places you walked. My floors were clean."

Ruby sank into one of the hardback chairs and Angie followed suit. "We rented a car. It's not too far from the airport to this place but we didn't want to take a bus or a cab," said Ruby. "How have you been? Are they treating you OK?"

"They treat me like royalty," he said. "Three times a day, they ask me, 'Mr. Merlino, what can we get you?' I've got it pretty good."

"Your lawyer, Frank DeSenzo, told me to give you his best and to tell you he's working hard on your appeal," said Angie. "Nunzio came with us and he's waiting outside. He'll come in to see you after we leave. He can tell you all about what's going on."

"Good. Good. If anybody gives you a hard time, just tell Nunzio and he'll take care of it."

Vinnie closely eyed Ruby, following the curves of her body. "You look good," he said. "I guess Carla isn't keeping you up all night."

"She's sleeping better. I left her with my aunt because it's too hard traveling with her."

"Well, give her a big hug from me."

"I'll do that," Ruby said. "She misses her father."

Angie crossed her ankles and then nervously re-crossed them. "How's the food? Do they make anything Italian?"

"Any kind of food you want," he said. "But it's nothing like your lasagna."

Angie blushed, pleased by the compliment. "That's because they probably don't put enough ricotta in it."

"So what else is new?"

"Carla has three teeth. They came through last month," said Ruby.

Vinnie didn't seem to know how to respond. "That's fantastic. By the time she gets all of them, I'll be losing mine," he said, trying to lighten the mood.

"Teething is painful. It keeps her up a lot, but now she's sleeping better."

"She's a very sweet baby," said Angie, reflexively grabbing for her purse that was in a locker outside the entryway.

Vinnie sat back in his chair and studied both women. "It seems like you two have become friends."

Angie and Ruby glanced at each other and both connected as though they had some secret agreement. "We're looking out for each other," Ruby said.

Angie rubbed the beads of her rosary. She still wore her wedding ring. "I've gone to the cemetery a few times to see Rocco and put flowers on his grave," she said. "I miss him."

Vinnie lowered his head as though he understood her pain. "Rocco was a good boy," he said. "It's sad what happened."

Ruby handed Angie a tissue before the latest wave of tears spilled over her cheeks. Angie blew her nose and stared at the floor, her whole body quivering.

"Crying won't bring him back," said Vinnie, ignoring Angie's outburst of emotion. "Has anybody heard from Nicholas?"

"Nothing," said Ruby. "Last we heard he was back at the farm."

Vinnie suddenly seemed agitated. "I guess he liked those pig farmers better than us."

The mood in the small room took on a brittle quality and for several moments nobody said a word. Ruby broke the silence. "Do you want me to get Nunzio?"

Vinnie looked up as though in a stupor. "Please. It was good to see you."

Vinnie hugged Ruby tightly and kissed her on both cheeks before thrusting his tongue into her mouth. He kissed her passionately and relentlessly. Ruby seemed startled but didn't break it off. Angie was uncomfortable and looked away as Vinnie caressed Ruby's behind. The guard cleared his throat to signal everyone's discomfort.

"I asked for a private room, but they don't allow that in this joint," said Vinnie. "So you better behave. I'll be out of here in no time."

Ruby grinned and rested her forehead against Vinnie's right shoulder.

"Angie, come," he said. "Let's all have a big family hug."

Angie didn't move until Ruby reached out and gently grabbed her by an elbow so they could all embrace.

Once the women were escorted out, Nunzio Carlucci swaggered into the visitors' room and locked Vinnie in a bear hug. They greeted each other in Italian, which seemed to put the guard on edge.

Carlucci filled Vinnie in on the latest underworld news, speaking in vague terms that only an insider would understand. Vinnie was relieved to learn none of the mob bosses had taken any action against his men or his family. Eventually they moved onto a discussion about what went down in Cuba.

"It's was a good plan," said Vinnie. "I've been thinking about how we can still make it happen. I know where I went wrong."

Carlucci looked at Vinnie as though he was crazy. "Not everybody would be happy with that," he said. "There are some people looking for repayment. They want their investment back."

"I've got that figured out, too."

"How's that?"

"The films."

"General Sanchez is dead. Nobody will care if you show his film collection to the world. They don't have any value."

"If we find the right collector, they might have lots of value."

Carlucci grinned. He was amused that Vinnie was scheming even while behind bars and especially after taking such a trouncing with his original plan. "I'm listening."

"I can easily get six figures for the collection," he said. "People pay big money for that kind of thing."

"And you'd use the money from the sale to pay back the investors?"

"That's what I'd do. Make it right with them. If they want to get in on the new deal, we can talk about costs."

"And if they show no interest, you'll be broke."

"Not if we increase the vig on the loans and we look into selling certain products like all the other families."

"That would require permission from Jerry the Joker who, like you, is still in the can," said Carlucci. "You'd also need approval from Junior in Providence, and maybe from the Dapper Don in New York."

"Once I explain it, I think they'll go for it," Vinnie said.

The guard glanced at his watch. "Time's up."

Carlucci gave Vinnie a friendly embrace. "See you soon, my friend."

"I'll look forward to it. And if you hear anything from Nicholas, you let me know right away. I think he'll come over to the family when he's ready."

62

BACK TO THE DESERT

JANUARY 1990
BOSTON, MASSACHUSETTS

Decker thought long and hard about possibly going back to the Middle East or, more specifically, to Iraq where he sensed global conflict was about to break out once again. The buzz going around at Langley had made it evident that seasoned operatives were welcome to join the fray and the list of missions was steadily growing.

Ever since returning from Cuba, Decker had been filled with a need to strike out on his own, the lone wolf with sniper rifle in hand. For months he'd been surrounded by fighting men and most were far less skillful at their profession, with the exception of Trevor Rainsford, Chad Taylor and a few others. Decker disliked amateurs, especially those who played the dangerous game of espionage and dark ops.

The more he considered going back to the desert, the more confused he became because it meant leaving Hannah for six to eight months, maybe longer. He wasn't sure if she was up to the separation. Wars did funny things to people, both those who functioned within the combat zone and those left behind. He had only to recall Selena Delgado and the rainforest passion they'd experienced. In his memory, it was a primal attraction mixed with the smell of gun oil, diesel fumes, roasted pork and endless talk of fighting. He'd need more than ten fingers to count the ugly divorces and separations he'd been privy to while deployed overseas.

When it came to the Middle East, the soldiers didn't have many options for infidelity. The troops often joked about "going Taliban," which implied sexual intercourse with goats and other livestock. But spouses left behind in the so-called civilized world would be exposed to far greater temptations, often putting their marriages at risk.

Decker gazed out at Boston Harbor from the condo he'd rented with Hannah more than a year ago, feeling the pang most travelers do when they realize the place they're leaving is beautiful and probably better than where they're going. He knew he'd miss that panoramic view of tankers, freighters, water taxis and sailboats, and his old haunts in Eastie directly across the water. He'd also miss the change of seasons that was synonymous with New England.

The Middle East promised heat, sand and baked rock, an inhospitable landscape filled with people trying to kill him. During a previous deployment as an Army Special Forces Ranger, he'd been shot twice while fighting Syrian soldiers and hit with shrapnel during a clash with Iraq's Republican Guards.

So why was he considering going back to Sandland, lugging his long-barrel Barrett sniper rifle on missions he was never truly convinced had any military value?

Decker wasn't sure he had the answer. All he knew for certain is that he felt at home in the wasteland, not so different from Mad Max. Every day was a struggle for survival, but where some people might crumble under such circumstances, he reveled in it.

The possibility of death at any moment pumped a weird blend of adrenaline through his body, putting him on edge while simultaneously providing him the situations and challenges he needed to feel alive.

Decker decided to tell Hannah about his voluntary deployment before she heard about it through the Langley grapevine or, worse, at a classified strategy meeting about the pending Persian Gulf War.

Hannah was equally stir-crazy after her return from Cuba. She had conflicting feelings about having slept with Carrington, though the guilt she experienced was less than she had anticipated. Their lovemaking had been flawless, like a couple tuned to each other's wants and needs. She enjoyed running her fingers through his blond hair and feeling the hardness of his athletic body as it overtook her. It had been an absolutely wonderful night in Havana but she swore she would avoid going down that path again. After all, Carrington was married, even if the relationship was unhappy and discordant. The man had a house somewhere and two kids in their early teens and probably a dog and a cat and a lawnmower.

Hannah also had recurring visions of shooting General Sanchez through the head but felt no deep emotion. It made her wonder if she was becoming too hardened. She chalked it up to payback for all the little boys the general had abused and tortured. She doubted the general had seen her, the woman he knew only as Mariel Becker, pointing a rifle at him. If he had, it undoubtedly would have been quite a shock.

The snow was falling in large flakes when Hannah and Decker traipsed from their harborfront digs to the Oceanaire restaurant near Government Center. The place had a good vibe. It was where they'd enjoyed a wonderfully contentious lunch when they first met. So much had happened since that afternoon of wine, oysters and laughter in the summer of '86.

"Are you going to force me to drink wine like you did last time we were here?"

"Did I do that?"

"You certainly did," she said, her lips forming a smile as she let loose the husky laughter Decker loved so much. "I should have known better."

"Any regrets?"

"We've come this far."

"We have indeed."

"So I guess that begs the question, 'Where are we?' I know we're here in Boston, but I can't help feeling you're going to tell me something I might not want to hear."

The waiter appeared at their table, politely clutching a pen and pad.

"I think we should order some wine."

"I already know you're going to say Amarone."

"You know me well."

"Sometimes."

The waiter pointed to an Amarone on the wine list and Decker gave him a thumbs-up.

When the wine was poured, Hannah held up her glass. "To Emmett Decker and everything that goes with him."

Decker's eyes closed nearly to squinting as he studied her face. "To Hannah Summers and the wonderful light she brings to my sometimes dark life."

"So when are you going to tell me?"

"Tell you what?"

"That you're going to Iraq?"

"That's a rather big presumption."

"But I'm right."

"Yes."

Hannah felt compelled to ask the one question that had been nagging her since she first heard Decker was volunteering for hazardous duty. "Did Bill order you to go?"

"Absolutely not. He knows my story. I don't think he wants to pile another long assignment on top of it."

"Is that the truth?"

"It is. He wouldn't do that. It's not his style."

"But you're going?"

Decker stared up at the ceiling skylights and inhaled deeply. "Yes. I'm going."

"Why?"

"Because it's what I do, and what I do best."

Looking around the restaurant before speaking in an amplified whisper, she said, "Oh, Decker. There are other operatives capable of carrying out the same assignment. Langley if full of people who can hide and shoot."

"I've been there before. I know the terrain. Besides, I've got black hair and lots of dark facial stubble so it's easy for me to blend in. Not so easy if you're blond with blue eyes."

"Do you also know that Barlow is over at Hill & Knowlton and he's the one pumping out those baby-killer rumors?"

"So I've heard. He was always a liar so his new desk should fit him just fine."

"But the American people believe the rumors they're being fed and it's getting them all fired up."

"Isn't that the point?"

"If the people really think Iraqi soldiers are ripping tiny infants from their incubators in a Kuwait hospital and burying them alive, it won't take long for the war drums to start beating."

"You overestimate the American public. First they have to be told where Kuwait is on the map and why it's our ally, even though it's just another sand lot from which we extract oil. Once they're down with that, the emotion needle will spike."

"What you're saying is, America will come to the rescue and invade Iraq."

"Precisely. And I need to be there before that happens so that certain high-value targets aren't on the defensive. Going now makes my job easier. I'll get to take out some of those babykillers before the shit hits the fan."

"Oh, Decker. You seem so out of sorts," she said, sliding a hand across the table and intertwining her fingers with his.

"I'm fine. I'll be in and out of the sand box before you know it."

"The last time you came home from there, you weren't so fine. I don't think you've ever faced the fact that you suffered some serious PTSD."

"Of course I have. I talked to all the shrinks at the VA about it, none of whom had ever been in combat, by the way."

"You need to rest."

"I don't do well with that."

"Everyone needs to rest every once in a while. My nerves were on edge when I first got back from Cuba. I think it was all the deception that took its toll."

Decker affectionately squeezed Hannah's hand. "I never honestly thanked you for saving my life when General Sanchez was about to put a bullet in my head."

Hannah leaned across the corner of the table and gave him a lingering kiss. "Thanks accepted," she said, the tiny scar twitching at the right corner of her mouth.

"It was a tough situation."

"I'm sorry about your friends Homer and Selena."

The mention of Selena brought a chill to the conversation because they'd never before talked about how close Decker had been to her. His valiant attempt to rescue her from the clutches of General Sanchez spoke loudly, yet it was his deep sadness following her death that had caught Hannah's attention.

Decker swirled his wine glass. "To better outcomes."

Hannah wasn't sure what he meant by the toast, but she clinked his glass and repeated his words.

Shifting quickly and unexpectedly from solemn to all business, Decker said, "I may be gone six to eight months. Could be longer. If anything happens to me, you're the beneficiary of my life insurance policy. I've paid the rent on our condo through June, presuming you intend on staying there, so you should be set financially. Otherwise, that would be a lot of monthly expense for one person. I also stocked the kitchen cupboard with chocolate bars, cashews, dried cranberries and several other snacks you've been known to covet, and three cases of wine."

Hannah loved him most at these moments, when the hard shell of Decker the warrior unveiled softness and vulnerability beneath.

"Shall we order some oysters? They're aphrodisiacs," he said.

"Do we need them?"

"Probably not. I was hoping this wine would do the trick."

Hannah let out another husky laugh. "Always scheming, aren't you?"

Decker inhaled Hannah's grayish-green eyes, her full lips and the shoulder-length honey-blonde hair that framed her face.

"I'll miss you."

"How will I know if you're safe?"

"You won't, but trust me, I will be," he said. "Every minute I'm there, I'll be thinking of coming back home to you."

A NOTE FROM THE AUTHOR

If you've enjoyed Blood Sons, I hope you'll read my previous novel, the serial-killer thriller *DEADLY FARE*. Follow Hannah Summers and Emmett Decker as they chase down a serial killer on the streets of Boston.

ALSO BY DAVID LISCIO

DEADLY FARE

A SERIAL KILLER THRILLER

Fans of James Patterson and Nelson DeMille won't want to miss this page-turning thriller set in Boston...

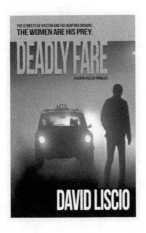

FIVE WOMEN MURDERED. A CITY PARALYZED BY FEAR. ONLY A MATTER OF TIME BEFORE HE STRIKES AGAIN.

When beautiful young women begin to vanish from Boston Logan International Airport, State Police Lt. Hannah Summers is the only one who sees a pattern amidst the cold case files. She knows a killer is on the loose, and she's determined to make her chauvinistic bosses believe her hunch about a gypsy cab driver -- before it's too late.

As the body count rises, so does the public's panic. Under pressure from the district attorney to make the killings stop, Summers soon finds herself rubbing elbows with ex-Special Forces soldier Emmett Decker, a private investigator hired by the wealthy family of a missing local girl. The more their paths cross, the harder it is to deny they may be chasing the same monster -- and that the tension between them is more than purely professional.

One thing is certain: the Boston Butcher must be stopped before any more women climb inside his cab... and wind up paying the ultimate price...

———

Now available for purchase in ebook and paperback.

ABOUT THE AUTHOR

David Liscio is an international, award-winning journalist whose lengthy experience covering crime stories led to the writing of his debut novel, the serial killer thriller DEADLY FARE.

An investigative reporter, David's work has appeared in dozens of magazines and newspapers. The recipient of more than 20 journalism honors, his feature stories have earned first-place awards from the Associated Press, United Press International and many regional news media groups. He has reported extensively on organized crime in both the United States and abroad, in addition to writing about environmental and military subjects.

David is an avid sailor, outdoorsman and adjunct college professor. A father of two, he lives with his wife and dog on the

Massachusetts coast, where he is a volunteer firefighter and Ocean Rescue team member.

You can contact him on his website: _www.davidliscio.com_. For book news and updates, please subscribing to his monthly newsletter: http://eepurl.com/dtek75

For more information:
www.davidliscio.com
david@davidliscio.com

ACKNOWLEDGMENTS

I'd like to thank my wife Christine for her continued support of my writing, knowing all the while it does not heap mounds of gold upon our doorstep. My unbridled thanks extends to my daughter, Julie, a talented author who understands more about this business than I do. Her emotional and professional support made this book possible. And to my son, Zack, who provides insight and cares that I succeed at doing what I love.

My appreciation also goes out to the FBI special agents from field offices in New York and Boston who shared stories and explained the intricacies of a bureau investigation into organized crime; to the Massachusetts State Police detectives who often pointed me in the right direction; and to the many colorful underworld figures who generously allowed me a glimpse of their lives.

A big chunk of my thanks is also reserved for the readers of my first novel, the serial-killer thriller Deadly Fare, who contacted me to say they were looking forward to my next book. I hope you enjoy *BLOOD SONS*.

CPSIA information can be obtained
at www.ICGtesting.com
Printed in the USA
BVHW04s0219111018
529871BV00025B/465/P